CHANGA'S SAFARI

Volume I

A Novel By

Milton J. Davis

MVmedia

Fayetteville, Georgia

ISBN 13: 978-0-9800842-1-4
ISBN 10: 0-9800842-1-0

Cover art and interior illustrations by Winston Blakely
Maps by Jason Zampol

Cover Design by URAEUS
Layout/Design by URAEUS
Edited by Lyndon Perry

Manufactured in the United States of America

First Edition

A DIFFERENT SAFARI

By Charles R. Saunders

Once there was a world in which sea lanes and trade winds connected scores of exotic kingdoms on opposite shores of a great ocean. Nations of black, brown, yellow, and white people interacted in rivalry and harmony, war and peace, trade and treachery. This world was not conjured out of a storyteller's imagination. It was real – the world of the African and Asian lands washed by the Indian Ocean. This world reached its peak during the 14th and 15th centuries, only to experience a downfall that lasted half a millennium.

During the best of this world's times, a vast and intricate commercial network stretched from the interior of Africa to the farthest reaches of China and India. That net-work ultimately unraveled with the coming of the Portuguese and other European nations bent on conquest and colonization. That was the downfall of a trade that was likely the richest in the world – a fact glossed over or ignored in subsequent history books.

That world lives again in Milton Davis's *Changa's Safari*. The title character, Changa Diop, is a merchant who drives a hard bargain, and can back it up with a sword-blade when necessary. Of West African ancestry, Changa fights his way out of slavery in the glittering cities of Africa's East Coast, and becomes a force to be reckoned with on two continents.

With his companion Panya, an enigmatic Yoruba sorceress, Changa goes to places whose names echo in the halls of history:

Mombasa, Calicut, Zimbabwe, the Middle Kingdom of China, Sofala and Indonesia. Larger than life but hardly super-human, Changa contends with mercantile rivals and political intrigue – not to mention supernatural perils – malevolent sorcery and mythical beings that come to terrifying life.

The word "safari" means "journey" in Swahili, the lingua franca of the East Coast. These days, that word is associated with khaki-clad white men and women chop-ping their way through the jungle, accompanied by black porters bearing bundles of supplies on their heads. Changa's safari is a journey of a different kind: an epic passage that makes the Odyssey look like a walk in the park.

With this novel, Milton restores a world of magic and mystery that is nonetheless the real world of our past – a past that centuries of colonialism obscured, but could not destroy.

Changa's ship is about to depart. Get on board, and enjoy the ride.

To Mom and Pop
Thank you for everything.

Kitabu Chakwanzaa

(Book One)

The Jade Obelisk

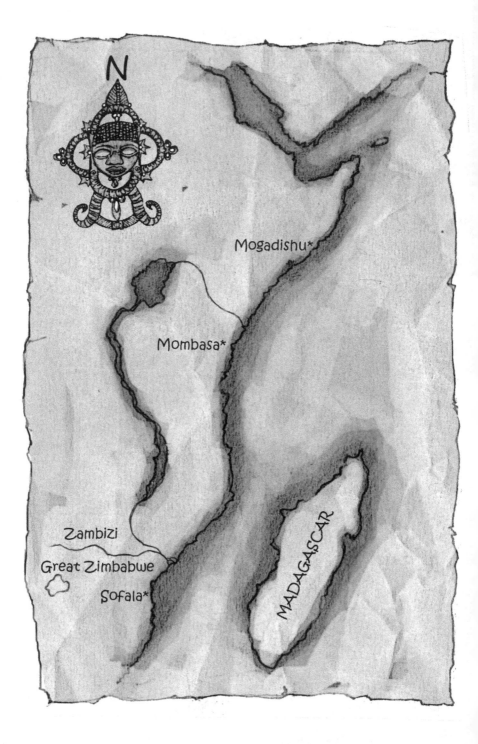

PREFACE

This was not the way for a prince to die. Amir Zakee ibn Basheer teetered at the edge of the cliff, his bloody fingers clinging to the hilt of a rusted scimitar as he clutched the precious bundle underneath his arm. His muscles had given up long ago; only hate and anger kept him on his bare feet. His black hair was matted to his forehead by sweat and blood, dungeon filth smeared across his young face and ragged clothes. Behind him the wind hissed through the leaves of the forest canopy carrying the urgent voices of his pursuers to his ears. Below him colorful birds darted through the branches, oblivious to his plight. Three days of flight and pursuit had finally ended. There was no way out.

His hunters emerged warily from the foliage, their cowhide shields protecting their leather clad bodies, their assegais leveled. A grim smile came to the young prince's face. They were being careful this time, the deaths of their comrades fresh on their minds. He summoned the last dregs of his strength and attacked, knocking the closest warrior's shield aside with the scimitar then dodging the point of the warrior's assegai. He stabbed the man's throat, turned and ran before the others could close the gap. The edge of the cliff rushed closer and closer with each step, but Zakee did not hesitate. He would not be a sacrifice. He closed his eyes, whispered a prayer, and jumped.

Chapter 1
The Unexpected Guest

Changa Diop stood at the bow of the *Sendibada*, a broad smile on his rugged brown face. He took a deep breath, raising his massive chest and shoulders in exaggerated ceremony, then let the air out like the monsoon winds pushing him south. For the first time as far back as he could remember, he was at peace. Mombasa and its mix of memories faded with each day sailed. Ahead lay Sofala and the promise of a new beginning. He glanced behind him for a check on the rest of his fleet. Eight dhows sailed in his wake, each of them laden with a wealth of goods. Changa intended to buy his way into the Sofala merchant guild just as his mentor Belay would have done. A sad shroud descended over him as he thought of the old merchant. He owed his life to Belay, this kind man that saved him from the fighting pits of Mogadishu and made him a free man. He closed his eyes and banished the bad thoughts to the winds. Sofala was a new beginning; the past would stay buried in Mombasa.

The jangling of bracelets brought a smile to Changa's face. He opened his eyes to see Panya beside him. She stood a head shorter with long beaded braids framing a face whose beauty displayed her royal Yoruba blood. Like Changa, Panya's origins lay far west of the Swahili Coast. Fate and circumstances brought her to Mombasa; her special skills brought her to Changa's attention. Their high status in a Swahili society that excluded outsiders was a testimony to their special abilities. In Mombasa,

Panya normally wore traditional Muslim garb, but on the sea she dressed practically. The cotton pants and loose shirt she wore looked much more alluring on her than on the men.

"Are you sure this is the right decision?" she asked.

"Of course not," Changa replied in his deep rumbling voice, "which makes it more exciting."

Panya folded her arms across her chest. "Mogadishu is a better choice. It's closer to Hormuz and the trade is well established."

Changa looked at Panya, his eyebrows raised. "So now you're a sorceress and a merchant?"

"Some things are obvious to anyone with a sharp mind."

Changa shrugged. "That's true, but the winds blow south so south we go. If we waited until the northern monsoons Mombasa would be in civil war. I have no desire to be involved in a war."

"I've seen enough of it myself," Panya agreed.

"Besides, Sofala is prospering. My friends say the iron trade with Benematapa is strong. We have enough goods to buy dock space and a trade house. The rest will come."

They were interrupted by a tall, lean man covered from head to toe in blue robes of concealment, his eyes the only visible part of his face. He bowed to Panya then focused intensely on Changa, pointing to the shore.

"You're right, Tuareg. Send a party to shore for fresh water and food. We'll take the Kazuri into the harbor. Will you lead the men ashore?"

The Tuareg nodded.

"Good."

Panya followed the robed man with suspicious eyes as he walked away.

"How do you know what he wants?"

Changa shrugged. "We've been together a long time."

"I don't see how you trust a man that never speaks."

"I saved him from the fighting pits and gave him his freedom, just like Belay did for me. Instead of going back to his homeland he chose to follow me. Over the years he has done much to earn my trust. In time you will learn to trust him."

The fleet sailed another hour before reaching their destination, an obscure harbor hidden by a hook of land. Changa used it many times as a destination for replenishing water barrels and food stock. The thought of hunting excited him, and he left Panya to find the Tuareg.

He found his silent friend overseeing the boat loading. "I'm coming with you," he said.

The two went to the bow and climbed down to the boats waiting to take them to the *Kazuri*, Changa's favorite dhow. It was small, fast and armed with the best cannons he could afford. The *Kazuri* was the perfect dhow for missions such as gathering fresh water, running blockades or chasing pirates. The crew consisted of Changa's best bahari, men hand picked for their fighting skills, seamanship, and bravery.

Changa's fleet anchored as the *Kazuri* set sail for the harbor. A good wind carried them quickly into the deep, calm waters. As they anchored, Changa appeared on the deck, sword at his waist, a crossbow in his arms, and his leather throwing knife bag on his shoulder. The Tuareg walked beside him, his takouba hanging from his shoulder, a hunting spear in his hand. They boarded the smaller boats with the others and rowed to the shore. They split into groups; one group would hunt while the other group gathered whatever edible plants were available. Changa's group went inland with gourds to gather water at a nearby freshwater stream they knew well. The stream was also a watering hole for the abundant bush dear and boars, which they hoped to bag to add to their stores.

Changa led the way, hacking through the thicket with his machete. The plan was to gather water first, of which the dhows were in the most need, then return to hunt for fresh meat. As they descended the slope leading to the stream, Changa could hear the grunts and growls of nearby *mambas*. The man-eating lizards slid silently into the waters as the men approached.

"Keep an eye out," he said. "We are here to gather food, not become it."

A grim laugh rose among the hunters as they reached the banks of the stream. The men filled their water urns as Changa and the Tuareg worked their way further down the bank until they found a shallow spot.

"Let's cross here," Changa said. "Maybe we'll find bull or boar. Either would be a feast."

No sooner had the words left his mouth when the sound of thrashing branches rushed towards them. They crouched, the Tuareg raising his spear while Changa rushed to load his crossbow. A man burst from the woods clutching a bundle of cloth to his chest with his left arm, his right hand holding a scimitar. He bled from cuts on his head and legs as he ran towards them with eyes full of desperation.

"Help me!" he said in Arabic. "They are after me!"

Changa raised his crossbow, aiming at the man. The Tuareg knocked it down, pointing his spear to the woods. More men appeared, tattooed, bare-chested warriors brandishing short spears and tall broad-leaf shields.

"This is not our fight!" Changa said. The Tuareg looked at him then turned to the attackers. He threw his spear, striking the closest man square in the chest with a force that knocked him back into his brethren. He drew his takouba and charged.

"Damn it!" Changa exclaimed.

He raised his crossbow and sent a bolt into another man. Two more went down to his fire before he threw the weapon aside, running to join the Tuareg. He twisted to his right, dodging a spear thrust aimed for his chest. Grabbing his attacker's shield, he twisted again, ripping the shield away and driving his sword into the man's gut. Changa yanked his sword from the man, kicking him into the warrior behind him. Another assegai flicked at his face; Changa knocked it away with his wrist knife then lowered his shoulder, absorbing the warrior's shield blow. He reached low, gripping the man between the legs and lifted him over his head. With a grunt he slammed the man on his head. A spear tip pricked his neck; Changa grabbed the spear shaft with his right hand, snatching the weapon from its wielder. He turned it about and rammed it through the shield and the warrior. Stepping back as the warrior crumpled to the ground, Changa's eyes darted about for more attackers. There were none.

The companions stood over their grim effort for a moment, making sure they were thorough in their task. Changa glared at the Tuareg as they approached the man who began this confrontation.

"You have no idea what you've gotten us into," he said. The Tuareg looked back, his gaze steady and unremorseful.

They halted before the man sprawled on the ground. He struggled to his feet, a grateful smile creasing his dingy face. He was younger than Changa first thought, his smooth face clear of the lines of wisdom. He was Arabic, possibly Yemeni. Despite his condition he seemed in good shape.

"Praise Allah for you both!" he exclaimed. I am Amir Zakee ibn Basheer, son of Sultan Saheed ibn Mamud Basheer.

Allah truly blesses his faithful, for he sent you to my aid."

"You're not much of an amir to look at," Changa replied.

Zakee looked at himself. "I have been held prisoner for weeks, I think."

"And I am to assume that bundle you hold is of some value."

The prince clutched the package. "If you seek ransom I'm sure my father would make my return worth your while."

Changa's banter with the prince was interrupted by at jolt on his shoulder. The Tuareg jabbed his finger to the stream. More warriors spilled out to the woods, assegais raised and swords drawn. Changa and the Tuareg pushed Zakee ahead of them and ran. There were too many to fight; if they could make it to the shore they stood a chance. Branches and vines flailed them as they ran down the narrow trail to the shore. Breaking out to the beach, they came upon the others loading the boats for the trip back to the *Kazuri*.

"Arm yourselves!" Changa yelled. "Yusufu, sound the drums!"

The bahari dropped the provisions and scurried to their weapons. Yusufu's hands blurred across the drum skins; his rapid rhythms were answered by the *Kazuri's* drummer. The dhow raised its sails and pivoted, exposing its broadside to the beach, the gunners working furiously to load and aim the cannons.

"Tuareg, get the supplies to the *Kazuri*," Changa shouted. "Bowmen, form a line and wait for my signal."

Changa raised his sword high enough for the gunners on the dhow to see. He waited until all the attackers were out in the open then snapped his arm down. The bow-men fired, their bolts felling the first line of warriors as the *Kazuri's* cannons barked in the distance. Changa and his men fired another volley of bolts then switched to their swords as cannon shells whistled overhead and exploded, throwing men and sand into the sky. The Mombasans fell upon the remaining enemy like lions. The unknown warriors were skilled, but against Changa's best they were no match.

As the last attacker fell, Changa and his crew hurried to the remaining boats. If this attack was like the earlier assault at the river, there were more warriors on the way. No sooner had the thought emerged in his mind when another wave of warriors appeared. The *Kazuri* fired another volley, ripping apart more sand and men. Changa grabbed Zakee by the arm and dragged him to the nearest boat.

"I hope you're worth the trouble!" he said as he shoved him into the boat with the Tuareg.

The bahari added their crossbow fire to the *Kazuri's* barrage while the others loaded the canoes and rowed away. One empty boat remained; at Changa's signal the remaining sailors sprinted for it. Changa scanned the beach as his men filled the boat, right hand holding his Damascus sword while the other held his deadly throwing knife.

Despite the barrage, the determined warriors broke through. Changa sent the closest one spinning to the ground, a throwing knife buried deep in his forehead. He ducked a spear thrust to his head, slicing the next man across the abdomen. Standing, he blocked a sword with his wrist knife and kicked another warrior back into the crowd of attackers.

"Changa, come!" his men shouted. Changa turned and high-stepped into the waves, the bowmen covering him the best they could from the rocking boat. Spears fell about him as he swam, nipping at his legs. He reached the boat and was lifted over the side. The rowers set pace immediately, climbing the surging waves to open water. The unknown warriors continued to pursue them, diving into the water and swimming furiously until there was no hope of catching the boat. The bahari cheered their escape as they pulled alongside the *Kazuri*, hoisting up the wounded before climbing into the safety of the armed dhow.

"Let's get back to the fleet," Changa ordered. The anchor was lifted and the dhow headed for open water. Zakee crouched on the deck drinking a cup of water, the bundle clutched under his arm. The Tuareg sat beside him, watching the young man with sym-pathetic eyes. Changa approached his unexpected guest, folding his arms across his chest as he looked down skeptically.

"I think it's time you showed us why our friends on the beach fought so hard to capture you."

Zakee put down his cup. "Yes, yes. You are correct."

He placed the bundle gently on the deck and pulled back the cloth, revealing a jade obelisk covered with symbols Changa did not recognize. The object emitted a mysterious glow that casted a faint green light on the prince's pale face.

Changa rubbed his chin. "Interesting, but it doesn't seem worth the trouble."

"That's what I thought," Zakee replied, "until I saw the sorceress use it with the others."

"Other obelisks?"

"No. I saw an elephant tusk, a blue diamond and a jeweled goblet. Together with the jade obelisk, the priestess was able to summon terrible evil."

"We'll show this to Panya," Changa decided. "Maybe she will know the story behind this thing."

The *Kazuri* met the *Sendibada* at the mouth of the harbor in full sail. The crew apparently had heard the cannons and broke for the harbor for assistance. The Tuareg, Changa, and Zakee transferred to the larger dhow, and were greeted on the deck by

Panya. Basheer looked at Panya and froze, his face losing color.

"Who is he?" she asked. "And what is wrong with him?"

Prince Zakee dropped to his knees. "If there was ever a reason for women to wear the burka, it is because of the beautiful women of this land. A man would truly go mad among such splendor."

"He is a flattering prince," Changa answered. "We found him fleeing a group of warriors I didn't recognize. He carried this."

Changa extended the obelisk to Panya. Her eyes went wide as she reluctantly reached out and touched the object.

"By the ancestors!" she said. Her amazed expression caught everyone's attention; there was very little Panya found interesting.

"Where did you get this?" she asked.

"It belongs to our family," the amir answered. "My great-grandfather Mamud acquired it during the Desert Jihad. He led an army against infidels dwelling at the Kahar oasis. The amir leading them was formidable, but no one can defeat the warrior carrying the shield of Allah. The infidels worshipped the obelisk, so my grandfather took it and brought it to our family mosque, locking it away."

"You know nothing of its potential?" Panya asked.

"I am a man of faith. I have no need of such things. But there is one who does. Her name is Bahati." The amir sat hard on the deck, his head falling into his hands.

Panya's eyes bulged at hearing the name and she looked at Changa. "We must take the obelisk to Zimbabwe. It is the only place it will be safe. If Bahati is attempting what I suspect, we are all in danger."

"Wait, who is this Bahati and why..."

They were startled by the clanging of the dhow bells.

"Everyone to their stations!" Changa ordered. He ran to the stern of the ship.

"Dhows approaching behind us," Mikaili said. The tall, bearded Ethiopian pointed, his piercing eyes focused on the horizon. Changa saw the ships in the distance and raised his spyglass. Five warships approached rapidly, faster than the winds that pushed them. Men scampered about the deck, preparing for boarding. At the bow of the lead ship he spotted a figure draped in a dark cloak, arms outstretched.

"It's her," the amir spat as he came to his feet. His face contorted in anger. "I will give you a thousand dinars for her head!"

"If she and her friends catch up to us, we'll be the ones losing our heads," Changa replied. "Were outgunned and out manned."

Panya came to his side and looked for herself. "She's raising a wind spell to speed their dhows."

"Can you stop her?"

"I can raise a counter spell with the obelisk. Amir Zakee?"

The prince handed over the talisman. Panya reached into the medicine pouch tied around her narrow waist, selecting a few choice ingredients and a stone pestle. She dropped the herbs into the mortar and ground them into a fine gray powder.

"Hurry, Panya," Changa urged. "We'll be in cannon range soon."

"Don't rush me, man!"

The thump of cannon fire crossed the distance to their ears. Moments later a plum of water erupted a hundred yards from the *Kazuri*.

"They're calculating range," Changa said. "Panya?"

"I'm almost done."

She sprang to her feet with the gray powder in her right fist, the obelisk in her left. She trotted to the stern of the dhow with Changa close behind.

"Will this work?"

Panya glared at the worried merchant captain. "Pray that it does."

Another cannon boomed and a geyser of water exploded a few feet from the ship. Panya extended her arm and dropped the powder into the sea. She spread her arms, reaching for the waves with the jade obelisk clutched in both hands.

"Oya, your daughter calls you! Great mother of the rivers and seas, mistress of the winds, give me your strength and your favor!"

Panya grasped the obelisk with both hands, pointing the tip towards the waves. A blast of wind shot from the object and she fell hard onto the deck. The wind struck the waters and the sea swirled. Panya scrambled back to her feet and pointed the obelisk again, this time preparing with a stronger stance. The obelisk blasted again, emitting a powerful stream of wind that churned the waters, pulling it upward into a wide spinning column. The column churned away, increasing in intensity and height as it meandered towards their pursuers. The peak of the watery spiral widened, forming a dark cloud that reached even higher as it darkened the sky. Lightening flashed and the clouds roared in response. The column became a storm, assaulting the enemy fleet with malicious fury. A towering wave rose before it, dwarfing the ships in its path. Panya convulsed and the wave crashed down on the hapless objects, burying them in water and foam. The water spout followed close behind, slashing about like a wounded snake. Storm clouds threw bolts into the maelstrom, the dhows vanishing from the sight of Changa's terrified crews.

"That's enough, Panya," Changa said.

The storms continued to pummel the area where the dhows were last seen.

"Stop it, Panya!" Changa yelled.

"I can't! I can't!" she cried.

Changa gripped the obelisk and jerked it from her hands. The storm waned, the clouds dissipating as the column of water collapsed into the sea. The commotion on the ocean surface diminished until the waves resembled those that lapped against the side of the *Sendibada*.

"Are you okay?" Changa asked Panya.

"Now you see why that thing must be destroyed," she answered, her voice coming out between gasps.

Changa extended the object to Zakee but the young man refused it.

"That thing reeks with the smell of Shaitan. I will have no part of it!"

Changa shrugged then went below to his cabin. In the corner hidden behind his map chest was a small box made of ivory, gold, and iron. Changa unlocked the box and placed the jade obelisk inside. He closed the lid tightly and locked the box with a key that he hung about his neck. Panya entered the cabin as he hid the box.

"There are eleven more talismans just as powerful," she said. "If Bahati has them, all her power will be unimaginable. We have to turn back to see if there are any survivors who could lead us to where the other objects are hidden."

Changa said nothing as he strode back on deck. "Turn us around, Mikaili," he ordered. "Let's see what we can find."

The *Kazuri* cruised among the wreckage. Broken wood and bodies bounced off the side of the dhow as it cut a wake through the carnage. Sharks searched for food among the dead, their fins slashing the surface.

"There," the prince said, pointing starboard. "It's Bahati."

The *Kazuri* veered starboard. Bahati lay still on a piece of wood just large enough to hold her.

"Come, Changa," Panya said.

Changa shrugged his shoulders and followed her to the boat. The oarsmen paddled them to Bahati as Panya worked on another concoction, rubbing the leaves together in her hands into a paste. They pulled alongside the plank and hooked it, pulling it close. The Tuareg jumped into the water and swam close to the body. He stopped trance-like as he looked upon her intense, unnatural beauty. The veiled man placed a hand on her neck then extracted a dagger from his robes.

"Tuareg, no!" Panya shouted.

The Tuareg glared at her as he pressed the blade's edge against Bahati's neck.

Panya pounded Changa's arm. "Stop him! We need her to locate the other talismans!"

Changa frowned at Panya then signaled his friend with a slight lift of his head. The Tuareg's eyes protested but he obeyed. He swam with her to the boat and the others lifted her inside. No sooner had they pulled her aboard did Panya rub the mixture on her lips. Bahati licked instinctively, sighed and was silent.

"I'll keep her sedated until we reach Zimbabwe. I hope Chipo can discover what we need to know."

A crescent moon rose over the calm night seas, its frail light barely staining the black waves. Changa paced the deck, his mind too muddled to rest. The intrusion of the amir and his mysterious nemesis worried him. As a merchant he was used to the unanticipated, but this situation involved powers beyond his knowledge.

A sound caught his attention, a painful moan drifting on the slight breeze. He hurried to the bow and saw the prince standing alone, his hands covering his face. Changa wasn't sure but it seemed the young noble was crying.

"Allah punishes me," he whispered.

Changa touched Zakee and startled him. The amir wiped his face and nodded his head.

"Forgive my display of weakness," he said. "It seems I have lost Allah's favor."

Changa shrugged. "Gods can be fickle. Tell me of this Bahati. I sense you have a deeper history than you've revealed."

"You are very perceptive," the amir confessed. He leaned against the bulwark then took a deep breath.

"My brothers and I were raised in my father's harem to protect us from the world and each other. When I turned twelve, my father took us into the world. We traveled the sultanate for two years, educated by tutors from as far as Timbuktu and learning the ways of our various subjects. After two years my father selected three of us, Yaseem, Abdul, and myself. Each of us was given a province to rule. It was our chance to show him if we were worthy to be his heirs.

"I was given Aden. I governed over the province and its port city for two years with the help of Hakim, my vizier. Under my rule the city prospered mightily. I was sure of my father's favor and knew my chance of becoming sultan was great indeed.

"One day a strange ship approached the harbor in a shroud of fog. For two days it sat motionless save for the rocking caused by the waves. No one walked its deck; no person climbed its masts to tend to the sails. A number of small craft tried to approach it but were held at bay by some strange current. Larger dhows attempting to approach were steered away by the winds.

"On the third day a boat was lowered over the side. It crept toward the dock, its occupants obscured by the distance. The harbor guard sent a message to me on the boat's approach, asking my advice. I decided to meet these mysterious visitors myself.

"I reached the docks the moment the boat arrived. Eight muscular men manned the oars on either side of the boat, their naked chests covered by a strange circular tattoo, their bare heads crowned by a simple gold band. The true surprise waited at the center of the boat. She stood almost my height with skin like the sky on a moonless night. She wore no veil, exposing her lovely face for all to see. Her garments fell about her in a sensuous way, clinging to her wide hips and full breasts with the rhythm of the sea breeze. I spent most of my life in the harem of my father surrounded by the loveliest women of the sultanate, but never had I encountered a woman as exquisite as her.

"She said her name was Bahati and she came to Oman as an ambassador of her people, the Zanj. She heard tales of the power of our land and was anxious to discuss the possibility of alliance and trade between our kingdoms. I greeted her as an equal, sending for my carriage to take us to my palace. She asked to see our city and I obliged."

A wistful look came to Zakee's face. "I must admit, by the time our tour ended I was in love with Bahati. I was determined to make her my wife. She seemed to feel the same, for she suffered my company with extreme grace and attention. For two weeks I courted her with lavish feasts and grand entertainment. She captivated me with exciting tales of her land and her people. A month after her arrival we traveled to my father's palace in a grand procession, a fine caravan loaded with gold, ivory, and exotic shells from Bahati's homeland and accompanied by the finest nobles of Aden. My father was taken by Bahati's beauty and impressed by the gifts she presented in his honor. We met later as father and son, and I expressed my intentions. Though he had reservations because she was an infidel, he understood my feelings for her. Before everyone he announced our engagement and promised a lavish dowry for his future daughter-in-law.

"I remember well the day we stood on the balcony of my father's palace, looking at the city when she took my hand and looked into my eyes.

"'Zakee,' she said, 'I came to your land seeking friendship and have discovered love instead. I am truly a happy woman.'

"But a melancholy shadow dulled her beauty.

"'What is wrong, my flower?' I asked her.

"'There was one task I hoped to accomplish here, but it seems I will fail like the others.'

"'Tell me.'

"'Two thousand years ago my people lost an object sacred to us, an artifact we consider essential to our future. Our priests decreed that anyone leaving the borders of our kingdom is obligated to search for this object and if found, return it to its rightful place.'

"'What is this object?' I asked.

"'It is a jade obelisk,' she told me."

Zakee smiled as he relived the memory. "My friend, I was a man overcome with joy and sadness. I knew of this obelisk and I could take her to it. But I also knew that by giving her this object I would be feeding into her pagan beliefs."

"'I know of this obelisk,' I finally said to her.

"Her eyes shone bright against her dark skin and she

embraced me.

"'I will take you to see it tomorrow,' I said.

"'No, no, we must go tonight,' she insisted. 'You have no idea how important this is to my people.'

"I took her to our family mosque. The imam led us to the secret room then handed me the plain oak box holding the obelisk. I showed it to her and her eyes glowed with her smile. She looked at me and I knew what I had to do. I closed the box and against the protest of the imam, I took it with us.

"The next day we set off for Aden. I wasted no time making preparations for the journey to her homeland when I arrived at the port city. In two weeks, three dhows were loaded with Bahati's dowry, supplies for the journey, and the belongings of my retinue.

"A great celebration was given in our honor the day were departed. We paraded to the docks through the decorated and crowded streets, boarded the dhows and headed to the Zanj.

"That night, far out to sea, Bahati came to my cabin.

"'I know it is your custom not to touch the bride before marriage,' she told me, 'but that custom does not apply to mine.'

"She removed her clothes and came to my bed. That night I knew I made the best choice."

Zakee's face turned grim and he said to Changa, "The next day I awoke in chains. The smell of death surrounded me as I struggled to rise from the floor of the dhow. I heard creaking and caught a glimpse of light. Footsteps came my way and I tried to raise my head to see. Bahati loomed over me, smiling.

"'My husband awakes,' she said.

"'What is going on?' I asked. 'What kind of game is this?'

"'This is no game, Zakee. I have what I want, so you are no more use to me. Your people are dead and your dhows burn.'

"'Why are you doing this?' I shouted. 'I love you!'

"Bahati laughed. 'That was your mistake, fool. I will keep you until we reach Zanj, then I will decide how you will die.'"

Zakee looked into Changa's eyes, his pain apparent.

"That was the last time I saw her. They took me ashore not far from where you found me. There was an altar on which I was to be sacrificed before the obelisk, just as those who possessed it had done for centuries before they were destroyed by my forefathers. But my ropes were loose and I broke free. I stole the obelisk and fled for my life."

"And then we found you," Changa finished. Zakee nodded. Changa walked to the bulwark and gazed into the night.

"An interesting story, but I wouldn't worry. Panya has knowledge of this Bahati. If anyone can solve this mystery, she will. She is a woman of many talents."

He reached down and lifted Zakee to his feet. "Get some rest, amir. You've had an eventful day."

Zakee managed a smile. "I will try, Changa. Thank you for listening."

Zakee went below. No sooner did he disappear when Panya came into view.

"How much did you hear?" he asked.

"Enough," Panya replied. "This is more serious than both of you realize, Changa."

Changa shrugged. "It may be, but I'll think no more about it tonight. It can wait until we reach Zimbabwe."

Changa left Panya standing alone on the deck. He hoped this all would end soon, but something in Panya's eyes told him this was just the beginning.

Chapter 2
Changa Loses a Dhow

The fleet continued to Sofala with its exotic passengers. As the sun climbed over the horizon, Changa sat at his desk in his cabin, revising the ship's log after the previous day's events and trying his best to shake an uneasy feeling about the amir and his mysterious wife. He was not the type of man to take chances without a reward. The amir was an easy decision. Once he was returned to his father there was money to make. But the sorceress? This was the situation that unnerved him.

Panya entered the cabin, her face serious. "Changa, believe me when I tell you we must go directly to Zimbabwe."

Changa put down his quill. "I trust your judgment, Panya, but you've got to give me a better reason than a feeling."

"You saw what the obelisk can do. That should be enough. The priests of Zimbabwe have the knowledge to destroy it and the others."

"Right now I don't know if there are others," Changa replied. "I do know that if I waste time chasing a hunch, I'll lose time establishing my merchant house in Sofala. My men need to be paid soon or they'll scatter to the highest bidder."

"Is that all you care about? Your money? Your time?"

Changa's expression softened. "I care about you. Your opinion means much to me. But I need more to go on an adventure which you describe."

Panya turned and stomped away.

"Panya, wait," Changa called out. He rose from his chair and walked to her. "I didn't say we won't go to Zimbabwe."

"Later is not soon enough," she said, jerking away from him. She strode away, pushing past the Tuareg and Zakee as they approached. The Tuareg looked at Changa, his eyebrows close.

"Yes, she's angry," Changa said.

"Pardon me, but I assume Panya wishes to go directly to this Zimbabwe?" Zakee asked.

Changa nodded.

"Maybe she is right. I don't know about you, but I have never seen anything with such power. It is an evil object and needs to be destroyed as soon as possible."

"I agree with you to a point," Changa replied. "I am a merchant, young amir, and as I told Panya I only take risks if there is a substantial reward. I don't deal in good and evil, only profit and loss. Let the priests handle such matters."

"Let us hope you are correct," Zakee replied. "If not, the world that allows you to make your profit may cease to exist."

"Get some rest, amir," Changa replied in an irritated tone. "In a week we will reach Sofala and discuss the terms of your ransom."

The remaining day crept by for Changa. He spent a restless night, the words of Panya and Zakee spinning in his head. The talk of spiritual matters dredged up a more personal memory, the recollection of a day that ripped him from a life of privilege to one of slavery; the day his father, ruler of Kongo, was slain. His life forward was cruel and brutal before Belay rescued him from the fighting pits and taught him the ways of the merchant. It was a life that at times could be just as brutal but always more rewarding. He never had time for spiritual matters and didn't understand them. Every situation he ever faced could be solved by either a handshake or a sword. In the end, he believed this obelisk matter would be no different.

He woke early the next morning and left his cabin for the deck. A dome of sunlight peeked over the horizon, extending an orange-red beam over the waves to the fleet. Mikaili waited for him at the helm, greeting him with a grunt, his face sporting his perpetual frown.

They walked the deck together, greeting men and shouting orders. Changa scanned his fleet and frowned.

"Where is the Kazuri?"

"Panya set out with the Kazuri hours ago," Mikaili replied.

"What?"

Mikaili stepped away from Changa. "Don't you remember? You sent the Kazuri ahead to take the obelisk and the sorceress to Zimbabwe."

Changa stormed off to Panya's chamber.

"She said she had your approval!" Mikaili shouted.

Changa kicked the door open. Panya was gone. A note sat on her desk; Changa snatched it up.

Changa, I did what I had to do. I will meet you in Sofala. Trust me.

"She steals my dhow and asks me to trust her?" Changa crumpled the note and flung it across the room. He spun and saw the Tuareg and Zakee standing in the doorway.

"Did you two have anything to do with this?"

Both men shook their heads.

"Good. That's two less people I have to kill."

Changa stomped back on deck. "Mikaili, get these dhows moving! I have a thief to catch!"

Changa could harangue his men but he could not influence the winds. The monsoon breezes took them south at a brisk pace, but not fast enough to catch Panya. His advantage was she did not know how to get to Zimbabwe. She would have to go to Sofala to find a guide.

The merchant fleet sailed relentlessly throughout the passing days, squeezing out extra speed from whatever wind they could harness. Changa remained awake, driving his crew to exhaustion as they attempted to narrow the gap between them and the *Kazuri*. As the sun climbed over the horizon on the fourth day, Changa stood at the bow, looking for signs of the *Kazuri*. Zakee cleared his throat to get Changa's attention.

"I am not experienced in sailing," the amir said. "Can we catch the Kazuri?"

"No," Changa replied. "She's is too fast and her crew is skilled. She's my best dhow."

"Panya chose well," Zakee replied.

Changa answered him with a glare which Zakee either didn't notice or ignored.

"She is a fascinating woman. Is this a common quality of Zanj women?"

"All those years in the harem and you learned nothing," Changa said.

"I learned countless ways to please a woman," the amir argued.

"But you learned nothing of a woman's mind," Changa countered. "If you did you would know how much women are like men, and how they are so different."

"Is Panya your woman?" Zakee asked.

Changa laughed for the first time since the *Kazuri's* disappearance. "Panya belongs to no man. She is a member of my crew. A senior member, but a member nonetheless."

"How did she come to deserve such an honor?"

"She saved my life," Changa replied. "I was an apprentice to Belay Gochi, a merchant in Mombasa. Belay considered me a son, so when he died he willed his business to me. His sons protested but the law is the law and they could not contest Belay's will, nor did any of them have the strength to challenge me. So they did the next best thing; they tried to poison me. I was having dinner with Kabili from Mogadishu on my birthday when a belly dancer appeared claiming to bear gifts from the Sultan of Malindi, an old friend of Belay. An army of female servant marched before us with trays of food, serving us by hand and entertaining us with dancing and magic. All of us were poisoned. Kabili died on the spot, as did the dancer and others. I don't remember much, but I was told it was the Tuareg who found Panya and persuaded her to help me. After I recovered I asked her to join my crew. I thought having someone around with her talents could be useful. I didn't know she would end up stealing my best dhow."

"Are you sure it is the dhow you're concerned about?"

"I think it is time you let working men work, young amir," Changa warned.

Zakee bowed. "I apologize for my curiosity." He strolled away, losing himself in the flurry of activity around him.

The morning light brought signs of civilization. Villages peppered the coconut palm lined shore, the adventurous man or woman waving items of trade to attract the attention of the passing fleet. Under other circumstances Changa would send a crew ashore to barter, but his focus was on Sofala and the *Kazuri*. The water traffic increased; soon the city of Sofala came into view. It was modest compared to Mombasa or Kilwa, but its success was new compared to those old Swahili trading cities. The major trade was ivory and gold, but recently iron had become just as important, for it was in high demand by the merchants of Calicut.

Changa anchored the fleet just outside the harbor. He and the Tuareg boarded a small boat and made their way to the docks. The dock master marched down the board-walk as they approached, flanked by a duo of serious looking enforcers armed with orinkas.

"What is your business in Sofala?" the dock master asked.

"I am Changa Diop of Mombasa, master of the fleet before you. I seek trade rights from your harbor."

"The traffic from Mombasa has been heavy of late," the dock master replied.

"What do you mean?"

"There was another ship from Mombasa two days ago. They came looking for a guide to take them to Zimbabwe."

"Was the master a woman?"

The dock master smiled. "Yes, a very beautiful woman. She took on a group of Shona seeking a passage home."

"Listen, I don't have much time," Changa said. "I need to land my cargo and set up a merchant house immediately. The woman you met is a thief. That was my dhow."

"I'm sorry Bwana Diop, but these matters take time. There are procedures that must be followed, taxes that must be paid, and approvals that must be received. The process could take weeks."

Changa reached his hand back to the Tuareg who gave him a heavy pouch.

"I don't have weeks. I need this matter resolved today."

Changa tossed the pouch to the dock master. He opened the pouch and nodded.

"I'll see what I can do, Bwana Diop."

The dock master left them in the company of the guards then returned with a companion. The man was as tall as Changa though not as well muscled. His darker skin told he was not Swahili though he dressed in the manner of a resident of Mombasa. He smiled as he came to Changa.

"Mbogo!" he shouted. "It's been a long time."

"Mulefu?" Changa's luck had taken a turn for the better. He hugged his old friend and laughed.

"I thought you were dead," Changa said. "I heard your dhow went down near Kilwa three years ago."

"The stories of my demise were false as you can see," Mulefu replied. "The storm did destroy the entire fleet. I managed to work my dhow close to the shore before we sank. I made it ashore with three other crewmembers."

"So how did a half-drowned sea rat end up dock master of Sofala?"

"We salvaged enough goods to buy a place in the market. The rest was Allah's will."

Changa was excited seeing his old friend but the urgency of his situation dampened his joy.

"Mulefu, I need your help."

"You have it. Come with me."

Mulefu led them to a large square building opposite the harbor. Its white walls stood three stories high, overseeing the harbor commerce. His office occupied a corner room on the highest level, the window offering a panoramic view of the harbor.

Mulefu sat at his desk and opened a thick, tattered ledger.

"There is a free warehouse where you can store your goods. I can arrange a meeting to get you started. You have a man to handle your affairs while you are away?"

"Yes."

"Good. As far as your other problem, your friend has a good head start, but the Zambezi will slow her down. There is a pilot, Kibwe, who can take you up the river. From there I'm sure you will find someone to guide you to Zimbabwe."

They returned to the docks. Changa's dhows were moored and unloaded. Crowds gathered as the cargo was counted, recorded and moved to the warehouse. Mulefu sent a man who brought Kibwe, a small, thin man with hard eyes and an intense smile.

"Kibwe," Mulefu said. "My friend Changa needs a pilot to navigate the Zambezi."

"It is my pleasure to help any friend of yours, dock master. I'm embarrassed to say, however, my price is high."

"Name it," Changa replied.

"Twenty dinars and a pound of salt," Kibwe answered.

"Is Sofala a city of merchants or pirates?" Changa bellowed. "I'll give you ten dinars and no salt!"

Kibwe bowed. "Bwana, I am a simple man of simple means. My only talent lies in reading the river, which takes me away from my wives and children for many days. How will they survive while I'm gone?"

Changa glared at Mulefu. "This is how you help a friend?" He turned his attention back to Kibwe. "Twelve dinars and a half pound of salt. I'll pay you half now and the other half when we return."

Kibwe bowed again. "Bwana is most generous. I will return with my belongings immediately."

Changa and his crew were loading supplies when they heard a commotion on the docks. Kibwe walked briskly, babbling to the three women and countless children swarming about him. He laughed, yelled, soothed and kissed his way to the dhow's walkway. After a boisterous farewell full of lamentations and ululations, Kibwe boarded the *Sendibada*.

"I am ready," he announced, ignoring the wailing of his family.

"I see why you were eager to guide us," Changa said.

The *Sendibada* set sail, taking advantage of the strong winds of an approaching rain. They sailed north, back to the mouth of the Zambezi River.

"You must be careful here," Kibwe warned. "The waters are shallow."

"Take the helm, Kibwe," Changa ordered. "That's what I'm paying you for."

Kibwe obliged, guiding the dhow into the river. He was an expert steersman, working the large dhow through the narrow stretches of the river with ease. Changa paced the deck, looking ahead for sight of the *Kazuri*, hoping that whatever they found would not be what he feared.

Kibwe looked up into the darkening sky. "We should stop for the night," he said. "There is a cove ahead with deep water. We will be safe there."

They sailed a few miles further before Kibwe steered starboard. The cove opened before them; resting in the center was the *Kazuri*.

"There she is," Changa shouted. "Let's move!"

"Wait, bwana," Kibwe cautioned. "Your dhow sits in shallow water. I suspect it has run aground."

"Dammit, Panya!" Changa yelled. He lifted his eyeglass and scanned the deck. "I see no one. They may be below deck or on shore. Kibwe, take us as close as you can. We'll free the dhow then search the area for Panya and the crew."

* * *

Deep within the forest, Panya and the crew followed their guides along a narrow road. The deeper they penetrated the woods the more she regretted her decision to take this precarious land route to Zimbabwe. Their guide assured her he could lead them with no problem. The more progress they made the less certain he seemed. The bahari obeyed her orders, although it was obvious they were uncomfortable in the dense forest with the fading light and unfamiliar ground.

Then there was the sorceress. Panya lifted her sedation to allow her to travel on her own. Though shackled by her hands and feet, Panya knew better than to think this woman was not dangerous. As an extra precaution the sorceress was gagged to prevent her from chanting spells.

"You do a foolish thing, sister."

Panya jumped, startled by the venomous voice coming from the bound sorceress.

"How do you speak to me?" Panya demanded.

"I speak mind to mind. Such is the power of the Jade Obelisk."

"Get out of my head!" Panya said.

"You are in no position to demand, daughter of Oya," Bahati replied. "The other talismans are in place. The obelisk completes the circle. You cannot stop the Joining now."

"I might not be able, but Chipo of Zimbabwe can."

Bahati's laugh rattled inside Panya's head. "Even he is not strong enough now."

The sorceress looked upward. "Your time is ended, daughter of Oya. My children are here!"

The canopy exploded in a cacophony of haunted laughter

as large figures scrambled through the branches like monkeys. Panya shifted her staff to a defensive position as the others drew their swords and bows.

"Give me the obelisk and I'll spare your life," Bahati said.

Panya raised her staff as a creature dropped in between her and Bahati. Its mottled body resembled that of a man except for large hyena head perched on its shoulders. Panya stumbled away as the creature's cackle bared its fangs. Though she had heard the stories, she'd never seen a *fisinaume*. Others fell from the trees like treacherous fruit among the terrified sailors. Panya gathered her wits quickly enough to dodge the metal covered paw swinging at her head. She struck back with her staff, knocking the beast to the ground with a blow to its hideous head. More fisinaume fell around Bahati, breaking her chains with their teeth and tearing away her gag.

"Forget the others," she commanded, pointing at Panya. "She has the obelisk!"

The beasts stopped their attack on the others and charged Panya. She ran to her crewmen, the beasts charging at her. She planted her staff into the ground and jumped over the beasts and landed among the crew.

"Give them the obelisk," Bantu, the bahari captain urged.

"No!" Panya shouted. "If Bahati gets this obelisk, everyone dies. Now fight!"

The beasts charged. They were steps away when the lead beast crashed to the ground, a familiar Kongo throwing knife buried in its head.

Changa jumped into the path followed by the Tuareg and the crew of the *Sendibada*. A cheer went up among the Kazuri *mabaharia* and they attacked the beasts with renewed vigor.

Panya smiled with relief despite the angry glare from Changa.

"I'll deal with you later," he said before jumping into the fray.

Panya stepped forward but was lifted into the air. She swung her staff upward, striking flesh and bone. She fell then crouched as more beasts surrounded her.

"Take it, take it!" Bahati shouted. The sorceress had climbed into the canopy with her companions. Panya swung her staff, clearing the beasts away but there were too many. Bahati landed on her feet before her, a victorious grin on her face.

"Give it to me," she demanded.

Panya jabbed her staff at the sorceress's face. Bahati sidestepped and kicked Panya in the stomach. She never saw the second blow; she fell to the ground in darkness. The next sound she heard was the urgent voice of Changa.

"Panya! Panya!"

Consciousness brought blinding pain. She moved her hand to the back of her head and felt blood.

Changa reached down and picked her up.

"Put me down!" she demanded.

"We need to get you to the *Sendibada*," Changa replied.

"Put me down I said!"

Changa eased her to the ground.

Panya frantically searched herself and let out a moan.

"She took it! She took the obelisk!"

"Good," Changa said. "That trinket has caused enough trouble."

Panya grabbed Changa and spun him about.

"You don't understand at all. That obelisk is the last piece of a puzzle that will mean the end of us all."

Changa looked skeptical. "Panya, I'm sure this talisman is

powerful. I saw what you did with it on the sea. But are you sure this obelisk is worth the trouble?"

"Do you know of the Mfecana?"

"Of course I do," Changa replied. "The war of Gods and Wizards."

"Remember what you were taught," Panya said. "The Gods defeated the rebellious wizards. They stripped away the wizards' power and buried their bodies in the center of the earth. But their power could not be destroyed. So the gods divided the power, locking it into twelve amulets which they hid throughout the earth."

Changa's face transformed from anger to concern. "What are you saying, Panya?"

Panya's eyes glistened. "The obelisk is one of those amulets. I don't know how she did it, but Bahati has them all."

The silence that fell among the Mombasans came from the implications of Panya's words. Changa knew what Panya would say; the thought was more terrible to imagine.

"We cannot catch her," Changa admitted. "We don't know where she is going."

"I have an idea, but I must confirm it with Chipo. Bahati will be difficult to defeat with the amulets in her possession. It will be impossible if she combines their power. Our only hope is Zimbabwe."

"Everyone back to the dhows," Changa ordered. "We sail to Zimbabwe."

They gathered the wounded and hurried back. The crew that remained behind managed to free the *Kazuri* but nightfall delayed their departure from the cove. While the others slept, Panya paced the deck of the *Sendibada*. Terrible images flashed in her mind, images she wished she could shake away.

"Lady Panya?" Zakee presented himself, bowing slightly. "The night is late and you still worry."

"I let her get away," Panya replied. "You have no idea what I may have unleashed."

"The burden rests on my shoulders, not yours," Zakee said. "If it were not for my lustful heart, Bahati would have never known about the obelisk. May Allah forgive me for my weakness."

Panya smiled at the naive prince. "Bahati knew you possessed the obelisk; that is why she sought you out. If she had not seduced you she would have killed you for it. It is because of your lust that you still live."

Prince Zakee grabbed Panya's hand and fell to his knees, startling her.

"For such a sin I must make amends," he announced. "Until we reclaim the obelisk and destroy Bahati, my life and my sword are yours to command."

"That may or may not be a help," Changa said. He strode over to Panya and Zakee.

"Both of you need to get some sleep," he said. "We have a hard day ahead and we all need to be sharp."

"He's right," Panya agreed. "I am grateful for your help, amir. I pray that it is only your sword we make use of."

Zakee stood, bowing to Panya and Changa before leaving the deck. Changa watched him disappear below.

"That boy follows you like a puppy," he said.

"Are you jealous, bwana?" Panya asked with a smile.

Changa's face remained serious. "I can't be jealous about someone who is not mine. Come now, to bed with you."

Panya followed Changa below deck. Before she entered her cabin she looked back, gazing into the night sky.

"What is it?" Changa asked.

"Nothing," she replied. "Nothing at all." She entered her cabin, keeping the knowledge of the darkening heavens to herself.

Chapter 3
The Fallen

Bahati and her fisinaume horde made good time through the forest, running at a brisk pace to the coast and the ships awaiting their arrival. She smiled as she recalled surviving Panya's destruction of her fleet. Amazing still was the fact that the witch had taken her hostage instead of allowing her to die among the debris. If she had done so, the obelisk would have disappeared into history again. Though Bahati suspected Panya was an intelligent and talented sorceress in her own right she was amused by the mistakes the woman committed. Did she actually think by binding her she would prevent her from summoning her children? Bahati laughed aloud and the fisinaume answered, their wicked noise echoing through the trees.

They emerged from the foliage to the secluded harbor. Her remaining ships rested just beyond the mouth of the bay, their white banners waving defiantly with the wind. The fisinaume recovered their boats and rowed to the ships. Bahati couldn't help but smile. After ten thousand years the amulets were together, ready for the Joining and the return of the Age of Priests.

Amra stood on the bow of the lead ship, his arms folded across his wide chest. He stared at her with his coal-black eyes, wrinkles forming on his bald head as he attempted to perform a mind-reading spell. He was another stupid man standing in her way, another fool underestimating her power. He too was a necessary evil in a world where a woman's strength had to be hidden to avoid fatal consequences. But those days were fast coming to an end. She relaxed, allowing the wizard to enter her mind and see only what she permitted him to see.

"You were successful," he stated.

"Of course," she replied.

They climbed aboard the ship and the fleet immediately set sail.

Bahati took the obelisk to her cabin and locked it away in an iron chest beside her bed. Placing her hand on the lid, she whispered a warding spell. She felt Amra's eyes on her and was annoyed.

"Go back to the deck," she hissed. "You're more useful there."

"The master told me to keep my eyes on you."

"Then you have already failed him," Bahati retorted. "Shall I tell him that you let the amir escape with the obelisk and that I had to retrieve it?"

"It was my dhows that pursued the Mombasans!"

"And it was your dhows that did not catch them. Were it not for my fisinaume the obelisk would be lost."

Amra backed away to the cabin door.

"Leave me be, Amra, and I will see to it that your death will be swift and merciful."

Amra slammed the cabin door and ran for the top deck. Bahati settled into her cushion stool, pleased with herself. There was only one more obstacle between her and the lost power of the old wizards, and she would deal with him soon.

*   *   *

The village of Katura sat so close to the banks of the Zambezi it almost spilled into the black waters. The villagers rushed to their dugouts as the *Sendibada* and the Kazuri approached. Katurians were a proud people and experienced traders, so they were jaded to the arrival of newcomers. What captivated them was the ocean going vessels crowding the river currents.

Changa marched about the *Sendibada*, working his massive arms as much as his mouth.

"Let's go!" he shouted at the crew. "Get these sails in and clear the deck!"

Panya appeared beside him, her urgent expression annoying him.

"We must hurry," she insisted. "Time slips through our fingers."

Changa's grimace didn't seem to disturb her. "I must secure the dhows," he answered. "Who knows how long we will be gone?"

As the crew finished preparing the dhow, the first trade canoes approached the ship. Kibwe stormed the bulwark.

"This is not a trading mission," he shouted. "Go away!"

"You have the tact of a drunken bull," Changa said. "These people have to tell us how to reach Zimbabwe. Let them board."

Kibwe frowned and lowered the cargo net. The villagers scrambled aboard, their goods hanging from their backs and dangling from their necks. His crew responded eagerly, happy that the villagers understood Swahili. Changa mingled among them but could find no one who either knew or was willing to lead them to Zimbabwe.

"This is impossible!" he finally said.

"I know a man in Katura that can lead you to Zimbabwe, bwana," Kibwe said.

Changa threw up his hands to keep from striking Kibwe. "Why didn't you say that before?"

"You didn't ask, bwana."

Changa, Panya, the Tuareg, and Zakee climbed down the ropes with Kibwe, boarding a canoe that waited for them on the water. They rowed to the docks of the town and the waiting horde of traders. Changa was pleasantly distracted, wishing he had time to barter. He felt a tug at his arm and turned to see Panya's serious stare as if she read his mind.

"Come," Kibwe signaled. "I will take to you to my friend."

They followed the little man down the narrow streets to a small wood and thatch house on the edge of the village.

"Kamali!" Kibwe shouted. "Come out and greet your brother!"

The door swung open and Kamali emerged. He was the exact reflection of Kibwe but many times larger. He stood at least a head taller than Changa with muscles that seemed chiseled from stone. His long arms swayed as he loped to his smaller sibling, scooping Kibwe off the ground like a child and pressing him against his massive chest.

"My brother!" he rumbled. "You have come home at last!"

"Yes, yes, Kamali. Now put me down before you kill me!"

Kamali placed Kibwe down, giving him a moment to catch his breath.

"How are my nieces and nephews?" Kamali asked.

"Mean and hungry," Kibwe replied. He turned to

Changa.

"Kamali, these are my employers from Mombasa. They need you to lead them to Great Zimbabwe."

"I will pay you well, but we must leave today," Changa added.

Kamali's smile faded. "The road to Zimbabwe is dangerous these days. Only the richest merchants can afford the journey, for mercenaries are expensive."

"We have our own protection," Changa replied. "We need only porters and supplies."

"That can be arranged," Kamali said. He turned to his little brother. "Are you coming?"

"No, brother," Kibwe said. "I've had enough adventure for one trip."

"Then come with me, bwana" Kamali said. "You and your friends are welcomed to rest in my home until I return."

Changa looked at the sad structure with a frown. "We will wait at our dhows, thank you."

"You brought dhows down the river?" Kamali looked at his brother with wide eyes. "You said you would do it one day!"

Kibwe's eyes sparkled. "And I did."

Changa grabbed the little captain by his shoulders and spun him about. "You told me you sailed dhows down the river before."

Kibwe smiled and bowed to Changa. "I did not lie to you, bwana, at least not completely. As you know, I am an accomplished dhow nahodha and I have taken ships larger than yours up many rivers. As for sailing the Zambezi, though I had never done it before, I always knew it could be done. I never had the opportunity to attempt the journey until you came along."

Changa gritted his teeth. "Did Mulefu know this?"

"Of course, bwana."

Changa tried his best to be angry but the urgency of the situation wouldn't allow it.

"I'll deal with Mulefu when we return to Sofala," he said. "As for you, Kibwe, stay away from my dhows!"

Changa turned his attention back to Kamali. "You have been to Great Zimbabwe, haven't you?"

"Yes, bwana, many times. Don't confuse my brother's ways for mine. Though I love him dearly, I am not the adventurous type, nor do I play with others' lives and property."

"Meet us at the docks when you have our supplies," Changa said. "Thirty dinars should suffice. I'll pay you half before the trip and half when we return from Zimbabwe."

Kamali shook Changa's calloused hand. "It is a fair deal. Come brother, we can catch up as I gather porters."

Kamali and Kibwe scampered off while Changa and the others made their way back to the dhows.

"Do you trust them, Changa?" Zakee asked.

"I don't trust anyone," Changa replied. "But money has a way in making men honest."

"Changa offered him twice what his help is worth," Panya said. "With that amount he's better off protecting us than killing us. It should also speed our departure."

The dhows were anchored before the village and swarming with townspeople. It was a boisterous scene; crew members haggled over prices on anything from sea turtle shells to jackal skins while the townsfolk gesticulated in mock frustration with the prices offered for their goods.

"Tuareg, stay with Panya," Changa ordered. The Tuareg nodded and Panya smiled.

"So you believe me?" she asked Changa.

"You stole my dhow," he answered. "You wouldn't have done so unless you really believed in this obelisk."

Kamali and the porters appeared at the shore hours later. The men pleased Changa; they were well-built professional porters instead of the maltreated slaves used by many Swahili merchants. His disdain for slave porters was as personal as it was practical. He would never put another man through what he had suffered most of his life.

In moments the porters packed the items and were ready to depart. Changa was disappointed when he saw the number of men burdened with the provisions for the trip. He was doubtful they would make it out of the village.

"Are you trying to cheat me, Kamali?" he demanded. "I paid for more porters than this."

"You said you were in a hurry, did you not, bwana?" Kamali replied. "We will carry half the normal provisions so we can cover more ground per day. The smaller group will allow us to take the smaller trails that will speed our travel."

Kamali patted one of the porters on the shoulder. "These are good men. They hunt as well as they carry and they are good fighters. If you ask me, I've given you more than your money's worth."

"Let's go then," Changa said. "We are wasting time."

They set out for Great Zimbabwe in the early afternoon, the sun high and hot. Kamali and the porters walked briskly despite their huge packs. Changa soon realized if anyone would be the cause of slow travel it would be one of his own. Months at sea had weakened their legs and stolen their wind. It was Changa who called for the first rest, much to the disappointment of Kamali.

"This is not a good place to rest," he protested. "There is a clearing a few miles ahead that is better."

"We may not live to see it at this pace," Changa replied.

Kamali frowned. "Please, bwana, be patient. It is not far."

It was Changa's turn to frown. "We'll continue, but if I die consider the rest of your payment forfeited!"

They reached Kamali's destination at dusk, a clearing surrounded by large mukwa trees. Changa and his crew collapsed where they stopped.

"Praise to Allah!" Zakee exclaimed. "Another step and my legs would shatter."

The Tuareg nodded to Zakee, pulling up his pants and rubbing his knees. Changa lay on his back, his chest heaving.

"We shouldn't stop," Panya argued, still on her feet. "We have to keep going." She disappeared into the forest as the porters built a fire for the night's meal. The Tuareg struggled to his feet and followed. They returned a few minutes later with armfuls of plants as the porters finished preparing the meal. Panya dumped the foliage by the fire, unpacked her cutting and cooking stone, and went to work chopping, grinding, and boiling the plants into an aromatic stew. She spooned the concoction into a cup and drank.

"Excellent," she whispered. "Everyone gather around."

Changa sauntered over to her, a bowl of steaming stew in his hand.

"What have you cooked up now?"

"Drink this," she said as she shoved the cup to his mouth and poured the liquid down his throat. Changa shoved the cup away, choking on the hot brew when a wave of energy swept his entire body. He placed his bowl of stew on the ground and took the cup from Panya, finishing the elixir with one swig. The soreness disappeared from his muscles replaced by a strange rested sensation, as if he had been carried the entire journey. His eyes saw his surroundings in crisp detail.

"What is this?"

Panya smirked. "It will keep us fresh during our journey, but we will pay a price later."

Panya and the Tuareg handed a cup of the elixir to everyone. Zakee held his suspiciously.

"Allah does not approve of such witchcraft."

The Tuareg placed a hand on Zakee's shoulder, sharing a look of concern with the young prince before drinking the brew.

The prince looked at the Tuareg doubtfully. "I don't know what caused you to take a vow of silence my friend, but I suspect you are a man of deep faith. I believe you would not commit an act without being sure of the consequences."

With that Zakee whispered a prayer and drank. He jerked, his eyes rolling back and he fell backwards to the ground.

Changa looked down at the amir. "I think you killed him, Panya."

Panya knelt beside the sprawled prince, putting her ear close to his nose.

"He's still breathing, he will be fine. The dose was probably too strong for him. He will recover soon enough."

The prince sat up suddenly as if raised by her voice. "I am ready to journey. In fact, I feel as if I could walk to the end of the earth!"

"Good," Changa replied. He made his way to Kamali and the porters who sat by the fire eating their meal.

"We are ready to leave when you are," he said.

"That is good, bwana," Kamali replied. "We have lost precious time."

"How much father to Zimbabwe?" Changa asked.

"If we set a good pace we can reach the kingdom in four

days."

"And what of the bandits following us?"

"Bandits?"

"You need to be more observant, my friend. They've trailed us since we left Katura."

"We must break camp now," Kamali urged. "The trees are too close."

"No, we are safe, for now," Changa replied. "They won't strike until nightfall. Keep your weapons close and be diligent on sentry duty."

"We will, bwana."

Two of the porters immediately took up sentry positions, scurrying into the low branches of the surrounding trees. The goods and supplies were moved to form a perimeter around them.

Changa made his way back to the others.

"Panya, go to the center with the porters." He turned to the young prince. "How good is your sword arm?"

"I was taught by the finest swordsmen of Aden," the amir answered proudly. "I also tutored under the great Andalusian sword master Al-Jafar."

"If you are alive in the morning I'll be impressed," Changa replied.

The travelers bedded down under the eyes of the sentries, but Changa did not sleep. He lay on his cot listening to the night, separating the sound of the camp from the sounds of the forest. As he expected, the sentries fell asleep soon afterwards, one falling from his perch and striking the ground with a muffled thud. The sounds of the interlopers emerged as soon as the sentries slumbered. Changa closed his eyes, concentrating on the sounds of the individuals creeping into their camp. It was a large group, ten to fifteen men total. Their urgent whispers spoke of a swift and deadly intent. Then he heard it, a low human-like laugh, rumbling from the throat of something he knew was not quite human yet not truly an animal.

Changa sprang to his feet, hurling a throwing knife at the laughing creature loping toward him. The fisinaume sidestepped the weapon and lunged. Changa braced himself but the beast was suddenly diverted by a sharp blow from Panya's iron staff.

Changa shoved Panya away from the fisinaume and the Tuareg caught her. Zakee leapt to his feet just in time to block the down stroke of a determined bandit. Before he could parry, the man's shrouded head flew from his body, dispatched by a stroke from the Tuareg's takouba. Panya, Zakee, and the Tuareg stood back to back, their arms, feet, and blades striking out at the bandits swarming around them. Changa went after the fisinaume alone. The beast had righted itself from Panya's blow and crouched, its thick legs curled under it. It leaped toward Panya and Changa threw his second knife. The whirling blade struck its mark this time, hitting the creature with enough force to bend it from its path. It landed in a heap among the bandits crowding around his desperate friends.

"Kamali!" Changa yelled. No help would come from the porters. A group of bandits held them at bay despite the hammering of Kamali's orinka and shield.

Changa knocked a bandit aside with a throwing knife as he sliced another with his Damascus. A bandit before him raised his iron sword to block Changa's down stroke. The man's expression changed from smirking to horror as Changa's blade shattered his weapon and cleaved his skull. Changa kicked the man off his sword. He saw his companions – Panya holding off her attackers with wide swings of her staff, the Tuareg's tandem swords a lethal blur, and the young prince struggling desperately, his life frequently spared by the timely intrusion of the Tuareg's skillful swordplay.

Changa stepped forward and was hit in the midsection and knocked onto his back, sword and throwing knife flying from his hands. The fisinaume straddled him, holding him down with one massive arm as the other raised a dagger above him. Changa threw up his left arm, taking the knife in the flesh of his forearm. He clinched his fist; the muscles of his arm tightening around the blade, and with a painful yell yanked his arm away, snatching the knife from the fisinaume's grip. Changa slammed his right hand into the creature's throat and the left hand followed. The fisinaume reached for Changa's throat but stopped, its eyes widening as it began to lose its breath. It clawed at Changa's hands, and then pummeled his wounded arm, attempting to break his grip. Changa's strength held as he dug deep into the depths of endurance developed from years of pit-fighting. The creature's flailing weakened then stopped. With its last breath it emitted a piercing shriek that cut through Changa's ears. The death wail took the fight out of its companions; the remaining bandits broke away and disappeared into the darkness.

Changa threw the dead hyena-man aside and struggled to his feet. The Tuareg set about the grim task of finishing off the wounded and dying bandits. Panya looked at the carnage around her then leaned heavily on her staff, wincing. Changa saw blood running down her calf and rushed to her side.

"Help me sit," she said.

Changa eased her to the ground beside Zakee who looked at the Tuareg with disbelieving eyes.

"It was like fighting beside a *sirocco*!" he gasped.

Changa smirked as he tore away the fabric of Panya's pant

leg, revealing a deep wound on her thigh. She grabbed his hand before he could inspect the wound.

"You have death on your hands," she said. "You'll infect it. Bring me my bag."

He found her bag close by and handed it to her.

"What about your arm?" she asked.

"I'll tend to it later," Changa replied. "I need to check on Kamali and the porters."

Kamali and his companions had not fared well. Of the eight only three survived. Kamali knelt beside one man who lay on his back, holding his abdomen and moaning. Kamali looked up at Changa, his eyes glistening.

"Can the priestess help him?" he asked.

Changa knelt and moved the man's hand aside. "She can ease his pain," he replied. Kamali whispered to his friend in their native tongue.

"He would be grateful," Kamali said.

The other porter leaned against a tree, staring at Kamali and his dying friend. He returned to Panya's side. The Tuareg had completed his chore and stood by, his arms folded across his chest. His eyes met Changa's and Changa nodded in agreement.

"If we want to make Great Zimbabwe we must leave tonight while the bandits gather their wits. I believe they followed the fisinaume. With it dead it may take them a while to revive their courage and attack again."

"I don't think we are strong enough," Panya said.

"We are closer to Zimbabwe than the village," Kamali said. "We should go on."

Changa smiled at the man, impressed by his resolve despite the loss of his friends.

"I can make potions to heal us," Panya said. She smiled

and went to work.

Changa finally sat down and tended to his arm. Only the Tuareg and Zakee went unscathed, but by the look in the Tuareg's eyes it was obvious he had second thoughts on saving the amir's life. The young noble followed the silent swordsman every step, talking constantly on the battle and the blessing of life the Tuareg bestowed on him.

"The potions are ready," Panya announced. They all drank and felt the effect, though not as intensely as the first round. They buried the dead porters and set out for Zimbabwe under the dim moonlight.

Four days later the dense forest loosened its grip, exposing the hilly rock-strewn kingdom Benametapa, the home of Great Zimbabwe. Changa walked beside Panya, the sorceress leaning on his shoulder as she limped on her wounded leg. She refused to be carried though everyone insisted, and she kept the pace in defiance of her pain. Zakee was quiet, resting his mouth after babbling throughout the night, much to the Tuareg's apparent relief. Kamali and the still unnamed porter kept their own company, their faces heavy with the death of their comrades.

Though the reason for this journey weighed on his thoughts, Changa could not suppress his ever calculating merchant mind. He memorized every twist and turn of the road, the small hills and tall trees, landmarks stored for a later date. Once he established himself in Sofala he would return to trade in this land, without the cost of someone like Kamali. Not only was Benametapa the homeland of Great Zimbabwe, it was also the home of the secret mines that held the gold dust, iron, and gemstones that spurred the growth of Sofala.

A long hill rose over the horizon before them, a rock-vested vanguard peering down on the road snaking through its shadow. As they came closer they realized the granite boulders were connected by walls. Changa spotted movement on the ramparts. "It is the first of many," Kamali said. "They are stone citadels, and they guard the road to Great Zimbabwe."

"The welcoming committee approaches," Changa said.

A group of men scurried down the hill, their assegais extended high over their heads, covering the distance with amazing speed. They stopped a few paces away, leveling their spears to chest height. The tallest of the warriors stepped forward, one hand resting on his sword hilt, a jeweled orinka in his right hand signifying his rank.

"You have entered the kingdom of Benametapa," the man said. "You shall go no further."

"We have urgent business in Zimbabwe," Changa replied. "I am Changa Diop, Grand Merchant of Mombasa..."

"Your title means nothing to me," the man interjected. "I am Siluwe, commander of this outpost. This orinka gives me authority and I say only the subjects of the Bene are allowed beyond this point."

Changa looked at Kamali for help.

"It is true," the guide replied. "The trading parties always stop here."

Panya came forward, her hand digging into her bag.

"We come on urgent business with the Shona," Panya declared as she stepped forward. "We demand safe passage to Great Zimbabwe under your protection."

Panya extracted a small ceremonial sword, its crescent blade plated gold, the hilt wrapped with silk and studded with diamonds, emeralds, and rubies.

"Where did you get that?" Siluwe demanded.

"Is this not the symbol of the Bene?"

The commander was confused and angry. "Yes it is, but how…"

"Then I demand safe passage to Great Zimbabwe for me and my companions."

Siluwe frowned. "I hope that sword was acquired honestly. If not, your visit to Great Zimbabwe will not be pleasant. The Bene is not a man to be toyed with."

"You're wasting our time," Panya said. "Our business is urgent."

The warrior spun and signaled his men. "Come with us."

The party followed the warriors to the outpost. Changa moved closer to Panya, a smirk on his face.

"I'm in no mood to be killed," he whispered. "Where did you get that?"

"I have been here before," Panya revealed, "though not from this direction."

"You must have made quite an impression on the Bene to leave with a passage totem."

Panya looked up at Changa, grinning. "He wished to make me his wife but I refused."

"And he just let you walk away?"

"Yes he did, though I'm sure he had a change of heart once the sleeping potion I gave him wore off."

The outpost was a modest camp consisting of a number of small cylindrical houses for the warriors and a large rectangular wooden storehouse. Beyond the walls cattle grazed while young boys tended plots of millet and yams. They were given a small but filling meal before setting out for the city. Kamali and his companion remained behind at the outpost. Changa shook the man's hand then handed him one of his throwing knives.

"Go to the Sendibada and ask for Mikaili," he said. "Show

him this knife and he will pay you the balance I owe."

"Thank you, bwana. I hope your journey to Great Zimbabwe is swift and safe."

Kamali's wish was not to be. Gloomy clouds appeared the morning they departed, their bulbous shapes hanging low over the landscape. By noon the clouds released their burden, turning the road before the travelers into a mess of mud and waterholes.

"This is Bahati's work," Panya said. "She has summoned the clouds to slow us down."

"The rainy season begins," Siluwe replied, "nothing more."

The rain increased, falling so heavy they could not see ahead. Everyone held their shields over their heads as they sloshed ahead. The sky became so dark it was hard to tell whether or not night would be soon upon them.

"There is a cave not far from here," the warrior shouted to Changa. "We should seek shelter until the rain ends."

Changa agreed. They made their way to another rock strewn hill. Siluwe led them through a narrow gap between two huge boulders into a massive cave. Water trickled into the roof of the cave through a small opening, a natural outlet for campfire smoke.

"I feel I've been wet all my life," Zakee exclaimed. "Praise Allah for this cave!"

The warriors started a fire with wood stored away for travelers. Zakee stretched out on the cave floor before the fire. Panya sat beside him, dropping her bag and massaging her exposed calves.

"Pardon me Panya, but may I ask if this is your homeland?"

"Yes, you may ask, Zakee," she replied, "and no, this is not my homeland."

Zakee sat up. "I thought it was because you possess the object for safe passage."

"I was here many years ago, more than I choose to remember. The Bene wished to marry me but I refused."

"I would think a proposal of marriage from a sultan would be an honor to one of your station."

Panya glared at the prince. "You no nothing of my station, boy. Besides, an unwanted proposal from any man, sultan, Bene or beggar is no honor at all."

She stalked away, finding an area isolated by large rocks to rest.

"You have insulted her, Zakee," Changa said as he approached.

"It wasn't my intention," Zakee replied. "I assumed since she was a sorceress she was born of the caste."

Changa sat beside Panya, taking a throwing knife from his satchel and inspecting the blades.

"Panya is a princess, a runaway bride from an arranged marriage. She is more than qualified to be a wife of a sultan."

Zakee bowed deeply to cover the shame on his face. "I apologize for any insult I may have bestowed upon you."

Panya wave her hand. "You didn't know. Besides, that was long ago and far away. I am as you see me."

"Your noble blood explains your beauty," the prince continued. "You would be well-received in Aden."

"Leave it alone, Zakee," Changa said. "Stop letting your loins speaks through your mouth."

The others laughed as the prince sulked away to another part of the cave.

Everyone settled into their corner to rest except Panya.

She sat by the cave entrance, staring into the clouds.

"The rain has stopped," she announced. "We should be on our way."

"It will be dark soon," Siluwe replied. "We will wait until morning."

Panya stormed up to the man. "Do you realize how important this mission is? We mustn't delay!"

Siluwe stood and Changa stood as well, his throwing knife in his good hand.

"Your sword gives you safe passage," he replied, his eyes on Changa. "It does not give you authority over me. Leave if you wish, but I and my men will remain here until the morning."

The warrior glanced at Changa then lay on his cot to sleep. Panya loomed over him, her shoulders rising and falling in anger, her small hands tightly fisted. Changa place his heavy hand on her shoulder.

"Let it go," he advised. "We are at their mercy for now."

"If only we came from the west," she hissed. "I would know the way myself." She marched away and sat before the dying fire, hugging her knees to her chest like an angry child, the waning flames dancing in her eyes.

"Get some rest," Changa said. "We can encourage our guides to leave at first light." With that he laid himself down and fell immediately to sleep.

It was instinct that woke Changa. He slowly opened his eyes to the darkness of the cave. The rain had subsided from downpour to drizzle, the fire embers casting a faint light which outlined his slumbering companions. Panya slept where she sat, her arms folded around her legs, her head resting on her knees. The others were scattered about the fire. He searched the cave with wary eyes, thankful for the heightened effect Panya's potion had on his senses. Something moved above, working its way among the stalactites hanging from cave ceiling. He slipped his hand into his knife bag and eased his hand around the grip of a throwing knife, concentrating his senses on the canopy. He could smell it, a damp, musky odor not much different from the cave except for the organic scent of an unwashed creature.

Debris fell into the embers and Changa sprang to his knees, locking his eyes on the dark space overhead. He followed the shadow creature as it scrambled across the ceiling towards him. Changa moved away from the others, leading the creature deeper into the cave towards an uncluttered space. His heel struck an object and he tumbled backwards, sprawling onto his back and dropping his knife. The creature plummeted from the cave ceiling, its features coming into view moments before landing on him.

It resembled the mountain apes Changa had seen in the markets of Kilwa, though instead of black its hair and skin were ashen like cave stone. Its red eyes were small and useless, its nose and ears much larger than its forest cousins. Changa lost his breath as the beast smashed against him, sinking its teeth into his shoulder. Changa bit back a yell, cupped his hands and struck the beast over its ears. It opened its mouth in a silent scream, releasing Changa's shoulder and falling away into the recesses of the cave.

Changa followed, yanking the leather straps from his wrist knives and snatching another throwing knife from his waist. He threw the knife at the silhouette of the creature and was rewarded with the sound of contact. Changa rushed forward to finish the beast and a shaggy gray arm bashed his shoulder, the force propelling him into the cave wall. He careened off the stone and fell hard on his back. The cave ape straddled him, the knife embedded in its chest. It lifted its massive hands over its head then brought them down. Changa rolled and the paws struck stone. He kicked out and smiled as the beast's knee snapped then sprang to his feet as the cave ape fell upon its back. Changa yanked the knife from the cave ape's chest and sank it into its throat. It flailed its arms, knocking Changa aside as its mouth gaped. Its chest heaved then the creature fell still. Changa kicked it to make sure it was dead then allowed the pain of his struggle to overwhelm him. As he fell to his knees, Panya called out to him.

"Changa, where are you? What's happening?"

He turned his head as she approached holding a small torch in her hand.

"You shouldn't be back here," she scolded him. "Bahati could be...Changa, you're hurt!"

Panya ran to him then saw the body of the cave ape.

"Oya protect us!" she exclaimed. Her shout woke the others. Siluwe was the first to appear, recognizing the beast on the ground and stumbling back.

"A *koloshe*! You killed this by yourself?" he asked, wide-eyed.

"I would have loved the help," Changa replied.

The other warriors appeared and were just as shocked. The Tuareg came upon the scene, looked at the creature and Changa, nodded his head in approval and went back to sleep. Zakee joined the Zimbabweans in wonderment.

"Great is the warrior that slays the demons of Shaitan!" he said. "You truly deserve the respect of your men."

"You can show your respect by dragging this thing outside before it starts to stink," Changa said. "Panya, can you do something about this?"

Panya fell to her knees and went to work on his shoulder.

"You could find an easier way out of this journey without taunting monsters."

"If I hadn't awakened this trip would have been over for all of us," he replied. "Just hurry up so I can get some sleep!"

He awoke the next morning with Panya asleep beside him. Though still bandaged his shoulder was painless, renewing his respect for Panya's healing abilities. The sun fought the receding clouds and made its way into the cave, a faint beam of light penetrating the gloom at the back of the cave. Changa grasped Panya's shoulder, shaking her gently.

"Come, it is time to go."

Panya was up immediately, gathering her items. The others moved about laconically, gathering their energy for the day.

"We should reach Zimbabwe today," Siluwe said. "Then we will see if the Bene will let you live."

Chapter 4
Kintu

The party made slow progress, the warriors apparently in no hurry to reach Zimbabwe. Villages grew more numerous along the road, the hillside herders tended cattle as women and children worked the terraced fields. The farmers were noticeably different from the warriors; short and stocky with broad features and dark smooth skin. They turned their eyes away from the warriors in respect, but Changa noticed the disdain as well. It was a look he'd held before, a gesture any ex-slave was more than familiar with.

The road climbed toward a large fortress resting upon a boulder strewn hill. Like the other forts along the highway, the granite slate walls joined natural boulders jutting from the earth, but these walls rose higher and grew wider. Large soapstone birds perched on pedestals atop the walls, staring down on them with lifeless eyes. The scattered villages gradually meshed into a continuous vibrant city, a metropolis that despite its different people and structures, reminded Changa of the Swahili trade cities.

The road was crowded with people making their way to the central market. Though the travelers respected the authority of Siluwe and made way, their progress was nevertheless slowed. They covered the distance from their first glimpse of the hilltop citadel to the structure itself in the same time it took them to reach Zimbabwe from the cave. They halted at the base of the hill.

"Muchese, go to the fort and ask them to send a runner to the Bene," Siluwe commanded.

A youthful warrior with a crooked smile and wide eyes sprinted up the causeway to the castle. Moments later he emerged, followed by two medicine-priests. They approached the travelers, pushing past Siluwe to stand before Panya. Both priests were bare-chested, medallions of gold hung about their necks, beaded head rings encircled their shaved heads. Long red kilts covered their torsos, extending down to just above their sandaled feet. The older of the two bowed slightly and smiled.

"Panya, it has been a long time," he said.

Panya smiled and returned the bow. "Lusungu, it is good to see you."

Siluwe's face crinkled with disappointment. Panya smirked.

"Zimbabwe has suffered long without your beauty, but it was foolish for you to return. The Bene hasn't forgiven you for leaving. He will not be happy to learn you have returned."

"The news I bring is worth the Bene's wrath," she replied. "The talismans of the Old Ones have been discovered."

Lusungu's mouth hung open. "You lie!"

"I possessed the Jade Obelisk myself. I tried to bring it here for your protection but we were attacked and it was taken."

"We will take you to Chipo. Come."

They began to follow but Siluwe stopped them.

"You and the Swahili can go. The white man and the covered one must stay with us."

"They are my companions," Panya insisted. "What is your problem?"

"It is our law, Panya," Lusungu replied. "I assure you they will be safe."

They passed through the gates and entered Zimbabwe. The road descended into a shallow valley of grass and trees. Stone homes with thatch roofs were scattered about the sloping hillside populated by medicine-priests and soothsayers serving the Bene. The road ended before the Great Enclosure, the palace of the Bene. The wall surrounding the compound stood the height of five warriors and was nearly as thick. It was elliptical, following the contours of the earth as it encircled sacred ground. Inside the secrets of the blacksmiths were hidden away, magic known only to the molders of iron and gold. The Bene was a member of their brotherhood, as were all Benes. Changa took his hand from his sword hilt long enough to remove the leather bands covering the blades of his wrist knives. If this Bene decided his personal feelings were more important than the fate of the world, Changa would make sure he and Panya would at least live beyond the day.

The council hall stood before the Enclosure, an expansive structure built of woven grass, the floor glittering brightly with gold-flecked granite squares. The dome building rose as high as the enclosure walls, the woven geometric patterns painted with contrasting reds, yellows, blues, and greens. The Royal entourage held council at the center of the dome, the Bene resting upon his royal stool, his slim muscular build a perfect representation of his people. A leopard skin cape draped his shoulders, cascading down to the floor. A matching crown with diamond studded gold bands rested upon his head. A gold bar hung from his neck, the pictograph in the center an exact replica of the image imprinted on Panya's sword. The Bene's orinka mirrored the opulence of his wardrobe. The ebony wood shaft sported bands of gold that spiraled down the ivory handle. The head of the club was a sphere of polished iron crusted with large diamonds.

On either side of the Bene were his personal guards, each man naked to the waist with a gold band wrapped around his right bicep. Each one wore a leopard-painted wrap around his waist; each man's sword rested in finely decorated wooden scabbards. They each held tall spears crowned with large broadleaf spear heads and narrow leaf shaped shields of rhinoceros hide. The Bene's interpreter stood beside him covered in a simple tunic that hung low to his knees. Beside him sat Chipo, the grand priest of Benametapa. Like the griot, Chipo dressed simply, a white tunic covering his narrow build. He leaned against his staff, his gray eyebrows rising as he smiled at Panya. A pointed gray beard covered his sharp chin, joining the thin gray moustache that spilled around the corners of his reddish lips.

The elders and visitors seated before the Bene made way for the approaching strangers. As Changa and Panya stepped into the hall, the Bene turned his back to them. The two of them followed the lead of their escort, dropping to their knees and touching their foreheads to the volcanic stone.

"Rise and be recognized," the interpreter said. "Bene Showe Maputo, father of the Shona and Bull of Zimbabwe, welcomes isiPanya back to his kingdom. He realizes you bring a message of grave consequence and he will not delay your meeting with Chipo."

"Great is the wisdom of the Bene and deep is the well of his kindness," Panya replied.

"Who is the man who comes in our presence with our adopted sister?" the interpreter asked.

"He is Changa Diop of Mombasa, a merchant whom I serve as a healer. He has pledged himself and the lives of his men to aid us against this threat."

The interpreter tilted his head towards Maputo before

speaking again.

"He wears the clothes of a Swahili but his name and face is Bakongo. It is a face well known by our warriors to the west."

Changa looked up, his hand moving to his sword hilt. Panya grabbed his wrist before it reached the ivory handle.

"You grace us with your wisdom," she replied. "Changa is Bakongo by blood but he is Swahili by tradition. He was taken from his homeland as a slave when just a boy and has since lived his life among the Swahili."

The interpreter stood silent for a moment. "A friend of Panya is a brother to us all. Go and have your time with Chipo. May the ancestors aid us in this quest."

Maputo stood and his bodyguard gathered about him. They blocked the view of the monarch, but not before Maputo turned, his eyes meeting Panya's. He smiled and then turned away as the warriors concealed his departure into the Great Enclosure.

Changa grasped Panya's hand. "It seems the Bene still carries feelings for his adopted sister."

"Be quiet, Changa!" Panya warned. "Chipo will hear you."

"He only states what is obvious to us all," Chipo said as he rose. "My daughter has finally returned."

They embraced, Panya holding the old wizard close, burying her face in his beard.

"It is so good to see you, baba," she said. "I only wish it was under better circumstances."

"Come, child," Chipo said. "We will talk as we walk."

Changa and Panya followed the priest up a narrow road that meandered over a small rise to his home. The building was similar to the Great Enclosure but modest in size, the stone walls much lower and half as thick. They sat before a fire outside the compound, the body of a young goat roasting slowly over the open flame tended by Chipo's servants. Panya shared the story of their adventure before coming to Zimbabwe. Her words seem to add weight onto the old man's shoulders. He slumped on his stool, his free left hand massaging his wrinkled forehead.

"It is as I feared," Chipo said. "For years I have seen the signs but I denied them. I convinced myself no one could know where all the totems lay hidden. Not even I have such knowledge."

"You can stop her," Changa said, his voice hopeful.

Chipo's brow wrinkled. "If she has all the talismans, she is too powerful for me to confront."

Panya's head sagged; Changa's heart raced on hearing Chipo's words. He had assumed all along this priest would be able to finish this business. Now he feared this nightmare was just beginning.

"So Bahati will come to destroy us?" he asked.

"We still have a chance," Chipo replied. "I cannot defeat her, but there is one who can."

Panya came to her feet. "You would do this? You would summon him?"

Chipo look at Panya with sadness. "We have no choice."

"He is as dangerous as she. He betrayed the gods!"

"If you know a better way, Panya, please tell me."

Panya opened her mouth as if to answer, then dropped her head.

"It is settled then," Chipo said. He grasped Panya's hand, his eyes on Changa.

"Come. There is much to do."

*   *   *

The Bene enlisted the aid of the entire city to help Chipo and Panya prepare their summons. Talismans, amulets, and all types of gris-gris were gathered into carts. The day was spent in ceremony which included the sacrificing of bulls and goats and the preparation of the feast to come afterwards.

By dusk everything was assembled before Chipo's compound. Torch lamps surrounded the structure, the light dancing on the painted patterns on the shields of the Bene's bodyguards. Drummers surrounded the granite base of the compound, their faces hidden by spirit masks carved from ebony wood. The compound had been evacuated of everyone except for Chipo, his acolytes, and the Bene's entourage. Changa, Panya, the Tuareg, and Zakee sat with the priest.

The drummers' pace increased as dancers leapt into the center of the torch circle, summoning the presence of the gods and the ancestors with their reverent movements to the furious rhythm. The tempo eased and the drummers hummed, their deep voices resonating in Changa's bones. Though there were no words to their song, the intent was obvious. Changa felt a change in the air, a sensation that seemed to increase with each moment.

"We shouldn't be here," Zakee whispered to Changa. "This is evil. If I had known the obelisk would lead to this, I would have destroyed it."

"But you didn't, young prince. I don't believe in many things, my life has been too harsh to allow much for faith. But I do believe in fate. We were all meant to be here at this moment for some purpose. So the choice was never yours, Zakee. Let fate take its course."

The Tuareg placed his hand on Zakee's shoulder and

squeezed. He reached into his shirt and extracted a silver diamond shaped cross etched with geometric patterns, each corner tipped with gold beads. He touched it to his face veil then placed it back into his shirt.

"I understand, my brother. My faith is strong. I shall not be swayed by the events of this night."

Chipo strode into the center of the circle as the dancers disappeared into the darkness. Draped in a leopard skinned cape and a tall antelope mask, he walked with a power beyond his small frame. The humming faded and the drummers switched to a simple heartbeat rhythm. The attendants swayed to the primal pace, the timing of life within themselves.

Chipo threw his hands up, the cape falling from his shoulders. He wore only a loincloth, every inch of his body covered with intricate tattooed glyphs, the story of the battle between the gods and the rebellious wizards told on his skin. He stood motionless, staring into the night sky.

"Ancestors! I stand below you, humbled by your infinite wisdom. A storm comes, a maelstrom created by the greed of man. It has festered and spread beyond our feeble talents. We come to you, hoping you will grant us favor and save us from ourselves once again.

"We understand our summons demands payment. We know there is a price to be paid for your help. I offer myself to you, a humble servant, and a man whose spirit, while nothing in your sight, towers above the others before him like the giraffe over the bush mouse. Accept my gift so that my people may be spared."

Panya entered the circle, her upper body naked like Chipo's, a leopard skirt wrapped around her waist held in place by golden cords. A string of cowries encircled her slender neck, her hair braided Zimbabwe style. Braced between her hands was a jeweled calabash, the contents escaping in a dense, gray smoke. Changa watched her as she approached Chipo, her eyes glistening with reluctant tears. Chipo took the calabash, whispered to Panya and she stepped away. She halted at the edge of the circle and sat, folding her legs beneath her thighs and placing her hands in her lap.

Chipo removed his mask and drank from the calabash. No sooner did he take the container from his lips did he drop it, spilling the remaining contents. He collapsed onto his hands and knees, coughing as his body shook. Panya began to rise but Chipo extended his open hand to her.

"No," he ordered, "stay where you are."

He convulsed and the skin of his back split open, a spray of blood flung into the air over him. The slit coursed down his spine, divided at his buttocks and sprinted down his thighs to his heels. He jerked again and the slit made its way up his back and across his neck.

Chipo's hands gave way and he fell to his elbows, his body shaking violently.

"He is coming!" he managed to shout. "He is coming!"

He collapsed onto the blood stained stone. Bare muscles emerged from his still body, a strange metamorphosis emerging from a human cocoon. The figure rose, possessing a body that expanded beyond the size of Chipo. As he grew, Chipo's shell was absorbed into it, disappearing like spilled liquid wicking into dry cloth. The figure stood as tall as the old elephants of the forest, its massive limbs tight with hard muscles. Features formed on the face, a countenance that expressed the strength of the gods and perfection impossible among ordinary men.

"Who speaks for you?" he asked. The sound of his voice

reverberated inside Changa's head – not in Swahili, but in his native Bakongo.

Panya rose to her feet and walked timidly to him. Before she could speak, the warrior smiled.

"Priestess, I have use of you. Make the potion I give to you."

Panya bowed and strode away, though Changa saw nothing pass between them. She signaled the acolytes to follow and they did so, staring back at the demi-god.

The man turned towards Maputo. The Bene prostrated himself before him.

"What do you wish?" Maputo asked.

"One hundred of your best warriors."

"I can summon a thousand times more."

"One hundred is all I need," the massive man replied.

Maputo scampered backwards and faded into the darkness, shouting orders along the way. The warrior strode to the center of the courtyard, his body still wet with Chipo's blood.

"Hear me! Your world is in danger. The ancestors have answered your pleas, but you must continue to pray for their strength. The wheel that spins this fate has turned long and is almost spent. Pray that it keeps spinning until I return."

The warrior walked away to the Great Enclosure. The doors swung wide as he approached, the mysterious blacksmiths face down along the granite path leading to their secret workshops.

"Come with me, brothers," he said to them. "We have work to do."

The night roared with the sounds of day as the Zimbabweans prepared for a different kind of war. The acolytes continued to drum, pushing the dancers with their tireless rhythms. The strange sounds emanating from the Great Compound were ever present, kindling curiosity about the motives and skills of this celestial warrior.

Panya sweated over a large iron cooking pot set up hastily before Chipo's compound, concocting the potion given to her by the warrior. Changa helped, dumping the various ingredients into the boiling brew, sweating from the intense heat.

"Is this the same potion you made for us in the forest?"

Panya paused, placing her hands on her hips and dropping her head in exhaustion. Grief was clear on her face although she had mentioned nothing of Chipo's sacrifice.

"Yes it is."

Changa stirred the brew. "I don't see how this is going to help us fight a sorceress."

"We have to trust him," Panya replied as she wiped sweat from her forehead. "He has done this before."

"Is he a god?"

"No, but he is as close as we'll ever be to a spirit while we live. He is Kintu, The Betrayer."

Changa laughed despite his weariness. "We place our hope in a betrayer?"

Panya did not smile. "Kintu fought for the ancestors against the old priests," Panya explained. "He was their greatest champion, defeating any challenge the priests set against him. But the spirits are like men, and like men even the strongest has its weakness. The priests discovered Kintu's."

"What was this flaw that brought him down?" Changa asked as he stirred.

"Kintu was created for war," Panya continued. "The priests knew that love and hate can sometimes be the same emotion, so they created someone for Kintu to love."

Changa stopped stirring. "Bahati?"

Panya took the paddle from Changa and continued to stir.

"Yes. She was the most beautiful woman in the world. Kintu dropped his weapons as soon as he saw her. Bahati whispered into Kintu's ear as they made love before the gods and the priests. Afterwards, Kintu denounced the gods and left to fight for the priests. Despite losing Kintu's strength the gods still prevailed. Bahati was destroyed, or so it was thought."

"Kintu was spared despite his betrayal?"

"The ancestors still loved him. They banished him to the Zamani to stay unless he was summoned to serve their purposes. Only when he has proven his loyalty to them will he be allowed to leave and move on to the spirit world."

Panya stopped stirring then stuck her finger into the brewing mix. She tasted it and nodded her head.

"It is done."

The gates of the enclosure swung wide and the massive warrior emerged. He was no longer naked. Kintu wore cloth breeches covered by iron studded leather strips. His chest was still bare, his head covered by a metal cap studded with spikes. Metal bands gripped his biceps with the familiar wrist knives protecting his thick wrists. His left hand held the largest broadleaf shield Changa had ever seen. It was all metal, covered with the cow skin leather pattern of Maputo's herd. He held a massive orinka in his right hand, a studded war club of solid iron. A bow and wooden quiver rested on his back, the quiver holding one arrow. A tall assegai with a wide blade separated the bow from the quiver. Kintu strode to the boiling pot and gazed at its contents.

"Is it done, priestess?" he asked.

Panya nodded, extending a gourd of the brew. The warrior drank and nodded his head in approval.

"You are skilled, daughter of Oya," he said. Kintu placed his weapons down and picked up the paddle. Bending over the cauldron, he spit into the elixir and stirred. Taking the calabash, he dipped into the elixir and tasted again.

"Give this to all the warriors," Kintu ordered. "As soon as they finish we leave for Madagar."

Kintu picked up his weapons and marched away to the compound followed by the blacksmiths. The Bene arrived moments later with his hand-picked warriors, one hundred as Kintu had requested. They were hard bodied men with serious faces and the scars of battle visible on their bodies.

"We are here to serve you," Maputo said as he lay on the ground before the warrior.

"Take your place with the others and drink the potion," Kintu ordered. "It will give you strength for the battle to come. You will not be immortal, but you will have a chance to see the end of this adventure."

Changa was the first in line, the Tuareg and Prince Zakee behind him. He was raising his calabash to drink when Kintu approached him, placing his massive hand on Changa's shoulder. "You will stay with me, Bakongo, as will the priestess. Your strength will be useful. Once you drink, lead the warriors to the Great Enclosure. My brothers have prepared your weapons."

"Who will we fight?" Changa asked.

Kintu smiled. "I don't know. Bahati will not disappoint us, however."

Changa drank, hoping to drown the dread Kintu placed in his heart. The sensation of the potion was similar to what he'd consumed earlier, but the effect seemed more pervasive. The earlier potion masked his fatigue; this concoction eliminated it altogether. Pains from his years as a pit fighter dissipated. He looked in amazement as old scars on his body disappeared. The calabash in his hand became so light that as he passed it to the Tuareg he almost threw it.

"I feel reborn," he whispered.

"You are," Kintu replied.

The others filed past the cooking pot to receive their dose of the elixir. Changa gathered them as they finished and led them to the Enclosure where the blacksmiths stood before a pile of newly forged weapons as fine as those in the marketplaces of Mombasa. He chose a metal spiked shield and assegai, but preferred to use his own Damascus sword. He was pleased to see a stack of throwing knives molded into the Bakongo style, duplicates of the ones he carried on his waist.

"For you, bwana Changa," one of the blacksmiths said.

Changa hefted the weapon and was pleased. "Your work rivals the best Bakongo blacksmiths."

Changa went to Kintu. The celestial warrior stood before the gates of the enclosure as the other warriors gathered. They formed an armored ring, each man radiating the mystical energy of the potion. Kintu looked among them and nodded. Changa felt a brush on his shoulder and saw Panya at his side, dressed in armor and carrying a metal staff similar to Kintu's spear.

"This is no place for you," he said.

"That's not your decision," Panya replied. "Kintu says I must come."

Changa was not happy. "This is foolish. How can so few men stop a goddess?"

"We may not be able to," Kintu answered. "Long before your grandfather's grandfather walked this land the gods and priests fought for control. Now you must fight for the gods, not to control the world, but for its very existence. Your ancestors and your families depend on you to honor them with your bravery in battle."

Kintu crouched then sprang over them, landing on the road with a crash that shook the ground. Changa broke the circle and followed, joined by the other warriors. Together they ran up the hill leading to the gate. The doors swung aside and the army passed through Great Zimbabwe in an instant, spurred by the elixir in their veins.

Changa ran full speed throughout the night with his cohorts, his breathe coming as easy as if he was sitting under a shade tree. His legs pumped at a speed beyond his natural capacity, alien to the quick fatigue running at such a pace was bound to bring.

The warriors entered Katura as the sun broke over the horizon. The villagers, emerging from their homes to go about the day's chores, fled back inside upon the sight of them. Kintu led them through the winding streets as if born to the town, his destination clear to Changa and the others. They arrived at the docks, the sails of the *Sendibada* and *Kazuri* still secured to the masts. The crew shuffled about on the deck until Mikhali spotted the warriors headed for the dock. The crew sprang into action, clamoring up the masts to release the sails, scrambling to load the cannons. Crossbowmen lined the deck as Mikhali took his place behind them.

Changa ran ahead of the group, raising his hands.

"Mikhali! Hold your fire!"

"Changa?"

"Yes, it's us!"

The crossbowmen lowered their weapons as the others came to the deck to watch the advancing warriors, amazed at the giant that led them. The dock rumbled with the drumming of scores of sandaled feet. Everyone stared at Kintu as he halted at the edge of the docks. The boarding planks were extended and the warriors boarded the *Sendibada*.

"We should take the Kazuri," Changa suggested. "It is fast and better armored."

"Our battle won't be fought on the sea," Kintu replied. "As far as speed, don't worry. The ancestors will supply all the speed we need."

Kintu's words stirred the breeze, the sails billowing as they unfurled.

"Panya," he said. "We could use the help of your orisha."

Panya nodded and ran to the bow of the *Sendibada*, raising her hands to embrace the light winds.

"Here me, Oya! Once again your daughter begs for your help. You know our task and you know what the cost may be. Give us your strength and your blessing!"

Panya was answered by a surge of wind that fueled the swirling river. Both ships strained at their anchors, anxious for freedom.

Changa worked his way through the dhow, reassuring his nervous crew. They made room for the additional bodies and loaded extra provisions. After a final inspection he gave Mikaili the signal to weigh anchor. The ships pounced forward into the spirit driven wind and current. Changa, Kintu, and Panya stood at the bow gazing down the Zambezi in the direction of their destination.

"Your wait is over, Bahati," Kintu said. "I am coming for you at last."

Chapter 5
Lovers' Embrace

Bahati's impatience for power grew with every day at sea. As her dhows came into sight of Madagascar she shook in expectation. The other talismans waited in the bowels of the heavily fortified city of Rabenja, deep in the forest interior. The time of deception was over. The talisman's power surged through her, a pleasure unmatched even by the embrace of Kintu. The thought of her former lover broadened her wide smile. She'd been created to seduce him, to lead the greatest warrior of the gods to betrayal. The two of them were uncontrollable together, a tangle of unquenchable lust. Kintu's betrayal brought the end of the medicine priests as the gods awakened to the real threat these ambitious men presented. Their wrath was swift and omnipotent, destroying everything and everyone associated with the priests except Bahati, for even the gods could not resist her beauty. On a barren landscape one speck of life survived, a small patch of grass which contained the mercy of the gods and the spirit of Bahati.

The dhows ran aground on the sandbars of the shallow harbor. Fisinaume leaped over the sides, splashing into the water and wading ashore, shields and spears held high. Bahati waited for a boat to be prepared, her human bodyguards forming about her. Though the hyena-men were useful for mass battles, Bahati preferred human slaves close to her. They were easier to control and more loyal, whereas the fisinaume had a tendency to succumb to their animal hungers. Her boat was lowered into the surf and she returned to Madagar with her new army.

The fisinaume waited on the beach, pacing about and fighting in anticipation. Bahati stepped out of her boat on the backs of her men. As she placed her foot on the sand, her handlers gathered about her.

"Get the beasts in order," she commanded. "We should reach the city by nightfall. If you fail me you will die. Serve me well and your pleasures will be endless."

The men fanned out among the beasts, shouting and striking them with bullwhips as they formed them into ranks. Bahati's litter arrived and she climbed inside. With a wave of her hand the army advanced, running down the narrow road leading to the city and her final steps to power.

Fisinaume swarmed the landscape, killing all in their path. No one and nothing escaped their ruthlessness. The carnage was unnecessary, but it was what the creatures were created to do and Bahati had no desire to restrain them. They drove entire villages before them as word of the slaughter spread, the people fleeing for the safety of the city walls.

Bahati's horde reached Rabenja at daybreak. The capital of Madagar was a collection of stone buildings speckling the island's only mountain. A defensive clearing ringed the city, a recent expanse littered with fresh tree stumps and hidden treachery. Formidable walls hid most of the city but Bahati's destination towered over the thick barrier. She smirked as she gazed at Aran's citadel. At least he was intelligent to know she would betray him. He had prepared well, but not well enough.

A wail rose from within upon the sight of the creatures, the warriors scrambling to the ramparts with crossbows and spears. The fisinaume swarmed out of the forest and charged across the clearing, ignoring the moats filled with thorn bushes and spikes, running headlong through the myriad of traps that would have thwarted a human army. The mass rammed the stone walls with a force that staggered its defenders, the beasts in the vanguard of the unruly charge crushed by the horde behind them. The city panicked as the distorted laughter of the hyena men poured over the walls. They leaped at the men above them, digging their claws into the mud as they attempted to climb the smooth surface. The warriors responded in desperate fury, shooting into the mass with lethal effect, dropping stones on them and pouring hot oil. The fisinaume came still, each one using the dead creature before it as a foothold. The defenders could not see the bodies of the slain piling higher and higher, slowly forming a ramp of flesh to the top of the walls. The creatures finally spilled onto the ramparts and the warriors fell back, the battle to defend the walls degenerating into a fight for their own lives.

Bahati and her entourage crossed the morbid field to the city gateway. The huge gates were torn from their hinges, sprawled on the ground to either side of the arch. Blood stained the ground but no bodies lay before them, each slain warrior resurrected as a fisinaume that charged toward the palace with its new brethren.

They arrived as the fisinaume assaulted the palace. Some beat their swords and spears against the granite walls while the newly converted clawed with bloody hands and crashed their bodies against the hardened volcanic stone. Bahati's bearers eased her litter down and she emerged before her objective.

"Drive the beasts back," she said. The handlers waded into the horde, pushing and striking the fisinaume into ranks then leading them away from the palace. Bahati strode to the palace door flanked by her warriors and acolytes. She gripped the obelisk with both hands and raised it high.

"Open," she whispered.

The gilded door exploded inward, crushing the palace guard waiting behind it. Bahati's warriors rushed into the citadel and a fierce battle ensued. Bahati walked into its midst surrounded by her priests, ignoring the violence around her. She made her way to a stone stairwell twisting down into the underground level of the palace. An acolyte passed a torch to Bahati and she led the group into the chamber. Her footsteps echoed off the damp walls as the passage leveled and expanded, the darkness swallowing the feeble torchlight. She could barely see as they reached the base of the stairs. The passage took a sharp turn and they were greeted by a gauntlet of torches perched along the chamber walls in golden mounts. The flame light danced across the ebony marble floor, illuminating the piles of riches stacked against the far chamber wall. Wooden chests filled with gold coins lined the base with stacks of the finest fabrics resting upon them. Huge ivory bowls rimmed with gold overflowed with jewels of all kinds. An intricately carved mahogany table stood in the center of this collection of wealth, its polished surface adorned with the other talismans, the symbolic brothers of the jade obelisk. The collective power of the old wizards was only a few steps away.

The shadows moved. Bahati raised her torch as bronze armored warriors emerged from the recess of the treasure room, their brown faces hidden by grotesque warrior masks. Behind them was Aran, master of the castle, a smile on his handsome face.

"Did you think me a fool, Bahati?" he said. "You overestimate the effect of your beauty."

"You are the fool if you think you can stand between me and the talismans," Bahati replied. "Step away and your death will be swift."

"You think you are the only one aware of the power of the

talismans?"

Bahati's eyes narrowed. "What have you done, Aran?"

Aran laughed. "Don't worry, sweet one. I offer you the same mercy you offered me."

Aran put his palms together, fingers pressed against each other. He lowered his head and closed his eyes, his lips moving silently. The talismans glowed weakly then gradually intensified with a light that shrouded the efforts of the torches. The acolytes backed away, seeking the safety of the passageway. Bahati remained, the smile still on her face.

Aran looked up, opened his hands then thrust his arms towards Bahati. A ball of flame formed before his hands and surged towards Bahati, but she did not move. She raised the jade obelisk before her and the flame ball exploded, the force smashing Aran and his warriors into the treasures behind them. The acolytes that fled suffered the same fate, their bodies crushed against the stone walls. Only Bahati and those acolytes brave enough to remain at her side survive the explosion, their bodies unscathed.

Bahati stepped through the debris to the body of Aran, his arms and legs twisted like mangled sticks.

"I wonder who told you the power of the talismans were yours to command." She knelt beside him, her lips close to his lacerated face.

"They neglected to tell you, or maybe they didn't know that though each talisman contains its share of power, that power can only be fully used when it is joined with the others. That can only be performed by the one who possesses the jade obelisk."

Bahati stood and spit on him. "If only you had known, you would have lived a little longer."

She turned to her acolytes. "Gather the talismans and bring them to the upper level," she ordered. The surviving priests stepped over the bodies of Aran's warriors and gathered the objects into their robes. Bahati led the way with her torch held high. The upper chamber was similar to its lower counterpart, the floor littered with dead men and fisinaume.

"Clear this place," she commanded. "The time of the ritual is now. Tonight we will summon the strength of the old wizards. Tomorrow, the gods will die."

*　*　*

The *Kazuri* and the *Sendibada* skimmed the ocean at an incredible speed, carried by the grace of Oya. Changa stood on the *Sendibada* deck with Panya by his side, buffeted by the forceful wind. Kintu manned the helm, his large hands swallowing the wheel of the ship. Mikaili stood by, his face contorted by a mixture of awe and anger.

Changa and Panya stumbled as the ship crashed into a large wave, grabbing each other for support.

"I don't know how long the dhows can take this beating," Changa warned.

"It won't be much longer," Panya replied. "Look."

Land appeared before them over the choppy horizon.

"Prepare for landing," Kintu ordered.

The crew brought the landing boats to the deck and loaded them on the hoists. Warriors boarded and were lowered into the waves. Thick clouds lumbered across the sky, emanating from beyond the horizon of the island. Changa's skin became cold, not from the sea spray, but from the falling temperature around him. He sat beside Kintu who stood at the front of the lead boat.

"We must hurry," he said. "Time is running out."

The dhows surged into the same Madagar harbor used by Bahati. Her ships bobbed on the waves, completely abandoned. Changa, Kintu, and the others boarded the boats and paddled furiously to the beaches. They stopped short of land and Kintu leaped into the surf. The others followed, a cheer of confidence rising from their throats. Changa felt the rush as well as he high-stepped through the brine to the rocky shore.

Bahati's creatures wasted no time attacking them. A band of fisinaume charged from the palm trees and fell upon Kintu. With one stroke of his huge shield he swept them aside, their bodies landing in a lifeless heap a distance down the shore. His human companions hesitated, stunned by the casual display of his enormous power.

"Come," Kintu commanded, breaking their trance. He led the warriors through the surf and onto the rock and sand as another group of fisinaume charged them from the trees. They killed the creatures quickly, but lost sight of Kintu in the process.

"This way!" Panya said.

They followed the priestess to the woods' edge where a broad path appeared, the brush pushed aside by Kintu's bulk. Running as fast as they could, they made up the distance between them and their celestial leader. Kintu came into view, knocking the hyena-men away with his shield and orinka. Though the warriors behind him handled the stray creatures, they were slowed by the attacks and had to make an extra effort to catch up to Kintu. Their quick advance ended when they entered the village.

Fisinaume spilled from every house, climbing the compound walls, running through the narrow alleyways and roads. Kintu halted and the warriors ran to his side. The beasts slammed into their raised shields and the slaughter commenced. Changa swung his sword as fast as he could, slashing at the reckless attackers. The fisinaume fought with little skill but with frightening ferocity. Changa thanked the spirits for the elixir they drank as he battled with ceaseless energy and strength.

Warriors fell despite their magical advantage. Those separated from the protective circle succumbed to the swarm, beaten down by the creatures. The creatures piled on each other, climbing the bodies of the dead and leaping down onto the warriors.

"We have no time for this!" Kintu shouted. The celestial warrior lowered his shield and surged forward, crushing the fisinaume in his path. Changa rushed to his side.

"Close the ring! Close the ring!" he commanded.

The warriors drew together and locked shields, striking down the beasts that managed to survive Kintu's punishing advance. Their pace increased as they reached the outskirts of the village. The path before them cleared and they ran again down the broad highway leading to the city.

Bands of fisinaume attacked them along the road but the warriors simply out ran them. Changa struggled to keep up with Kintu despite his perpetual energetic state. The others suffered as well – the Tuareg running no faster than Changa, and Zakee straining to keep pace with them both. Changa pulled Panya along as she stumbled.

"Slow down, Changa!" she pleaded.

Kintu turned his head at the sound of her voice and slowed his pace.

"Sorceress, come," he gestured.

Panya ran to the warrior. He swept her into his arms and smiled.

"You must make it," he said. "You have an important role to play."

Kintu picked up his pace again, leaving the others behind. They ran for another hour, the attacks of the hyena-men subsiding. The forest thinned, the diminishing trees giving way to shrubs and tall grasses. Kintu stopped, holding up his shield to call the others to halt.

Changa came to Kintu's side, stunned at what he saw before him. The road angled downward into a barren valley. In the center a citadel loomed, surrounded by thousands of fisinaume. The ground seemed to move as the creatures paced about, their morbid laughter rising from the valley.

Kintu pointed his spear at the palace. "Our destination," he said.

Changa looked at the swarming fisinaume and shook his head.

"We won't make it," he said. "There are too many of them."

Kintu looked at Changa and smiled. "Your faith is weak, Bakongo. In times like these we must look to higher powers."

Kintu looked up into the thick clouds gathering overhead. He grabbed the massive bow on his back and took the arrow in his quiver.

"Priestess, bring the offering," he said.

Panya came forward with a small pouch. Kintu nocked the bow with the arrow. Panya tied the pouch to the arrowhead as Changa looked on.

"One arrow cannot stop an army," he said.

Kintu ignored him, raising his bow to the darkening clouds. The arrow sprang from the bow, streaking straight into the clouds. Lightening flashed where the arrow penetrated the ominous ceiling, punctuated by a tremendous thunderclap that startled the hyena-men, their misshapen heads jerking up to the black sky.

Kintu's arrow fell from the cloud, striking the ground before a puzzled hyena-man. Lightening erupted again and the subsequent thunder opened the clouds suddenly to a torrential downpour. Arrows streaked down from the heavens, impaling the beasts by the hundreds. They ran about frantically, seeking cover from the lethal deluge but none was to be found. Many fled for the safety of the forest only to be cut down before they could reach the trees. The few that made it were dispatched by the hidden warriors.

The arrow shower subsided then ceased. Changa looked at the slaughter in amazement.

"Be careful where you step, Bakongo," Kintu warned. He picked up Panya and strode out into the clearing. Changa and the others followed, avoiding the arrow riddled bodies of the fisinaume. The careful walk became a run again as Kintu increased the pace. The warriors ran across the clearing and up the hill to the broken citadel gate. No sentries stood on the wall and no armies charged out to meet them.

Kintu turned his head. "The ceremony has begun. We must hurry!"

He ran into the building. Changa and the others followed, running over the dead and dying strewn across the marble floor. The door to the hallway was open and they charged in, their footsteps echoing off the mask-covered mahogany walls. At the end of the passageway was another wide room; unlike the entrance this one was not empty.

Bahati's warriors attacked. These were not the half-man beasts depending on primal ferocity to overwhelm their enemies; these were skilled fighters and proved it immediately. Kintu stopped, protecting Panya while swinging his orinka to drive them back.

Changa jumped into the fray. He slammed his shield into one warrior while striking another in the leg with his throwing knife.

"Clear them away from Kintu," Changa yelled. They attacked Bahati's warriors furiously, forcing them away from the guardian spirit. The giant ran to the closed door, Panya in his arms. He stopped just before the door, placing her down.

"Your task is the greatest among us all," he said.

"What must I do?" Panya asked.

"You will know," Kintu answered. "Call the Bakongo and his friends. It is time to meet Bahati."

Kintu raised his shield, his orinka clutched in his right hand. He charged the bolted chamber door and slammed into it. The door exploded and Kintu was swallowed by a cascade of blinding light. Panya shielded her eyes.

"Changa!" she yelled.

Changa broke away from the melee and ran to Panya.

"Tuareg, Zakee! Follow me!"

The trio ran to their companion. The light spilling from the chamber room subsided as they reached her side.

"Kintu's inside," she said.

Changa ran into the room and froze at the sight before him. Bahati hovered above the center of the room, her nude perfection flooding his every sense and paralyzing him with desire. She was illuminated by eleven beams of light, each stream emanating from a different talisman placed in a circle on the floor. An acolyte attended each object. The jade obelisk stood in the center of the circle, its green light a wide band that held the priestess aloft.

Kintu's eyes were transfixed on the goddess that was created for him.

"You've come," Bahati said.

Kintu tried to look away. "You know why I am here."

"You think you've come to destroy me," she replied. "Look at me, my lover. The power I possess is more than the gods you serve. Share this power with me and we can rule the heavens and the earth."

Kintu blinked, confusion contorting his face. "If I do not stop you I will never be free."

"You are free," Bahati replied. "Do you fear I will fail? If you join me my victory is certain. All of this will be yours for eternity!"

She slowly swept her hand over her head, then slowly across her body. Kintu's eyes followed her hands and his arms fell to his sides. He placed his shield on the floor and dropped his orinka then unbuckled his weapon belt and tossed it aside. He removed his quiver, bow and javelin, placing them inside his shield.

"I am ready, my love," he said.

"NO!" Panya screamed. "You must resist her!"

Kintu looked at the sorceress, helplessness in his eyes. "I can't. She was made for me."

Bahati smiled down on Kintu and opened her arms. The obelisk's green aura enveloped him and he rose from the ground, his hands extended towards his lover. Panya ran to Kintu's discarded weapons, attempting to pick up his javelin. Even with her enhanced strength it was too heavy.

"Changa! Help me!"

Panya's plea shattered Changa's trance. He saw Kintu rising to Bahati, feelings of fear and jealousy twisting his heart.

"Changa!" Panya shouted. "You must stop him!"

Changa bounded to Panya and lifted the javelin. It was

heavier than he expected and he stumbled backward under its weight.

"Hurry, Changa!" Panya pleaded. "If he embraces her we are lost!"

Changa balanced the javelin on his shoulder then ran toward the celestial duo. Instinct told him to aim for Bahati's heart, but just as he was about to let the missile fly Kintu's body blocked his target. Changa picked up his pace as he drew his arm back.

"Forgive me, Kintu," he whispered.

Changa threw the javelin with every fiber in his body. It flew like a bolt from heaven, tearing through Kintu's back, bursting through his chest and impaling Bahati's heart. The cries of the deities stabbed him with pain and he tumbled to the floor, his hands clasped over his ears. The marble floor shook with the weight of the fallen lovers, deep cracks running from the impact like rivers. The cries ceased. Changa lay on his back close to unconsciousness.

"Well done, Bakongo." Changa cracked open his eyes to the image of Kintu hovering over him.

"You have succeeded where I was destined to fail."

Changa moved and it hurt. The elixir had worn off; pain and fatigue swept over him with enthusiasm.

"I'm glad you survived," he managed to say.

Kintu smiled. "No, Bakongo, I did not, but Bahati is no more. I am free to pass on to the ancestors. You saved your world, Bakongo. Cherish the gift."

Kintu faded, replaced by Panya's worried face.

"Thank the ancestors you are alive!"

Changa struggled to a sitting position. "For now, it seems."

He looked about and saw the Tuareg rising to his feet while shaking his head. Zakee survived as well, crawling about on his hands and knees and moaning. Panya helped Changa to his feet.

"It is done," she said. "Bahati and the talismans are destroyed."

Changa looked to the sacred circle and saw the talismans in pieces, the charred body of an acolyte sprawled on the floor behind each one. Bahati's body was gone.

"Are we sure she is dead?"

Panya shrugged. "You can never be sure with spirits. Even if her essence survived, it will be thousands of years before she can threaten the world again."

The Tuareg approached them and touched Changa's shoulder. He pointed at the treasures lining the walls of the chamber and a gleam came to Changa's eyes.

"You're right, Tuareg," he said. "It seems this journey will pay off after all."

Panya looked puzzled then startled. "You don't mean to take this treasure, do you?"

"I believe the former owners are in no position to complain," Changa replied.

"Besides, I consider this payment for services rendered."

Panya folded her arms across her chest, patting her foot. "Only you could save the gods and transform it into a business opportunity."

Changa placed his hand on her shoulder. "I don't understand these things the way you do. I realize what happened here was of great consequence, but when it is all said and done we must live our lives in this world. I'll deal with the next world when I get there. For now, we have a treasure to gather and a long journey home."

Panya smiled despite herself. "You are a great man, Changa Diop. You are also a fool."

Changa laughed. "I'll take that as a compliment. Tuareg, take Zakee back to the dhows and bring back the crew."

Changa looked at the remaining warriors as they milled about, still stunned by the destruction of Bahati.

"It is over, brave ones," he said. We have won! Now help us with the bounty left to us and you will all return home rich men!"

Smiles came to their worn faces and they made their way to the treasure. Changa watched them as they picked up what they could and carried it outside, a great smile on his face. Sofala was a good decision, he thought; a good decision indeed.

End Kitabu I

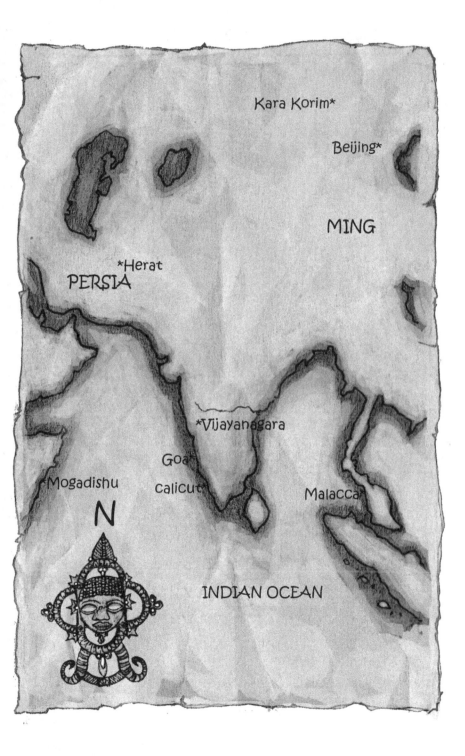

Kitabu Chapili:
(Book Two)

A Certain Spice

Chapter 1
The Treasure Junk

Sofala harbor teemed with dhows of every description, their lateen sails crowding the wharf view like a canvas forest. The northwest monsoon had pushed the bahari home, their holds packed with exotic cargo. Changa's dhows rested on the outskirts away from the crush, rocking with the languid waves. The swift *Kazuri* and the noble *Sendibada* were familiar sights, but the majestic dhow between them was a fresh vision to the jaded Sofalans working the dock. Below its sturdy deck a celebration took place. The revelers sat in a circle on gilded stools surrounding an exquisitely carved ebony table from the markets of Malabar. Elegant porcelain plates and bowls from the east brimmed with succulent fish, fowl, rice, and fruit, while gourds of local beer mingled with bottles of fine Mediterranean wines. Changa Diop stood and raised his gilded goblet high, a satisfied smile on his face.

"Welcome home!" he exclaimed. The others raised their goblets and cheered. A year had passed since he and his companions sat together for a good meal and a good drink. Changa surprised himself; he missed them all more than he imagined, especially Panya. She sat beside him dressed in the finest silks from Pate, her braided hair bouncing on her shoulders as she laughed at Amir Zakee. The young Arab made comic faces as he described the host of characters he encountered during his journey to Zanzibar. The Tuareg laughed in his own way, his hand pressed against his veil, his eyes squinting.

"By the ancestors!" Changa bellowed. "It's good to have you all together again."

"You act as if we've been gone for years," Panya replied, a playful gleam in her eyes.

Changa took a swig of beer, wiping his mouth with his sleeve. "It seems that way. While all of you roamed the world I've been stuck here counting money. I never thought success would be so boring!"

"I think our friend is getting land sick." Mulefu, the Grand Merchant of Sofala, descended the stairs into the dining cabin of the new dhow to join the revelers. He was dressed regally as always, his body covered in white silk robes, a royal blue turban crowning his head. Sofala had grown in size and importance because of the efforts of Mulefu and Changa. It showed in the prosperity of both former pit fighters.

Changa rose and met his friend with a magnanimous hug. "Well, what do you think?"

"She's magnificent," Mulefu replied. "A beautiful vessel indeed, but I question the size. This is a huge dhow, Changa. What are you up to?"

Changa led Mulefu to his seat. A servant filled Mulefu's goblet with millet beer and the Grand Merchant raised his cup to Panya.

"Panya, you are as lovely as ever."

"Thank you, Mulefu," she replied.

"I hear the Bene is just as impressed. The word in the market is that he has made a marriage offer."

Changa, Zakee, and the Tuareg looked at Panya in surprise.

"When did you plan on telling us?" Changa asked.

"Soon enough," Panya replied. "It is of no consequence. I plan on refusing him."

Changa's eyes narrowed. Her words were certain but her expression seemed unsure. "You haven't told him yet?"

Panya looked away from Changa's probing eyes. "It is a delicate matter."

"I should say so," Mulefu interjected. "The word in the market is…"

"Please bwana Mulefu," Panya interjected. "I would like to share my personal affairs with my friends, if you don't mind."

"Oh yes, of course. I do apologize. Anyway, we were talking about your very big dhow and what you plan on doing with it."

Changa's eyes lingered on Panya for a second before he responded to Mulefu.

"I named her Hazina. She's built to carry three times the normal cargo load. Her hull is constructed of the hardest woods available and her frame reinforced with metal for travel on the heavy seas."

Mulefu's face became serious. "What is the purpose of all this?"

Changa moved closer to Mulefu as if sharing a secret. "The Bene's iron is indispensable to the smiths in Calicut. Without it they cannot forge the wootz steel needed for the sword masters of Damascus. You know as well as I that we must ship the ore north to Mogadishu. The Arabs buy it and then trade directly with Calicut. The Hazina can handle the worst the sea can muster. She'll sail directly to Calicut. Imagine the profit we'll gain!"

Mulefu rubbed his chin thoughtfully before speaking.

"It's a dangerous gamble, Changa. The northern merchants won't be happy. They have allowed us our monopoly with Benametapa because we pass the ore through them. If we cut them out they will surely send their own emissaries to Maputo."

"The Bene made a deal with us," Changa answered. "He will not break it."

"Not as long as he thinks he has a chance with Panya."

"This is supposed to be a celebration," Panya reminded them. "Enough talk of business."

"Panya's right," Zakee said. "Today is a rare day, a day for friends and good thoughts. Allah has never made a more wonderful moment and we should enjoy it in peace."

Rumbling drums interrupted Zakee's speech.

"The harbor alarm?" Mulefu said. "What in the Prophet's name could this be?"

Changa sprang to his feet and climbed the stairs to the deck. He emerged to see Mikaili and the crew staring towards the horizon.

He went to the Ethiopian. "What is it?"

Mikaili turned to Changa and stepped away. Changa filled his space, looked out into the harbor and was stunned. The others finally reached the deck and were equally subdued.

"Praise to Allah," Zakee whispered.

A wall of ships sailed towards them, strange crafts that bore large square sails and mysteriously carved bows. Their variety rivaled their numbers; some were small one-sail boats that bobbed in the massive waves like corks, others monstrosities that looked like floating buildings. The *Hazina*'s signal drummers recovered from their initial shock and beat out a warning. The harbor watch answered, igniting a scramble on the docks and the harbor ships.

"Raise anchors and drop sails!" Changa commanded. "Send a signal to the Kazuri and the Sendibada. If they hurry they can escape the harbor and head south."

"Wait," Mulefu said.

"For what?" Changa asked. "Whoever these people are, they have come well prepared. A fool can see Sofala is lost."

Mulefu pointed at the fleet. "I see dhows flying familiar banners among these ships."

Changa raised his eyeglass. He spotted dhows from Malindi, Kilwe, Mogadishu, and even Mombasa. The sight of the Mombasans boats gave him pause, for he spotted the banner of his old mentor, Belay. His sons were among the fleet, which did not bode well.

The ships continued to approach, the true size of the fleet revealing itself as they sailed closer. One particular ship emerged from the horizon, its masts rising higher and higher until they threatened to touch the clouds. Eight masts ran from bow to stern supporting ribbed rectangular sails. The monstrous vessel dwarfed its escort, lumbering into the harbor like a wooden elephant. It was the largest ship any of them had seen in their lives.

The ship decks stirred with the movement of men as signal flags sent silent commands. The sails were hauled in as the fleet came to rest at the mouth of the harbor. A hatch appeared on the side of the behemoth ship and disgorged a fleet of small boats filled with men and oars. The oars smacked the water in unison as a drummer played a steady rhythm.

"So what do we do now?" Mulefu asked.

"Since you are aboard my dhow, Grand Merchant, we are the official greeting for Sofala," Changa announced. "Let's meet our new visitors."

Changa ordered his men to lower the sails and weigh anchor. The gesture was noticed by the ships and they altered their course, heading to the *Hazina*.

The occupants of the boat looked as strange to Changa as their ships. Their straight black hair reminded him of Arabs but their skin was much lighter with a golden hue. Their eyes were slanted as if in a permanent squint. One man stood in the boat, draped in a large silken robe whose wide sleeves hid his hands. His slim face seemed solemn, his eyes cast down as if in thought. An Arab sat at his feet, his mouth moving as he talked to the standing stranger.

The boat came into hailing distance and the robed man raise his head as he extracted a scroll from his wide sleeve. He read in a language Changa did not recognize. The Arab spoke soon afterwards in heavily accented Swahili.

"I bring greetings from Zhu Quizhen, Emperor of the Middle Kingdom and master of the fleet before you. I, Zheng San, have sailed thousands of li to present to you a small token of my master's wealth, an example of his blessings from Heaven."

Mulefu moved to the ship's bow.

"I am Mulefu, Grand Merchant of Sofala. I greet you and your magnificent fleet. Please follow us to the harbor where we can discuss the generosity of your emperor."

"Take the Hazina into port," Changa ordered. He stood by Mulefu as the ship turned about and returned to their fleet.

"What kind of trickery is this?" Mulefu whispered. "They bring a fleet large enough to pound Sofala into dust then offer us tribute. It makes no sense."

"Actually it makes perfect sense," Changa replied. "They want to trade and they are offering the easy way. The warships are sign that there is another option."

"So why not use it?"

Changa looked at Mulefu, disappointed.

"Because it is costly. Everything you destroy you have to rebuild. Best leave it as it is and cut in on the profit by making the deal mutually beneficial. Whoever this Zhu Quizhen is, I like the way he thinks."

Mulefu, Changa, and the rest of his crew debarked as the massive ship maneuvered as close as it dared into Sofala's harbor. The hatch opened again near the water line and eased into the water. Small transport ships disembarked and completed the journey into the harbor. Once they were secured the bounty of their holds was revealed, each ship laden with eastern treasures. Changa was dazzled not only by the variety of the items but also by the amount. His amazement was interrupted by a gentle nudge.

"It's been a long time, kibwana." Changa turned to see the face of an old friend.

"Yusef!" Changa bellowed. Yusef laughed, exposing his perfect teeth. The Mombasan towered over Changa with skin the color of night and eyes burning with life. They hugged and pounded each other on the back with a force that would break most men.

"What are you doing here?"

"I heard there was a fleet sailing to Sofala so I decided to visit an old friend."

Changa frowned at Yusef's obvious lie and Yusef shrugged.

"The *tembo* are becoming scarce outside Mombasa. I'm here to see what Sofala had to offer."

"You brought strange companions with you," Changa said.

"They call themselves Han. I told them if they truly wished to go home wealthy, they must visit my friend in Sofala as well."

Changa rubbed his chin. "So they call themselves Han?"

"Yes. They have stopped at every Swahili port with the same request and the same display. I think that treasure ship has a secret door to heaven."

"What do they want?"

"Your loyalty and your freedom. In exchange for this treasure they demand that you acknowledge the supremacy of their Emperor and become his subjects."

"That could be a problem," Changa mused.

"It was in Mogadishu," Yusef replied. "At least it was until the Han cannon destroyed the main stone house and convinced them otherwise."

So the Han were not beyond using force, Changa mused.

"I will warn Mulefu," Changa said. "But enough of this. You will stay with me of course."

Yusef frowned. "I'm not in the mood to sleep in a dhow's hull. I was thinking of renting a room in a hostel."

"You have no idea how good Sofala has been to me. Ask for me at the market when you are finished."

Yusef nodded to Changa. "I will kibwana. For now I must organize a safari." He slapped Changa's shoulder. "It is good to see you, rafiki. We have much to talk about."   He pounded Changa's shoulders and disappeared into the crowd.

Changa watched Yusef for a moment then turned his attention back to the harbor. A parade of cargo boats glided inbound propelled by bare-chested rowers, their long black hair twisted into single braids that ran the length of their backs. They were flanked by larger craft crammed with soldiers, grim faced men clothed in studded leather armor and brandishing elaborate crossbows. The soldiers disembarked and pushed away the eager and the curious while the laborers unloaded their goods. A nervous looking Yao servant met the Han and signaled them to follow him to Mulefu's vacant warehouse not far from the main docks. Sofalans cleared the streets, their faces angry and fearful. The Han took no notice, their eyes locked forward. Once they reached the warehouse the soldiers surrounded it, crossbows at the ready and swords drawn.

"This is not good," Changa said to Panya. "This feels like an occupation."

They pushed their way to Mulefu, who stood before Zheng San and his translator. The Grand Merchant was not happy.

"Your soldiers must leave the docks immediately!" he demanded. "I have summoned our craftsmen to construct an encampment for you and your men outside the city. Your soldiers can return when the camp is complete."

The Arab translated while the Han nodded, his eyes closed. He opened them suddenly, staring directly into Mulefu's eyes as he answered.

"The goods from our junks are still the property of my Emperor," the Arab translated. "We have the right to protect them."

"Our *Samburu* will guard your goods," Mulefu replied. "They are honest warriors."

"A union such as ours should be founded on trust," Zheng San replied in perfect Swahili to everyone's surprise. "I will allow the Samburu to protect our goods. Our soldiers will return to the fleet, but we will suspend unloading until our encampment is prepared. I believe this arrangement should be suitable to everyone."

Zheng San called out to his warriors and they formed ranks, marching back to the docks. The Samburu replaced them; familiar faces but just as grim.

"Can we continue our negotiations, elsewhere?" Zheng San asked.

Mulefu led the group to the merchant guild house, an elegant stone structure occupying a small hill overlooking the harbor. The house was surrounded by the villas of Sofala's wealthiest merchants, the myriad of designs a visual collage of the influences of many lands.

A crowd of merchants gathered about the house in anticipation of Zheng San's arrival. The Tuareg and Zakee mingled among them, the Tuareg standing out in his dark blue garb and Zakee in his bright colors and ever-present smile. Mulefu's guards cleared the way and they entered. Zakee and the Tuareg fell in with their companions, Zakee stepping in between Changa and Panya.

"This is so exciting!" he exclaimed. "Nothing like this ever happened in Aden."

"You forget your bride so easily?" Changa joked.

"I mean in a good way," Zakee replied.

"Let's not celebrate yet," Changa cautioned. "These Han brought warships and soldiers."

"They have a great treasure that needs to be protected," Zakee said.

"But at such a scale?" Changa rubbed his chin. "I'll feel better when I see their rudders and feel their money in my pouch."

Mulefu led Zheng San into the main hall. The room was built in a circle, the looping rows of wooden benches descending toward the stage. The crowd hushed as Mulefu took the center, Zheng San and his Arab cohort standing slightly behind him, their heads bowed.

"My brothers," Mulefu began, "you would have to be blind not to have witnessed the spectacle that entered our harbor this day. You are probably as overwhelmed as I by the size of this foreign fleet and the wealth below their decks. As I speak woodsmen clear the land outside Sofala to build a trading camp for our guests so they can reveal to us the full extent of their possessions.

"This is Zheng San, ambassador to Zhu Quizhen, Emperor of the Middle Kingdom. He bears a proposition which requires our attention, so please allow him to speak in peace."

Mulefu stepped aside and Zheng San stepped forward. He bowed deeply to the merchants then reached into his wide sleeve, extracting a gilded scroll. Zheng San took his time unrolling the document, taking full advantage of his audience's curiosity.

"I bring greetings and blessing from Zhu Quizhen, Emperor of the Middle Kingdom and Son of Heaven. I have been sent by my master to extend the hand of friendship and brotherhood to all Swahili. The token of my sincerity is the fleet in your harbor, a mere fraction of the wealth of my master. Great is his power, for he has treated his children kindly and punished his enemies mercilessly.

"My master offers you his protection and grace. Give your allegiance to him, accept him as your sovereign and your lands will prosper beyond your dreams, for Zhu Quizhen's generosity knows no end. It is an everlasting well from which life and prosperity springs."

"And if we say no to your emperor?" someone shouted.

Zheng San closed his eyes as he lowered his head.

"My master would be most disappointed. Emperor Zhu Quizhen opens his hands to his subjects, but he closes them to his foes." Zheng San made the gesture as he spoke, his open hands forming firm fists.

The hall was silent, the threat in Zheng San's words clear. Mulefu leaned close to Changa, his lips almost touching Changa's ear.

"He threatens us with attack. Do you think these Han will attack us?"

"Yusef told me they fired their cannons to gain access to Mogadishu when the sultan refused them," Changa said. "They'll use force if they have to, but this emperor has the mind of a merchant. He'd rather buy us than fight us."

"So what do I say?" Mulefu asked.

Changa leaned away and gave Mulefu an annoyed look.

"You are the Grand Merchant, it's your decision."

Mulefu voice was urgent. "I cannot decide the fate of this city!"

"Men do it all the time," Changa shrugged. "If the others disagree, they'll surely let you know."

Mulefu shook his head. "Why did this have to happen to me?"

He straightened his robes and strode back before the group and stood beside Zheng San.

"Bwana Zheng San, we are humbled by your Emperor's invitation. However, we need time to discuss this gracious invitation. Please accept our hospitality in the meantime."

"It would do me a great honor if Bwana Changa would be so kind to show me your city as you deliberate," Zheng San announced.

"It is done," Mulefu agreed. "Changa will see to your needs."

Changa glared at Mulefu.

"Changa," Panya whispered. "Say something!"

"I will be most honored to assist you, Bwana Zheng San," he growled.

"I accept your courtesy," Zheng San replied. He left the floor and worked his way through the crowd to Changa.

"Come," Changa said. "Let's get out into the open. The smell is better."

Changa led his unexpected guest to the chaos of Sofala.

"Thank you for your courtesy," Zheng San said. "I apologize if I upset you."

"I am no diplomat," Changa warned. "I don't see the purpose."

"It's obvious who the true master of this city is," Zheng said. "Mulefu seem to be a capable leader, but he is not a man of vision like you and I."

"You assume much, my friend," Changa said.

"You own the largest dhow in the harbor," Zheng replied. "Is this not evidence of a man with high ambitions?"

Changa smiled. "That doesn't make me a sultan."

"Cities like Sofala prosper because of men like you," Zheng San said. "Your dreams bring wealth and prosperity. The doubts and fears of men like Mulefu can kill the future like stagnant water."

Changa and Panya led Zheng San and his entourage away from the guild house to the cliffs overlooking the harbor. Changa's villa rested atop the highest rise, built tight against the edge and surrounded by a high coral stone wall. The stone house was much larger than his needs, with room for Panya, Zakee, the Tuareg, and four guests. A large dormitory stood opposite the house with rooms for his bachelor crew members. Those married either lived in the city or scattered about the forest in the villages of their wives.

Changa approached the gates surrounding his home and they swung wide. His servants appeared to relieve them of their gear.

"Take these men to the tower rooms," he ordered. Changa smiled at Zheng San.

"I'm not sure of the comforts of your homeland, Bwana San, but I can assure you that my guest rooms are the best in all of the Swahili cities. Once you are settled your servant will bring you to the dining hall. We can continue our conversation then."

Zheng San bowed. "I am grateful for your kindness." He followed the servant into the house.

"Be careful of that one," Panya warned. "He brings more than treasure."

"Divide and conquer," Changa replied.

"Exactly," Panya agreed.

"You talk as if Zheng San is an enemy," Zakee said. "All he offers is friendship."

Changa laughed. "Apparently this is a lesson you still have yet to learn, young prince. Remember your former wife?"

"Of course I do!" Zakee retorted.

"Zheng San is testing the waters, seeking allies and enemies. He'll use his treasure to divide and weaken us. When his emperor is ready to make good his claim to our city we will have defeated ourselves."

"You wouldn't stand against Mulefu, would you?" the prince asked.

"Of course not."

"So what will you do?"

Changa rubbed his chin. "I'll wait to see what Zheng offers. I'll play dumb and make him state his intentions clearly, and then I'll meet with Mulefu and decide what to do next."

Changa's home became a flurry of activity to accommodate his unexpected guests. His servants assaulted the marketplace and returned with extra food to prepare dinner for everyone. It was a lavish affair despite the short notice and everyone seemed to enjoy it. Zheng San commented on every item with praise; if his palate did not agree with anything before him he was expert at hiding it. They were halfway through the meal when a nervous looking servant scampered up to Changa.

"Bwana, there is a man demanded to see you, a very big

man with a goat."

Changa laughed. "He's late. Bring him."

Yusef strode into the courtyard, dragging a goat behind him. He looked at Changa and the others, a frown forming on his face.

"So these are the manners of Sofala? You invite a man to your home and start dinner without him?"

"You're late, Yusef," Changa replied. "Sit down and join us."

"What about the goat?" Yusef stabbed a thick finger at the animal.

"It will fill us another day. For now we have enough."

The excitement of the day abated with the descending sun. The woodcutters made impressive progress clearing the woods for the Chinese camp, laboring well into the night by torchlight. Changa rested in his chambers, his mind stirred by Zheng's words. He had not set out to distinguish himself in Sofala, but his exploits brought him special attention nevertheless. Griots recited the story of his adventure with Kintu and Bahati; and the alliance he instigated between Sofala and Benametapa brought more prosperity to the city. Many whispered that the balance of Swahili power was shifting to the south because of him. With the *Hazina* resting in the harbor to trade directly with Calicut, he was poised to break the northern Swahili monopoly and shower more prosperity on the region. To Changa this was a natural progression but to others it was a dangerous move sure to provoke a response.

Changa blew out his candles. He was thinking too much. Zheng was Mulefu's problem. He'd take the Han to him in the morning and get on with his life.

Chapter 2
Trouble in Threes

Changa couldn't sleep. He'd spent too much time thinking and now he was wide awake staring at the mahogany beams crisscrossing his ceiling. A deep, rhythmic rumbling punctuated by grating snorts made him smile. It was good to see Yusef again, good to share his company. In the morning he would talk to him about moving his family to Sofala. The tembos were still numerous beyond the city and the hunting would be much easier.

Changa slipped from his bed and donned his sword. A walk would do him good. He eased down the stairs and out of his house, his destination the citrus garden between the house and the bahari dormitory. The city slumbered under the clear sky, the air humid with the season. He was entering the grove when a shadow descended upon him, a sudden foreboding that stopped him in his tracks and sent his hand to his sword hilt.

The *tebo* coalesced before him. Alone in the darkness it had no need of its usual disguises, its massive bulbous form pulsing to the rhythm of a malevolent heartbeat. The foul servant of Usenge had found him and the fear and guilt accompanying it swept into Changa's mind. There was no need to call for help; the creature could die by his hand only. It was a personal curse against his bloodline only he could confront.

Changa was bracing for the creature's attack when a second *tebo* appeared to his right. It slithered beside its cohort, multiple arms waving spasmodically. Hope diminished in Changa's heart. He had defeated tebos before, but never had he faced two. That hope disappeared when the third tebo trudged up on his left, tall as the banana trees behind it and just as narrow. Never before had he confronted three tebos. One almost killed him years ago. Three was a death sentence. But Changa would not die easy.

"Son of Mfumu, your time has come!" they spoke in unison.

Changa eased his sword free, wishing he had brought his knives. The Damascus would inflict damage, but his knives were made of Bakongo iron. They held kabaka magic, the power of his lineage. A blow from any of the blades would do great damage to the tebos.

The tebo to his right lunged, its narrow arms spinning, the ends shaped like scythes. Changa dodged the whirling appendages and fell into the stubby arms of the behemoth before him. He sliced the creature across the face before it could crush him and it staggered away clawing at the wound. He was free for only a second when something hard slammed into his back, knocking him forward as his sword flew from his hand. He slammed against the ground and rolled away. The tebo landed where he had been, the jolt bouncing him into the air.

Changa was thankful once again for Kintu's gift. Energy surged through him as he jumped to his feet, the pain in his back subsiding. He had to act fast for the effect would only be temporary. He winced as the tebo's blade hand sliced his shoulder but managed to grab his sword. He spun, ducked under another blade hand then plunged the steel into the creature. Its mouth distorted in pain but no sound emerged as it fell back into the massive tebo.

A wet fist struck Changa, the force lifting him off his feet.

He hit a citrus tree and slid to its base. He smiled through the fire in his side for he still held his sword. He stood and stumbled away, dodging the tebo's swipe that clipped the tree in half. The huge tebo was working its way toward him; the blade beast still lay in its slime, shuddering. Blood ran down Changa's arm, his shoulder wound burning. Pain shot though his torso like sparks from a blacksmith's anvil. Kintu's gift was fading.

An object streaked from out of his line of sight. It smacked against the tebo and the creature shrieked. The tebo clutched the spot where the object stuck, a putrid green smoke sifting through its misshapen fingers. Changa looked at the object as it hit the ground and new vigor pulsed through his wounded body. It was a throwing knife.

"I am coming, kibwana!" Yusef rumbled out of the darkness in a loincloth, his scimitar in his right hand, Changa's knife bag grasped in his left. The wounded tebo rose and surged toward him, the others close behind. Yusef stopped and threw the bag over the tebos with all his strength then fled. The leather bag landed a few feet away from Changa. The tebos turned away from Yusef, shuffling as fast as they could to Changa. Changa reached the bag and threw it over his head, the strap falling over his shoulder and across his body. His hand flashed into the satchel and a knife spun out as if it flew on its own. It ended its flight in the head of the narrow tebo and the creature screamed. It quivered and crashed to the ground, continuing to quake as it melted into the soil.

His advantage did not deter the other tebos. They attacked him simultaneously, thick arms swinging at him from either side. Changa stepped closer to the small creature, bracing himself for the impact. Its fist crashed against his ribs and sent him flying toward its companion. Changa twisted to face the beast-spirit, knives in both hands. He drove them into the tebo's face and it fell onto its back. Changa rolled off the mass and staggered to his feet. He turned to face the final tebo. It stomped over its fallen cohort, its mouth wide and arms reaching out toward him. Changa reared back and threw his knives with all his might. The spinning blades disappeared into the tebos maw then burst from the back of its thick neck. The creature halted, still as a baobab, then fell to its side.

"The son of Mfumu still lives, Usenge," Changa rasped. The pain in his side flared and he grabbed at it. Strength left his legs and he dropped to his knees. The taste of blood seeped into mouth; the knives in his bag suddenly felt like ballast stones.

He was falling back when a pair of large, familiar hands gripped him under his arms and lifted him to his feet.

"It is a good thing you are so tiny, kibwana," Yusef said.

Changa was too weak to respond. Yusef half dragged, half carried him to the house. He kicked the door open and carried him inside. Panya appeared at the top of the stairs.

"What is all this…Changa?"

She rushed downstairs and grasped his cheeks with her soft hands. The Tuareg appeared beside her, takouba and scimitar drawn.

"What happened?" she demanded. "Who did this?"

"The tebos," Yusef answered. "They found him again."

"Tuareg, help Yusef take Changa upstairs," Panya ordered. "I'll get my herbs."

"I need no help, blue man," Yusef said. "Help the medicine woman."

Changa winced with each jolt as Yusef carried him upstairs to his room. Yusef placed him in the bed as carefully as he could. He stepped away, replaced by Panya's concerned face. She poked and prodded him, causing more pain than all three tebos combined.

"You have some broken bones and I think some internal injuries," she said. "What are these tebos? Why did you try to fight them alone?"

Changa opened his mouth to answer and almost passed out. He looked at Yusef and blinked his eyes.

"The tebos are bad spirits. They serve Usenge, the sorcerer that killed his father. This is not the first time they have found him."

Panya turned her anger at the big Mombasan. "Why didn't you help him?"

"I did!" Yusef replied. "I heard the fighting and took kibwana his knives."

"And that was all?"

Yusef frowned. "The tebos are his curse. Only he can kill them. But they can kill anyone. The best I could do was distract them."

The Tuareg arrived with a basket of gourds and cloth. He set them down beside Panya.

"Do you know of these tebos?" she asked the Tuareg. He glanced at Yusef then nodded his head.

"Everyone out," she said angrily. "I need silence."

"Maybe this will help."

Zheng San stood beside Panya, his eyes on Changa. He held a small vial between his fingers.

Panya's eyes narrowed. "What is that?"

"A most wonderful spice," Zheng replied.

He touched Changa's lips with the vial lid before Panya could stop him. Pleasure surged through Changa like a torrent. He closed his eyes, savoring the rush of euphoria. When he opened them the Tuareg held the Han by his hair, a knife to his throat.

"No," Changa said.

Panya's eyes went wide. "You can speak!"

The Tuareg let Zheng San free, his eyes showing confusion.

"Everyone out," Changa said. "Let Panya do her work." He trained his eyes on Zheng San.

"You and I must speak of this when I'm well."

Zheng San smiled. "I agree. We have much to discuss."

Changa spent the next weeks nursed by Panya and soothed by Zheng San's strange spice. He healed quickly as was his way, rising from his bed after three weeks against Panya's protest and taking solitary walks in his garden. The signs of his struggle against the tebos were barely noticeable but the images lingered in his mind. Despite his prosperity he was still a hunted man. Usenge would not rest until Mfumu's seed was either destroyed or under his complete control. The tebos also reminded Changa of another part of his past. The promise he made to himself was still unfulfilled. It had been years since he thought of his vow; that so much time had passed shamed him. He sailed the Swahili Coast, living the life of a wealthy merchant while his sisters and mother languished under the cruel hand of Usenge and his ghost men. Despite all of his success, he was failing at what mattered most.

"You are well, I see."

Changa turned to see Zheng San's calm face creased with a slight smile. He wore a green silk robe decorated with prancing white horses and golden birds, his hands hidden in his wide sleeves. The bottle of spice dangled from a golden chain around his neck.

"Thank you for your help," Changa said.

Zheng smiled. "My assistance was not needed. Panya would have healed you without me. The spice made the experience bearable."

"You said we would talk about this spice." Changa walked through the garden and Zheng San followed.

"It seems more like a drug to me."

"I assure you it is not, Changa. The spice leaves no desire nor does it leave a trace."

"Something like that would be very valuable," Changa stated.

Zheng sighed. "That is true. Unfortunately what hangs around my neck is all that exists in this world."

"That's impossible. Everything has a source."

"As does the spice," Zheng agreed. "But only one man knows its source. I know this man."

Changa's eyes narrowed. "Why are you really here, Bwana San?"

Zheng perpetual smile faded. "Just as Mulefu is not the true master of Sofala, Zhu Quizhen is not the true emperor of the Middle Kingdom. He is just a boy who inherited the throne after of the death of his uncle. I serve Wang Zen, Master of the Eunuchs. The emperor follows the council of Wang and no other."

"What does this have to do with the spice?"

"My master wants the spice. My man claims he knows the source of the spice. He is the one who gave me the sample you tasted. The spice grows in a land of pirates, rebels and stranger things. I sent two expeditions and none have returned. The men of my country will not take the risk at any price."

Changa rubbed his chin. This would not be a simple task. The Swahili coast was his domain. He knew every harbor and cove; the winds were constant and familiar. This task would place him in an unknown land at the mercy of the ancestors and the whim of strange gods.

"My master is desperate to find this treasure," Zhang

continued. "He is so desperate he sent me across the world to find the one man fearless enough to pursue it."

"Don't waste your flattery on me, San," Changa said. "You no more knew of me than I knew of your pompous emperor."

Zheng San grinned. "Let us be honest then. Sofala is no longer safe for you. Those creatures that attacked you have done so before. I assume they will continue until you are dead. The sorcerer who seeks you is obviously powerful, but with the wealth you earn from the spice you may be able to defeat him."

"Don't think I'll listen to your offer out of fear," Changa retorted. "Like you said, I've face the tebos before. You want me because I have no fear of your demons, not mine."

Zheng San nodded, his perennial smile returning.

"Sofala has been lucrative, but I do miss the excitement of a new adventure," Changa continued. "Book keeping is not my passion, nor is lounging around with a group of petty old men." Changa rubbed his chin. "I accept your offer on one condition. I'm your sole agent in Sofala. I'll control the trading between the Middle Kingdom and the Swahili merchants."

Zheng San frowned for the first time since meeting Changa.

"You ask too much. I can only offer payment."

"Then you can leave," Changa replied. "I am not a hired hand. I'm a business man. I control the iron trade between Benametapa and Sofala and soon my dhows will sail directly between this city and Calicut. I am in no need of payment."

"I must consider this," Zheng San. "My master did not expect the Swahili to be so sophisticated. We were wrong to underestimate you."

It was Changa's turn to smile. "I'm sure your master trusts your judgment. He would not have sent you otherwise. There's no need to decide now. The night is still fresh."

Zheng San gazed into the sky. "I must think on this, Changa. Yes, I must think on this."

Zheng San headed back to the house. Changa watched him leave as his bravado faded. The tebos did worry him. He had thought he'd become stronger since his days in Mogadishu, but he was still not strong enough. Maybe San was right.

"Kibwana! Panya said I would find you here."

Yusef strode up to him, his face graced with his usual smile. A canvas travelling bag hung over his shoulder.

"Yusef, you are leaving?" he said.

"Yes. My dhow sails today."

Changa looked up at his friend. "I was hoping you would stay longer. It's been a long time since we've seen each other."

"That is true, but I have a family waiting for me. You know how Kenda can be when she's angry."

Changa chuckled. "Yes I do."

"Well, my children take after their mother. Short and mean, every one of them, and they get meaner the longer I am away."

"Then I guess you should go."

The former comrades stood silent, the moment awkward for both.

"Thank you for saving my life," Changa finally said.

Yusef waved his hand. "I could save you a thousand times and still be in your debt. Be safe, kibwana."

Yusef bent down and wrapped his massive arms around Changa. He lifted him off his feet with a hug then dropped him.

"I will tell Kenda you wish her well." With that Yusef spun and strode away.

"Be safe, my friend," Changa said. "Be safe for both of us."

Chapter 3
The Lobola

Changa rose early the next day, eager to set his affairs in order before his new safari. He dispatched a servant to Mulefu, summoning his old friend to join him for a mid day meal where he would inform him of his decision. He was surprised to see the Grand Merchant return with his servant.

"Changa, what's going on?" Mulefu asked anxiously.

"I am going on safari with Zhen San," Changa replied. "We leave with the coming winds."

Mulefu eyes stuck out from his face "Leaving? Leaving! Changa, you can't leave!"

Changa tried his best not to laugh. "I thought you'd be pleased. Some say there's a rivalry between us."

"Of course there is! It is a friendly one that I enjoy. At least you haven't tried to kill me."

"The truth is I'm bored," Changa replied. "I'm anxious to see this Middle Kingdom Zheng San brags so much about." He said nothing of the tebo attack.

Mulefu stared at his old friend. "Don't give me that crap, Changa. Zheng San offered you a deal and you're taking it. Whatever it is, I want in on it."

"Sorry, Mulefu, that's not what I'm here to discuss. I want you to handle my affairs while I'm away."

Mulefu's eyes gleamed. "Me?"

"Who else? I'm ready to make you executor of my holdings

until I return. Fifty percent of my profits will be your payment."

"Though it is with great regret I receive this news, I would be more than happy to take on this burden, my friend."

"I thought you would be," Changa said with a smirk.

Mulefu managed to form a serious countenance. "You must make me one promise before I accept."

Changa's eyebrow rose. "What is it?"

"You must promise to share this secret with me once you return."

"Once I return it won't be a secret," Changa replied.

Panya burst into the room, interrupting their conversation.

"Changa, I need you now!"

"Please, Panya, Mulefu and I…"

"Now, Changa!" Panya shouted. She gripped his right arm with both hands, her nails digging into his skin as she dragged him to his feet and hauled him into the hallway. Changa planted his feet and pried her hands from his wounded arm.

"What the hell is wrong with you?"

"Maputo is here!" she cried.

"What do you mean by here?"

"His messenger is standing before the gates."

"He's probably delivering a message for you. Everyone knows you live here. What's the problem?

"You don't understand, Changa. I know that messenger. He is a court messenger, not a courier. If he is here, Maputo and his entourage are close by."

"Maybe he's come to see the Han."

"No, Changa," Panya objected. "He's here for me."

Changa stared at Panya in silence. He felt odd, as if he should be upset, but something inside him would not allow it.

"He's come to marry you?"

Panya's face was solemn. "I think so."

Changa placed his hand on her shoulder. "Isn't this what you wanted?"

"I thought so, but I'm not so sure now. Ever since we decided to go with Zheng San..."

"Hold on now," Changa replied. "We didn't decide anything. I gave you the option to stay here in Sofala and tend to my affairs."

Panya looked at Changa then dropped her head into his chest. "Please, Changa!"

"I'll talk to him," Changa conceded.

"Thank you." Panya looked relieved.

Changa scowled. "Don't thank me. I'm doing this for Maputo. He lives a life of tradition and obligation as a chief. He marries who he has to, not who he wants. Now he finds a woman whom he loves and he believes loves him and she toys with his heart."

"You don't understand," Panya said. "I like Maputo, but I don't love him. I considered marrying him only because it seemed we would settle down in Sofala and I'm tired of being alone."

Changa walked away without comment. Panya was the most important member of his crew, but it was apparent she didn't realize it. He shrugged his shoulders and returned to Mulefu.

"I'm sorry, Mulefu. I must end our meeting. The Bene has sent a messenger to my home and requests my presence."

"Maputo? This is truly a day of surprises. I will accompany you, of course."

"No you won't," Changa warned. "This is a personal matter. You can prepare the papers for our agreement. Take my scribe and Zakee with you. The young prince has a head for such things and he'll make sure you won't cheat me."

Mulefu feigned shock. "Changa, I'm insulted."

"Good." Changa grabbed Mulefu's hand then hugged him. "I'll meet you later at the guild house."

Changa went to his room, changed quickly into his ceremonial clothes and headed to the stables. The Tuareg waited holding the reins of two fine Arabians. The horses were a gift from a colleague in Mogadishu, two of a herd of twelve. Changa kept the animals in an enormous barn outside the city; he let them out rarely for fear the tsetse flies would kill them. The beasts would eventually succumb to the sleeping sickness but Changa had managed to maintain the herd for two years without a loss. The two would be his first losses, but they were necessary to make the proper impression on the Bene.

Maputo's messenger waited outside the gates, a rangy fellow clothed in a simple loincloth that contrasted with the elaborate gold ingot hanging from his neck by a gold chain glistening with diamonds and emeralds. A buffalo image filled the center of the ingot, the royal symbol of the Bene. The messenger dropped to his knees, touching his forehead on the ground as the gate opened.

"Master Diop, Bene Maputo requests your presence at his camp beyond the river."

"I accept his invitation," Changa responded. The messenger nodded and set off at a brisk pace through the city. Changa and the Tuareg followed, their mounts trotting to keep pace. Traffic was sparse until they approached the Han camp. It was a raucous scene, the din of haggling merchants and restless beasts raising Changa's adrenaline. This was his passion, the excitement of an open market where fortunes passed from hand to hand in an instant.

Halfway through the camp a squad of Chinese soldiers

blocked their path. The officer, a stout man with a weak beard and brandishing a red armband approached Changa and bowed.

His Arabic was coarse but understandable. "Bwana Diop, Master Zheng San wishes to accompany you on your journey to Bene Maputo's encampment."

Changa grinned at the soldier as he spoke to the Tuareg in Swahili. "I see our secret meeting has been discovered." He immediately switched to Arabic.

"Zheng San is most welcomed to ride with us," Changa replied. "We will wait for him beyond the west gate."

The officer bowed, rallied his men and they marched into the crowd. Changa and the Tuareg continued through the Chinese market to the city's outskirts. The road was filled with a constant flow of traffic as people from villages throughout the highlands traveled to see the visitors from the east. Zheng San and his men appeared a few moments later mounted on horses from their cavernous ship.

"Greetings, Changa!" Zheng shouted. "I thank you for allowing me to come with you. I hope I won't be in the way."

Changa smirked. "We'll see."

Maputo's camp rested a half day's ride from Sofala. Cylindrical grass huts peppered the low hills on either side of the road leading to the monarch's temporary dwelling. Maputo's reed palace commanded the crest of the highest hill. His personal guard ringed the structure, stern bare-breasted warriors in mud cloth kilts holding tall leaf blade spears. The messenger led them up the fresh road to the entrance of the palace. Maputo sat on his gilded stool surrounded by elders young enough to make the rigorous journey. Changa and the Tuareg dismounted and entered the palace. They knelt before the Bene, touching their heads to the ground.

"Rise, my friends," Maputo said, breaking custom by speaking directly to them.

Changa smiled as he came to his feet. The Tuareg's eyes gleamed in response.

"Praise to you, Bene," Changa said. "It has been a long time."

"Yes it has, my friend. I see you still have the girth of a bull."

Changa laughed. "I see you still have the mouth of a lion."

Maputo nodded to the Tuareg and he nodded in response.

"Tuareg, you are a welcomed sight. I always feel safer in your presence."

The Tuareg closed his eyes and bowed.

The Bene rose from his seat and approached Zheng San with curiosity.

"You are the yellow man we have heard so much about."

Zheng San bowed. "It is an honor to meet a man my emperor can call brother. I extend greetings from Zhu Quizhen, Emperor of the Middle Kingdom."

A Chinese warrior stepped forward carrying a jewel covered lacquer box and kneeled before the Bene. Maputo's guard stepped forward to receive the gift but the Bene waved him off. Maputo lifted the lid and a bright smile came to his face.

"Magnificent!" he exclaimed. Inside the jeweled box rested the most exquisite sword Changa had ever seen. The inch wide blade was obviously forged by expert hands, the flawless steel polished to a mirror reflection. The blade was punctuated by a hilt carved from ivory and banded with rings of gold. Inlays of green jade filled the space between each ring; within the ring bands silver dragons with ruby eyes danced. Bene lifted the sword from its cradle like a child.

Changa leaned close to Zheng San. "So I am not worth such a gift?"

Zheng San smiled. "Rank has its privileges. You are a great man, Bwana Diop, but you are not a Bene."

"I thank you for this gift," Maputo said. "Your Emperor is apparently a man of great wealth and power. My advisors have many questions for you."

Five elderly men wrapped in brightly colored robes and draped in gold came forward. They nodded to Zheng San and motioned for him to follow. They led the Chinese merchant to the sole tree standing at the crest of the hill and sat under the shady branches.

"Walk with me, Changa," Maputo commanded. The Bene set off at a slow pace, Changa and the Tuareg following at a respectful distance.

Changa decided to get to the point. "Great Bene, why have you summoned me?"

Maputo stopped, turning his head slightly. "Panya did not tell you?"

"We spoke, but our conversation was merely speculation. I would not try to know the mind of the Bene."

Maputo turned to face them. "Well, my friend. Let me bring your speculation to rest."

They stood at the edge of the summit. Below them a vast kraal held the finest collection of Zebu cattle ever seen in Zimbabwe. Each bovine was an exact copy, heads black from nose to neck, the rest pure white. The unique coloring was a result of careful breeding by Maputo's clan over generations. A herd of such caliber would bring a fortune in the Soafalan market; to the

Zimbabweans it was priceless.

"As you know, Panya is very special to me," Maputo said. "Years ago when she first came to my kingdom, I offered her marriage. I'm afraid I was too forceful and I drove her away."

"You were young," Changa replied.

"Yes, that is true," Maputo agreed. "When she returned, it was as if the ancestors were giving me a second chance. I have been patient with her this time. I feel I am closer than before."

Changa said nothing as he passed a concerned glance at the Tuareg. His companion responded, his hand moving close to the hilt of his takouba. Changa turned slowly and strolled towards the palace, his eyes darting about for the location of their horses. Maputo noticed and hurried to take his position in front of them.

"Something is holding her back," Maputo continued. "I sense she has feeling for me, but she hesitates."

They were back before the reed palace. Maputo's servant still held the sword box. He knelt as the Bene approached, extending the box to him. Zheng San had ended his meeting with the royal advisors and the group made its way to the horses. Changa's horse was tethered close by with the Tuareg's. It was then Changa took notice of the people in the camp. No women were present, only young men. Maputo had not come so far from home to negotiate a marriage. Changa and his cohorts were in the midst of a war camp.

Maputo opened the gilded box and extracted the sword.

"I spent many nights awake trying to discover this obstacle. Finally the answer rose one night with the full moon."

Changa rested his hand on the hilt of his sword, his throwing knives pouch hanging from his saddle, too far away to be of use.

"And what was your revelation?" he asked.

Maputo pointed his sword at Changa.

"You are the reason Panya will not marry me," he answered.

"I don't think so," Changa replied. "Panya is a strong willed woman. She makes her own decisions."

Maputo lowered the sword. "I'm asking for your help, Changa. Tell Panya that marrying me is best. Release her from your crew so she feels no obligation to anyone else. In return I offer you the herd as her dowry."

"I cannot accept your offer, Bene. My influence over Panya is not as great as you think. I will talk to her on your behalf, but I doubt she will listen. As I said before, she is of her own mind." Maputo's expression turned grim. "You act as if you don't see what is before you, like a bat in the daylight. Panya cannot love me as long as she loves you."

The accusation thrown from Maputo's mouth hit Changa off guard, so much so that he spotted the Han blade intended for his neck by chance. He threw up his right hand instinctively, catching the blow with his wrist knife. The blade cut into the iron ring, stopping short of slicing it in two. Changa twisted his arm, pulling the sword from Maputo's hand then slammed his open left hand into the Bene's chest, knocking him back into his bodyguards and onto the ground. The guards swarmed about him, shocked that their king had been pushed to the ground. It was the delay Changa hoped it would be. He ran for his horse, the Tuareg close by his side. The Han had witnessed the attack and were already mounted.

"Let's ride!" Changa shouted.

They galloped down the hill, hitting full stride on the sloping road leading from the camp. Zimbabwean warriors ran into their huts and emerged with swords, spears, bows, and orinkas. Changa kicked his mount to a faster gallop, the Tuareg beside him. They were halfway through the camp when Changa realized the Chinese were not with them. He turned his head to see them following, the warriors lined across the trail on their small, swift horses. They pulled small bows from their saddlebags, loading and firing with amazing speed and accuracy. Their fire was so devastating the Zimbabweans slowed to seek cover. By the time Changa and the others reached the perimeter of the camp, they were alone on the road to Sofala.

The Han increased their pace and caught Changa and the Tuareg. Zheng San rode up to Changa, a rare serious look on his face.

"What happened?" he asked.

"I underestimated Maputo's ambitions. He's going to attack Sofala."

"For Panya?"

"Panya may be a catalyst, but I think Maputo has been planning to take Sofala for some time. We must warn the city."

They rode full gallop to the city gates. Changa stopped at the guards, two menacing Samburu mercenaries.

"Sound the drums!" Changa ordered. "The Bene is coming with an army."

The guards looked skeptical.

"Do you know who I am?" Changa growled. The men recognized him and nodded.

"Then sound the damn drums!"

The men scaled the platforms holding the alarm drums and began pounding. The rumble was picked up by the prayer callers who yelled the warning from the minarets.

Changa, the Tuareg, and the Han rode through the streets

past curious people and city guards running to the gate in response to the call. They separated at the town market, the Han headed to their encampment, Changa and the Tuareg for the merchant guild house. Merchants gathered at the hall, rushing Changa as he arrived.

"What is going on?" they shouted.

"Maputo is coming with an army," he shouted back.

"Impossible!" Mulefu declared. "The Bene is a friend of this city."

"He's not anymore," Changa corrected. "We fled his camp a half a day's ride from the city. I don't know how soon he'll be here but he is coming."

"Shona are camped outside the city?"

Changa shook his head in disbelief. "You need to spend some time outside your counting house, Mulefu."

The merchants yelled and screamed, running away to their homes.

"Wait!" Changa yelled. "We need all of you to send your guardsmen to the gates. The city guard is not strong enough to stop Maputo alone."

"What about my goods?" someone shouted. A rumble of agreement swept the crowd.

"Listen to me!" Changa growled. "If we don't keep Maputo on the other side of the walls you won't be alive to worry about your warehouses. We live or die by what happens at the gates."

"That's easy for you to say, Changa," another voice replied.

"Your goods will be sailing away in your dhows before the Bene sees the gates."

Changa considered the man's words. There was no doubt he was going to load his ships and send them away as soon as possible. The Kazuri would stand by to remove him and the others if the battle turned for the worse.

"My dhows can only hold so much and I must consider my own. Bring your goods. My crew will load what we can but I make you no promises."

The merchants scattered back to their stores. Changa and the Tuareg rode to the docks. Panya and Zakee ran up to them.

"What's going on?" Panya asked.

"Your boyfriend is coming to pay a visit and he brought an army with him."

"Don't play with me, Changa."

"I'm not playing, Panya. Matupo's camp is a war camp. He offered lobola to me if I persuaded you to marry him. When I refused he tried to kill us."

Panya looked stupefied. "You refused?"

"Of course."

Panya punched Changa in the shoulder. "You fool!"

Changa was angry and confused. "What? Oh, now you want to marry him?"

"Of course not, you idiot!" Panya snarled. "If you agreed he would not be marching on us now."

"You're a beautiful woman, but you're not the sole reason Maputo is coming," Changa said. "I think he's been planning this for a long time."

Changa's anger transformed to curiosity. "Exactly what did you two talk about during your visits?"

Panya looked thoughtful for a moment as she recalled her conversations with the Bene. Suddenly her eyes widened.

"I told him everything," she admitted. "I thought he was only curious. He was using me for information!"

"We don't have much time," Changa said. "Zakee, go

aboard and gather the men. We'll leave a skeleton crew to take the ships out to sea. I need another team to go to the warehouse and move everything possible aboard the Hazina. The rest of the men will follow me to the south gate."

"As you wish, Changa," Zakee replied.

He ran up the plank onto the *Hazina*, yelling orders as he ascended. Changa's men from the *Kazuri* and the *Sendibada* dropped their boats over the sides and rowed to the docks. They gathered around him and the Tuareg waiting for their orders.

Before Changa could begin, Panya pushed her way to his side.

"What are you doing?" Changa asked.

"I'm going with you."

"Not this time, Panya. If Maputo's men see you it will give them incentive to fight to their fullest. I'm sure he's offered a reward to the man who brings you to him."

"I'll stay with the Hazina," she conceded. "But you send for me if you need me, Changa."

"I give you my word," Changa grinned.

Changa led his men through the streets of Sofala to the Western Gate. They met other armed men heading to the gate in groups and alone. Some were warriors, their taut, scarred bodies braced with chain mail, their swords, knives, and spears clattering against their shields as they marched. Others were hunters, masters of stalking and killing game but novices in the ways of battle.

Their worn spears and tattered shields would shatter when struck with Shona steel, but their numbers were welcomed. The rest were rabble, troublemakers and braggarts whose strength would last until the Bene's warriors appeared. Changa hoped their panic would not spread to the others when the time came.

Changa reached the gates with his men and smiled. The

Han had come. Zheng San stood by the gate with Mulefu and the other merchants brave enough to stand against the Bene.

"It is good to see you all, especially you, Zheng San," he said. "Did you bring your archers?"

"They stand ready, Bwana Changa," Zheng San replied. "I regret our commitment to your battle is not sincere."

"What do you mean?" Mulefu asked.

"We are here only to assist in repelling the Bene until our cargo is secure. Once that is done we will retire to the safety of our fleet."

"It is only fair," Changa said, disappointed. "We are thankful for your help, however brief it might be."

The hours passed swiftly as the makeshift army shored up the wooden walls and dirt mounds surrounding the city. The Swahili that settled Sofala never considered the inland chiefdoms a threat, sure in their natural superiority. They overlooked the wealth they passed to the Bene and the others, their eyes fixed on the ports of Arabia, India and beyond. So while the defenses of the harbor were strong and numerous, the walls facing the interior were few and weak. Only the main archway was built of stone.

The gate consisted of wooden planks held together by rusted steel strips, a pathetic defense at most.

The men rested as the sun fell below the western hills. Changa stood on the ramparts, gazing as far as he could into the bush. The hills stole away his light, making the task useless. Mulefu came to him, worried as always.

"Where is the Bene? He should have attacked by now."

Changa looked at Mulefu as if he was a fool. "So you're rushing him? Let's hope I'm wrong and he went back to his kingdom."

"You are not wrong, Bwana Changa. The Shona will come,

but they will not come now. It is too close to dark."

Changa turned to face the man who spoke. He was dark skinned with deep, serious eyes. His round body and broad shoulders barely fit his chain mail, a small conical helmet sitting high on his head.

"This is Shamafuta," Mulefu introduced. "He was once a slave of the Shona."

Shamafuta bowed to Changa. "The Shona will not fight at night. The spirits are too strong. Even the Bene's gris-gris is not powerful enough to hold back the spirits of his enemies at night."

Changa folded his arms across his chest. "When will his magic be strongest?"

"First light," Shamafuta replied. "That is the Shona's time."

"Good," Changa said. "We have time to rest. We'll divide the men into watches. We need to be alert during the night just in case Bene's magic has changed."

Changa left the details of the night watch to the city guard commander. He spent his night traveling back and forth between the gates and the docks, supervising the loading of his dhows and encouraging the warriors along the gates.

A crescent moon peeked down on Sofala, its feeble light swallowed by the torchlight flickering throughout the city. Despite his stamina, Changa was tired. He barely kept his eyes open while he watched the dock workers load the last of his cargo on the *Hazina*. The *baghlah's* capacity exceeded his expectations. The entire contents of his warehouse fit easily into its cavernous hold, leaving the *Sendibada* and the *Kazuri* free to receive the cargo of the other merchants.

Panya startled him when she placed her hand on his

shoulder.

"Come, Changa, you must rest. You're asleep on your feet."

She took his hand and led him to his cabin. Changa dropped down on his bed and removed his weapons.

"Always the mother hen," he commented.

"Someone must take care of you," Panya answered. "You won't take care of yourself, so until you find a woman stupid enough to marry you it's my job."

Changa smiled as he lay back on his bed. The feather mattress wrapped around his bulk like an eager lover, his tension soaking into its comfort. He was falling to sleep when he heard Panya's voice brush his ears like a tender wind.

"Changa, did you mean what you said?"

"What did I say?" Changa mumbled.

"You said I am beautiful," Panya reminded. "Did you mean it?"

Changa turned on his stomach. "Of course I did. So what?"

"Oh, nothing," Panya replied. "It's just good that you see me as a woman, not just another crew hand."

Changa turned onto his back then sat up, his face a picture of aggravation. "Why?"

Panya stepped back a bit, caught off guard by his angry tone. "Most men spill compliments like water just to get what they want. But you don't. It means more coming from you."

"A person should be aware of what they possess," Changa answered.

"Only then can they use their talents to their advantage. For a woman, beauty is strength. Add that to your other abilities and you are a very powerful woman, Panya. That's why I chose you for my crew. Only the best can work for me. Now let me sleep."

Panya beamed. "As you wish, Bwana." Panya opened the door then turned back.

"By the way, you're beautiful, too."

"Get out!" Changa snarled.

His eyes seemed closed only seconds when he was shaken awake. The Tuareg stood over him, his eyes urgent. Changa clamored out of bed and armed himself. They ran through the *Sendibada*, clamored down the plank and leaped onto their horses. They rode furiously to the gates, the city streets deserted in anticipation of Bene's attack.

Mulefu waved as they galloped up to the ramparts.

"Come, Changa, come quickly!"

Changa and the Tuareg followed Mulefu up the dirt and stone walls. Sofalan warriors lined the fortification, their nervous eyes following Changa as he reached the wall.

"Look!" Mulefu urged, gesturing toward the road. A lone man sat cross-legged in the middle of the road, his face hidden behind a large bull mask.

"The Bene's medicine priest," Shamafuta commented. "He is raising the spirits to guide the Shona to victory."

Zheng San scowled and called out in his native tongue. A Mongol archer stepped forward, loaded his bow and shot. The medicine priest's hand flashed across his face and he rolled away from the arrow. He sprang to his feet, holding the arrow in his hand. Raising the arrow over his head, he yelled and snapped the arrow in two.

The ground shook under the Sofalans feet. Panic swept the ramparts as the trembling increased.

"Stand fast!" Changa commanded.

He gripped the wooden beam in front of him and stared at the medicine priest. A dust cloud emerged behind the old man, rising higher with each moment passed. The city guard fell back behind the volunteers and brandished their orinkas, ready to kill any man that attempted to flee. Changa snatched his eyeglass from his waist belt and looked into the dirt storm.

"Brace the gate!" he yelled.

Cattle stormed up the road, a thick mass of bovine muscle and horns trampling everything in their path. The charging beasts parted only for the scattered trees and for the chanting medicine priest.

"Zheng San, order your archers to fire on the lead bulls!" Changa yelled.

Zheng San gave the order and his archers stepped forward with crossbows unlike any Changa had seen. They braced the crossbows against their waist and began working a lever attached to the weapon back and forth as fast as they could. The skies darkened as a shower of bolts spewed from the bows. Beasts stumbled and fell victim to their own. Other bulls spilled over the fallen as those behind began climbing the herd like a wave breaking over hapless boulders. Behind the sound of dying cattle Changa picked up the rising war chants of the advancing Shona.

The cattle continued their blind charge despite the carnage. They collided against the flimsy barricade and sent the bracers flying. Changa crashed onto the ground and blacked out.

For a brief moment he knew only pain and darkness then his eyes cleared to chaos. Men surrounded him, some dead, others injured. The wall leaned inward, the bellowing of the herd rising over the moans and curses of the confused Sofalans. The Tuareg appeared and pulled him to his feet, breaking his daze. His crew gathered around him while he struggled to his feet, their terrified eyes searching him for guidance.

"That wall is about to come down and when it does those damn beasts will trample everything in their path," he warned.

"Get to a building quickly and stay inside until they pass."

Like an evil prophesy the walls collapsed. Changa lurched for the nearest shelter, slamming his shoulder into the door and knocking it off the hinges. He and the others ducked into the house just as the herd poured into the streets. The cattle mass rumbled by, followed closely by Shona warriors advancing behind a wall of locked leather shields, their long assegais protruding from the gaps. Sofala's guardsmen spilled into the street from the surrounding buildings and charged the Shona, Changa and his men close behind. He smashed the leather and wood shield of the closest Shona warrior with powerful blows of his Damascus then finished him off with a head blow from his orinka. The Tuareg fought beside him, his takouba in his right hand, scimitar in his left, slashing and stabbing with his legendary speed and skill.

The Shona warriors realized there was no reward in attacking this group; there was easier prey in the city and a dead man collected no prize. They broke rank, scattering throughout the streets in small groups to hunt for loot.

Changa looked at the fighting around him and cursed. They had to make a stand; otherwise the Bene's warriors would wipe them out one group at a time.

"Fall back!" he shouted. "Make your way to the central market. Spread the word to all you meet to do the same!"

Changa and the Tuareg set out at a full run through the streets, fighting as they shouted to the cohorts to pull back to the market. Men struggled singly and in pairs, the rattle of swords and spears mixed with the cries and shouts and bellows of men and cattle. Changa ran from a narrow alley and was nearly trampled by a pair of bulls determined to continue their stampede.

They finally reached the central market. Other soldiers arrived, sent by the words of his men.

"Use the carts to form a barrier," he said. Changa turned to face the houses surrounding the market.

"If you can hear my voice, help us! Hiding in your homes will not save you!"

Men and women poured into the market. Changa directed them and the market transformed into a ragged line of carts, boxes and sheds, a reasonable line of defense. More soldiers arrived and were waved over the barriers.

Changa spotted the Han and called them to him.

"I see you are still with us," Changa said to a ragged looking Zheng San.

"I seem to have lost my way to the harbor," Zheng San replied.

"Place your men at the front of the barricade. Their arrows will slow the Shona down enough for us to mount a charge."

Sofala's defenders settled behind their barrier and waited. Half of the city was in Shona hands, the sounds of pillage echoing through the streets and alleyways to the central market. The din waned, replaced by the shouts of commands. The war chants began again.

The Shona emerged in formation. The Sofalans flung their spears and threw their orinkas in vain, the projectiles bouncing off the Shona's interlocked shields. The Mongols composite bows were deadlier, their arrows piercing the shields like ragged cloth. But there were not enough Mongol archers to stem the surge; the fallen warriors were dragged away as others took their place.

It was the Shona's turn. Throwing spears leapt from behind

the shield wall, arched through the sky and fell upon the Sofalans with lethal effect. No sooner had the spears come down did the Shona throw their orinkas. Theirs were not the hardened wooden clubs carried by the Sofalans; Shona orinkas were built of dense ebony wood crowned with a studded ball of iron the size of a fist.

The metal juggernauts smashed shields, heads, and arms, driving the Sofalans away from the barrier and giving the Shona the time they needed to charge.

Changa scrambled away, a metal orinka barely missing his head. He ran back to the barricade to see the Shona closing the gap. His stare was broken by a familiar sound; the boom of the *Kazuri's* cannons. Changa jumped for cover as the cannon shot exploded in the midst of the Shona. Five rounds slammed into the marketplace just beyond the barricades. Dust and dirt showered the market as Shona warriors staggered about dazed by the unexpected barrage. The Sofalans were stunned as well, scrambling about in the haze to reform their line for the expected assault.

Changa's shock was cleared by the clatter of hooves on stone behind him. He spun to see Panya streak by him astride his favorite Arabian.

"Panya, stop!" he shouted.

She rode on, urging the horse to the barricade. It jumped, clearing the makeshift wall and landed among the Shona.

"Maputo!" she shouted. "You have come for me so here I am!"

Changa scrambled to the top of the barricade.

"What the hell are you doing? Get back here now!"

Panya glowered at Changa then faced the Shona.

"Bene, show yourself!" she demanded.

The Shona warriors parted. Maputo approached in a gilded litter carried by eight broad shouldered slaves wearing loincloths and jeweled neck chains. He sat cross-legged, the bull helmet of his clan covering his head and obscuring his face. A leopard skin cloak fell from his shoulders; the golden bull symbol rested in the center of his chest, dangling from a thick gold chain. He held his jeweled orinka in his right hand, the sacred flywhisk in his left.

Maputo's calm face in the midst of battle radiated the spirit of a man used to power. Panya climbed down from the Arabian and sauntered towards him. They met between the ranks of Shona and Sofalans, the Bene's litter halting as Panya approached. She knelt and touched her forehead on the ground.

The litter was lowered and the Bene's linguist, Topwe, took his place beside the Bene.

"You think highly of yourself to imagine my master leads this army to claim you," he said.

"This is what you say," Panya replied, "yet we stand here because I called his name."

Topwe frowned before speaking again. "Sofala is a rich city. It has held my master's interest for some time now. A city of such stature deserves the care and benevolence of a strong bull."

Panya stood and marched to the Bene's side. Maputo looked at Topwe and nodded, dismissing the linguist.

"Taking this city is the worst thing you could do," Panya said.

"I listened to your stories," Maputo answered. "Your details were very accurate."

"You used me," she accused.

"As you used me," Maputo replied.

"If you take this city, yours will be destroyed. Zimbabwe's prosperity relies on a healthy Sofala."

"I will not harm the traders," Maputo said. "Their livelihood will not be interrupted. They will only answer to a new master."

"The Swahili will never accept a Bene. They will abandon Sofala as soon as they know all is lost."

"And what of you?" Maputo asked. "If I leave Sofala, do I leave with a wife?"

"Not now," Panya replied. "I respect your feelings, but I must go with Changa."

"You favor the Bakongo?"

"This is not about you or Changa. It's about what I need to do. I left before and I came back. I'll be back again."

Maputo's hard look fell away, replaced by a hopeful smile.

"You will accept my offer when you return?"

"Yes."

He raised his hand and his servants lifted the litter.

"I will leave Sofala. Consider this my lobola," Maputo said. "I give you two years, Panya. If you don't return by then I will come back to claim my bride price."

The litter bearers turned on the Bene's signal and strode away. The Shona warriors followed their Bene single file. In moments they were gone, disappearing down the road to Great Zimbabwe.

The people of Sofala broke out in celebration, hugging, kissing, and shouting in joy and relief. Panya slumped against her horse and let out a deep breath. Changa rushed over the barricade and down the other side, breaking Panya's brief respite.

"What were you thinking?" he said. "You could have been killed!"

P   anya smiled. "You're right, I could have. I didn't realize it until Bene spoke to me through Topwe. He's never done that before."

Changa was about to argue but was pushed aside by a horde of merchants led by a jubilant Mulefu.

"Panya you saved us all! Praise to Allah! Praise the ancestors!"

They carried Panya away, showering her with praise and promises of rewards. Changa watched in awe then laughed. It was no wonder the Bene was ready to destroy a city for her.

Chapter 4
Dragons and Spice

The citizens of Sofala spent weeks after the Shona attack rebuilding the city and preparing the dhows for the journey to the Middle Kingdom. Trade resumed between Sofala and Zimbabwe as if nothing had ever occurred. Panya refused to visit the Bene, fearing if she did he would not let her return despite his promises. She occupied her time treating wounded warriors and civilians.

Changa was in a foul mood for weeks after the attack. He learned he would have to pay for the damage done by his cannons to the central market. The entire guild ruled against him, ignoring his argument of saving the city and their cargo. When he finally returned their goods many merchants discovered a sizable portion missing. No one was brave enough to question the Bakongo, though it was assumed by all that the cost of the missing goods equaled the expense to repair the central market.

The winds finally shifted, blowing the flags atop the minarets northward. It was time to say farewell to the visitors from the East. Dhows and junks sagged with cargo, each pregnant with a wealth of ivory, leopard skins, gold and iron. In return the Sofalan market shimmered with silk, porcelains, medicines and spices from the East. The greatest gift arrived the day before the fleet's departure. A Shona procession appeared unexpectedly on a misty morning, rumbling drums announcing their arrival. As a gift of forgiveness, the Bene presented to the Chinese a menagerie of animals taken from the forests. Leopards, monkeys, and other animals were displayed, but the prize was a pair of giraffes captured in the scrublands to the south of Zimbabwe. Zheng San fell to his knees at the sight of the beasts, raising his hands in gratitude.

"Fortune smiles on us," he exclaimed. Changa and the others looked puzzled but kept their questions to themselves. Zheng San ran to Changa, his small eyes as wide as he could manage.

"Your land is truly blessed," he said. "The quilin roams your forests!"

"Quilin?"

"Yes, yes!" Zheng San replied. "In the Middle Kingdom this animal is a sign of good luck. The quilin assures us a safe journey home."

"You may not think so when you have to feed your good luck," Changa replied.

"That will be no problem," Zheng San said. "The quilin will be housed on the stable junk. We prepared special quarters for just a discovery. Stories of your land spoke of the sacred beast roaming free, and Bene Maputo has proven the stories true."

"Just how large is this stable junk?"

"You will soon find out, my friend."

A strong wind blew through the harbor, stirring the ships like waking children. Hundreds of ships dropped their sails and raised their anchors in unison. The smaller ships leapt forward like cheetahs, riding the wind to the front of the fleet. The larger ships were more patient, creeping forward as they gathered the wind in their massive sails. Soon the entire fleet was away, following the impatient winds eastward.

Changa stood at the helm of the *Hazina* and watched Sofala fade into the horizon. He was tired of the city, his restless spirit thankful for release and Zheng San's invitation. He gave the city another moment of his attention then turned away, looking ahead to the massive merchant fleet before him. Dhows and junks bobbed on the white-capped waves like fishing corks, each one at the mercy of the gods and the ancestors. In the center of it all was the Chinese treasure junk, the fantastic floating city laden with the wealth of Sofala. Changa spent the first day on deck, much to the disappointment of the crew. They were used to the scrutiny of the Tuareg, enjoyed the naïve exuberance of Zakee, and no one complained when Panya appeared. But Changa was a hard task master. As night reached out to meet them over the eastern horizon they realized Changa had no intentions of riding them.

Changa retired to his cabin at dusk. The space was much more opulent than his cabin on the *Kazuri* and *Sendibada*, a perfect complement to his position. A bed stretched the length of the wall opposite the cabin door, complete with a feathered mattress covered with silk sheets. His desk filled the corner to the left; the right wall supported a shelf crowded with maps and charts recently crafted in Zanzibar. His private chest rested below the shelf. The sound of the sea surrounded him, its calming rhythm occasionally disrupted by Han drums as the ships communicated with one another. Changa barely heard the knock on his door over the night sounds.

"Enter," he said.

The door opened and Panya stepped inside.

"Am I disturbing you?"

"No," Changa replied. "Come and sit."

Panya seemed relieved. She hurried to his bed and sat. Changa rested at his desk, curious at why she had come to his cabin.

"It's good to be away," she said.

"You mean at sea?"

"No, I mean away from Sofala. I couldn't stand another minute there."

Changa smirked. "The Bene was wearing on your nerves, I suppose."

"It wasn't just him," Panya replied. "It was everything – the smell, the sights, the people, everything."

"I didn't take you as the restless kind."

Panya leaned back on her arms and Changa found his eyes drawn to her breasts.

"Sometimes I forget I'm Oya's daughter," she said. "She is the orisha of water and wind, and she pushes me like a feather in her embrace."

"You should find another orisha to praise," Changa said.

Panya frowned. "You don't choose an orisha, it chooses you."

Changa was not about to be dragged into a religious discussion.

"How is your cabin?"

"It's okay," Panya replied with a shrug of her shoulders.

"Just okay?" It was Changa's turn to frown. "As I recall it's quite a space. I believe it's bigger than mine."

"It's not the size," Panya explained. "It's the company, or lack of it."

Changa's eyebrows rose. "You didn't sneak Maputo aboard, did you?"

Panya laughed. "No! I miss you."

Changa sat speechless for a moment. "Me?"

"Not you exactly, but your company," Panya explained. "We shared a cabin for a long time, you know."

Changa relaxed. "It was for your protection until the crew accepted you."

"I can handle myself," Panya replied.

"Against a few of them you could, but not all of them."

Panya folded her arms across her chest. "And I guess the mighty Changa Diop can slay them all with one swing of his mighty Damascus sword."

"Of course not," Changa admitted. "But they believe I can."

They were silent for a moment. Changa watched Panya, noticing her agitation. There was something else on her mind.

"Changa," she finally said, "why are you doing this?"

"That spice could make me a fortune," he replied too quickly.

"You are already wealthy," Panya observed. "You could have said no to Zheng San."

Changa didn't like the direction of the conversation. "But I didn't. I'm a restless soul, too. The east intrigues me."

"Is it the tebos?" she said.

Changa stood and let out a yawn to mask his discomfort. He was not going to talk about the tebos with Panya, at least not now. Their threat faded with every league sailed.

"You can't flee your fears," Panya said. "One day you must face them. It is the only way you can truly be free."

Changa fought back his anger. She did not know who commanded the deadly half dead shamans seeking his life.

"It's late, Panya," he said "Get some sleep."

Panya stared at him for a moment then stood. "I'll try, but I think I'd rest better under your protection."

Changa snarled and strode to his chest. He took out a hammock and strung it up across the room near his bookshelves.

"What a gentleman," Panya said.

Changa smiled. "The hammock is for you. Pleasant dreams."

*   *   *

The excitement of a new voyage inevitably gave way to the monotony of the open sea. The days were filled with the mundane chores required to keep a dhow above water and on course. A mood change permeated the fleet the further the vessels sailed away from the Swahili Coast. The boats gradually grouped themselves based on the origin of the occupants; Sofalans, Mombasans, and Malindians formed pods, the largest being the Chinese fleet.

Though the ships remained in sight of each other, the distances between them was noticeable. The tension eased when Changa and the other captains received an invitation to join Zheng San on the treasure junk. There was to be a feast celebrating their journey; the captains would dine on deck with the other Han dignitaries, but Changa and his cohorts received a special invitation to a private feast with Zheng San.

Changa, the Tuareg, Panya, and Zakee waited on the *Hazina* for the ferry sent to carry them to the treasure junk. A soft breeze caressed their robes as wisps of clouds sauntered above them in the sharp blue sky. The bahari went about their routine as their nahodha watched the bright colored junk make its way towards the *Hazina*.

"The others will be jealous," Panya whispered.

"Let them be," Changa answered. "Zheng San favored my company in Sofala. Why should it be any different at sea?"

"I don't have to explain that," Panya snapped. "Anyone close to the Han is close to his emperor and his power. That person, if they return to Sofala, would be the most powerful man in Sofala, perhaps among all the Swahili cities."

Changa roared with laughter. "I'm here for the spice."

The ferry pulled alongside the *Hazina* and the delegation

boarded. Changa and Panya sat in the center near the bow while Zakee and the Tuareg sat aft. The drummer flailed at the huge drum before him, the oarsmen falling in time with each other.

Despite the time with the fleet Changa was still in awe of the treasure ship. It loomed over the other ships like a mountain over the hills, its towering sails casting shadows over them all. The stern drummer ceased beating and lifted a large horn to his lips. He trumpeted and the hatch opened, easing into the water. Soldiers marched down the hatch edges holding red banners that snapped with the breeze. The ferry eased onto the hatch and the Sofalans disembarked. Zheng San waited at the top of the hatch draped in a splendid blue robe etched in red and yellow dragons. He greeted his guests with a broad smile and a respectful bow.

"Thank you for accepting my invitation."

Changa bowed. "How could I refuse? I have been anxious to take a safari through this behemoth."

"Of course, but first we must feast." Zheng San waved them forward. "Come, our dinner waits."

They followed Zheng San down the wide corridors to a cabin that rivaled the most ornate banquet hall in Sofala. An enormous ebonywood dining table rested upon a massive Persian rug, high back chairs surrounding it like small thrones. Lacquered squares filled with coiled golden dragons decorated the walls. A servant stood behind each chair. When the Sofalans entered, the servants snapped straight and pulled the chairs away for their guests.

They sat down to a sumptuous meal. The food came in quick succession, some familiar, others exotic. Changa ate with his usual gusto, laughing with old and new friends. The dinner ended with a dazzling performance of musicians and acrobats.

Zheng San escorted them through the treasure ship,

explaining each area in detail. They ended their tour above the stern, gazing out over the merchant fleet.

"You are a gracious host," Changa said.

"Thank you my friend. I feel it is always best to experience pleasure before discussing business."

He reached into his sleeve and extracted a folded map.

Changa's eyes gleamed. "Is this it?"

Zheng San spread out the map. "The island we seek isn't far from our current position. We should reach it in two days."

Changa leaned against the railing, looking into the distance. "We're not taking the fleet, are we?"

"No, my friend." Zheng San leaned beside him. "I hoped I could convince you to take us."

"I was going to suggest the same. I assume our cargo won't be large."

"No it won't. My source tells me there isn't much spice left. Those who hold the secret of processing it are long dead. What remains was created long ago and dwindles with each day."

"When do we leave?"

Zheng San smiled. "Tonight."

The remaining day crept by in nervous anticipation. Changa could barely contain his energy. Panya did not share his joy. She shadowed his every move, ready to share her objections but he wasn't interested in her opinion. The purpose of the journey was the spice; there was more value in a thimble of it than the entire cargo hold of the *Hazina*. He would listen to no challenge to his decision.

A Han cargo boat approached the *Hazina* at dusk, rowed by ten men in gray work clothes, their faces hidden by broad conical straw hats. The bahari dropped the cargo nets, lifting the workers and their cargo aboard. As the goods descended into the hold, the workers followed a bahari below deck to the mess hall where Changa and the Tuareg waited. The Han shed their disguises, revealing Zheng San and nine grim faced soldiers. The last man to disrobe resembled the Han but was much smaller; akin to a child except for the wisp of hair above his lip. Fear danced in his dark eyes as they darted between San and Changa.

Changa nodded at the man. "Is he your contact?"

Zheng San placed his hand on the man's shoulder. The man flinched and tried to step away but San's nails dug into his shoulder.

"He is Yongki. He will lead us to the spice."

Changa rubbed his chin. "Is this his decision?"

Zheng San frowned. "Does it matter?"

Changa began to protest but decided to drop the matter. He was more interested in obtaining the spice than debating the details of justice among the Han.

A moonless night shrouded the fleet in darkness that drank what little light the ships torches emitted. Changa and his crew worked in the void, easing the anchors up and turning their sails. Mikaili steered the *Kazuri* to the south. The sleek dhow fulfilled Changa's boast; the island rose over the horizon a day and a half later. A horde of hungry gulls swarmed over the ship, their constant cries adding to the tension on deck. Changa searched the shoreline for an obvious landfall but was disappointed. The dense forest ran up to the edge and spilled into the ocean. Changa had seen many forests in his travels, but never one as foreboding as the profusion of plants on the island.

Zheng San joined him, the diminutive island man by his side.

"Yongki says we are not far. There is a trail that runs from the water's edge directly to the *wat*, the temple that holds the spice."

Changa and the men loaded the boats and set out for the island, Yongki sitting at the bow of the lead boat with Zheng San.

They rowed along the shoreline for two miles before Yongki yelled, stabbing his finger at the shore. The rowers responded, maneuvering through jagged rocks to the dense shoreline. Yongki leaped from the boat and swam through the shallows. The boats glided forward, Changa and the others waiting until they ran aground before entering the warm transparent waves. Changa waded up Yongki who peered into the foliage. He stood beside the islander and looked, finally spotting a sliver of path obviously created by Yongki's small folk.

Zheng San came to stand beside them. "This is the path to riches," he announced.

Zheng San nodded and Yongki jumped into the jungle. Changa ducked under low branches, following the man into the trees. A sour odor assailed his nostrils as his large bulk was enveloped by branches heavy with broad, sticky leaves. Yongki waited, waving for them to follow. Changa and the others did their best but it was slow going. The pungent branches buffeted their torsos; thorny vines tore at their shins. Changa understood why Yongki was small. This land stunted his kind with its relentless density, weighing down a man so until it became a trait passed on through generations.

They covered two miles in a half day. Changa, a man of the forest, fared better that the Han and his companions. Zheng San and the others lay sprawled about among the trees, exhausted. Yongki looked at them all, disappointment on his face. He jumped up and down, waving angrily at the group.

"Save your energy, little one," Changa said. "This is as far

as we go today."

Zheng San stepped gingerly to Changa, his feet in obvious pain.

"We must camp here. My men and I can go no further."

"I'll scout out ahead a bit." Changa replied. "I don't trust your captive completely."

"As you wish." Zheng San bowed and returned to his men.

Changa walked on, Yongki stared suspiciously at him as he passed. The path remained difficult, becoming so narrow in some places he was barely able to follow it. He pushed on until dusk then headed back to camp, his stomach rumbling.

He was near the camp when terrified voices reached his ears. Changa snatched out his Damascus on the run, his brow tight with dread. He burst into the clearing and froze at the sight before him. Large reptilian creatures swarmed the camp, beasts as large as *mambas* but with smooth gray skin like snakes. They moved like simbas, jumping away from the frantic sword swings of the terrified Han soldiers then pouncing in to nip at their legs and arms. A soldier turned to run and a creature leapt on his back, its bulk slamming him into the underbrush. Other creatures swarmed around him like ants, ripping away flesh and lifting their heads to swallow their morbid prize.

"Komodo!" Yongki shouted as he ran back down the trail. The little man's yelling snapped Changa's daze and saved his life. The bushes shuddered near his feet; he jerked his leg high and a Komodo streaked past. Changa dived aside, avoiding the leap of a second beast. He hit the ground on his shoulder and rolled to his feet, his Damascus back in its scabbard, his throwing knives poised. The first Komodo was airborne, its mouth open. Changa threw the knife into its throat and it crashed into the ground. The second lizard jumped its companion, the smell of blood breaking whatever primal bond that existed between them.

Changa looked up to see Zheng San pulled to the ground by three lizards. He started in his direction but felt a tug at his arm. He spun, his sword raised and Yongki stumbled back, his hands protecting his face.

"No, bwana, no kill!" he squealed in broken Arabic. "We go, we go now!" Changa turned back to see a cluster of lizards where Zheng San had stood. Sounds of tearing fabric and flesh assailed his ears and he backed away from the carnage. All the Han were dead, the lizards fighting among themselves for the spoils. Yongki continued to pull at his arm and gesture for him to follow. They crept back until they were certain they were out of hearing range then ran as fast as their legs could take him.

The trail widened as a green mountain emerged over the canopy. The way became steeper; thick trees gave way to grass splotches and clumps of rocks littering the road. Yongki's slowed, his carefree expression replaced by nervous eyes. The constant drone of creatures unseen faded; an unnatural silence settled down around them. Instinct sent Changa's hand to his throwing knife bag. He took out a knife, comforted by the feel of its leather handle in his hand. Yongki stared at him, his eyes locked on the weapon. Changa shook his head and the man relaxed.

They continued climbing, the trail gradually disappearing into rock strewn, open ground. Yongki's gait became unsure with each step, his eyes darting right and left, forward and backwards. It was obvious to Changa he was unused to the open expanse.

Yongki stopped. Changa scanned the area and saw no sign of any temple, no indication of human settlement. He studied the stones and boulders for signs of workmanship but saw nothing. He returned to Yongki and shoved him, pointing ahead to the shrouded mountain.

"Keep going, damn you." Yongki sneered at Changa then ran. Changa raised his throwing knife, sighed and brought his arm down. Wounding the man would make him a burden; killing him served no purpose. He watched the man fade into the distance then continued alone.

The scattered stones yielded their secrets under scrutiny. Though they showed no signs of tooling, Changa suspected they once formed a road. Time and weather had dispersed them but Changa picked out the faint path through the grass and moss. The sun dipped into the western horizon, its light frayed by the tangled treetops. Changa picked up his pace, bounding over the road fragments and skirting those too large to leap. He hoped to find some type of shelter before nightfall. The memory of the Komodo slaughter gave spirit to his weary steps.

Dusk revealed the ruined temple grounds. Rows of knotted trees flanked the dilapidated road like ancient sentries, their order visible despite the undergrowth surrounding them. The arbor gated road led to a steep stone wall swathed in broad vines. The gate stood visible, a huge aperture of pitted stone and rusted metal. Changa crouched suddenly, his senses aware of what he could not see. He was not alone. He quit the road, slipping into the undergrowth with the stealth of a panther, feeling his way ahead until his calloused fingers grazed the temple wall. He gazed upward attempting to judge the wall's height but the dense leaves obscured his view. Changa shrugged his shoulders. He grasped a handful of vines and began to climb. He eased up the verdant barrier, stopping to reach out when he grasped an edge. He let go of the vines and heaved himself atop the wall. Changa stared at temple grounds as he rested. The courtyard spanned the size of a town, its gardens growing wild with neglect. Broken statues of heroes long dead lay prone in the grass, resembling the death throes of the men they represented. A faint smell of spice tickled his nose and he smiled triumphantly. He had found the source.

The wall pitched and Changa fell. He twisted as he plunged, grabbing at vines to stem his descent. A finger clamped around a vine and he jerked, pain shooting up his arm to his shoulder. He swung his body about, grabbing with his left hand until he found another vine. Changa shuffled sideways like a crab and a huge boulder struck the wall beside him, the impact knocking his feet free. He had no time to look for his attacker as he scrambled down the treacherous wall, stones crashing around him and showering him with dust and wood. A few feet from the ground Changa let go of the vines, landing in a crouch at the base. A large stone near him covered a gruesome sight; the body of Yongki lay broken like a selfish child's toy, his blank eyes staring upward. Changa looked away in time to see another massive stone hurtling towards him. He rolled away, the massive projectile landing where he stood.

The stones flew too fast to be launched from a catapult. Changa saw the hurler standing before the temple entrance, his fear checked by his desperation. The orange ape-like beast was twice Changa's size, a broad torso jammed on short thick legs. Its primal face looked almost peaceful as it lifted another stone with arms twice as long as its body. Its black eyes followed Changa then with a sudden lunge the stone flew at him. The shocking sight of the beast slowed his reflexes and the stone struck him a glancing blow. The world went black as Changa spun like a rag doll, landing in a heap in the moss. He struggled to his feet, his left arm hanging at his side, throbbing in pain, a throwing knife grasped in his right hand. The ape thing was charging, waddling on its stubby legs with a boulder looming over its head.

Changa threw his knife. The blade whirled through the

air, striking the creature's left arm at the elbow. The arm failed and the boulder crashed down on the beast head with a loud crack of skull and bones. It moaned and fell face first into the moss, jerked and fell still.

Changa kept his distance, walking wide around the beast, working his wounded arm as the feeling returned. Sword in hand he inched toward the beast, stabbing it to confirm its demise. Thin metal bands encircled its wrists, a sure sign the beast was trained by men to guard the temple. Changa jerked his knife from the creature's arm and its hand shot out to grip Changa's ankle. It stood, snatching Changa off his feet in the same motion. Changa winced, the flashing pain in his head blinding him. Then he was weightless, air rushing over him before the sensation ended suddenly and painfully. He attempted to stand but fell, overwhelmed by throbbing dizziness. His second attempt succeeded and none too soon, for when his eyes cleared the orange man-beast was almost upon him. Changa charged, leaping off his feet and into the beast. He wrapped his legs around its torso as he slammed his right forearm into its throat, his other arm hooking behind its head. He tightened every muscle in his body and the beast shrieked. It gripped at Changa attempting to tear him away but Changa clutched the beast like a python. Something inside the beast snapped and it reeled before collapsing onto its back. Changa winced as its weight crushed his arm but he did not loosen his grip. The beast's thrashing subsided; its last breath spewed on Changa's face.

He rolled off the beast and lay beside it, his body aching with each breath. The scent of spice reached him, dulling his senses. The aroma was irresistible; he stood despite his injuries and lurched toward the temple entrance.

A broad passageway of damp limestone stretched before

him. Torches leaned from the wall in equal intervals, some of them flickering dimly while others rested unlit. Odd geometric images decorated the floor and ceiling, their meaning incomprehensible to the dazed Sofalan. The bittersweet smell of spice enticed him deeper into the temple. He gripped his Damascus and stumbled onward, bracing for an ambush with every step.

The light wavered; darkness clung to his bare arms like a damp veil. Something moved in the distance and he strained to see in the dim light. Men were coming his way, their faces similar to Yongki's. They disappeared and the passageway transformed into an endless blue serenity. Changa looked side to side and saw nothing but sky until he looked below him and saw the gray stone of the passageway. His knees touched the stone and the passageway surrounded him again. The men were closer; blind smiles on their gaunt faces, their rotted teeth protruding from their thin mouths.

Another rush of pleasure seized him and Changa was in the sky again. He soared, the world passing beneath him like a swollen river. He flew higher and higher – and crashed onto the floor covered by his attackers, their stench mingling with the sweet odor of spice. Fists pounded his back, fingers pulled at his hair. Changa yelled and pushed to his feet, his attackers tumbling onto the stone floor. Two swipes of his sword sent four of them sprawling. The others tried to attack but Changa swept their emaciated bodies aside.

Spice burned his nostrils and his head ached. Charging down the corridor to his prize, he slipped in and out of consciousness, fighting the desire to succumb to the tantalizing images crowding his mind. The sensation was nothing like what he experienced in Sofala. This was pure spice, dangerous and addictive.

The corridor ended; the main chamber of the temple

opened before him. The rotund room reeked of spice. A dozen men sat cross-legged around a stone altar, swaying to the rhythm of a chant barely escaping their frail throats, rags hanging from their bony shoulders. Smoke rose from a massive stone mortar resting in the center of the altar, forming a hazy cloud obscuring the dome ceiling. The men were starving to death, enraptured by the hallucinations created by the burning herb. Changa realized if he stepped into the room he would be among them, wasting away to nothing under the enchantment of the spice. He backed away, fighting every desire in his mind for the survival of his body. He stumbled over the bodies of the slain, fell to his knees and crawled. He reached the temple entrance and the sun blinded him. He tried to stand but his legs would not allow it. The dreams overtook his mind and he ascended higher and higher until he was in the sky once more, soaring through the blue and entering the soothing blackness of oblivion.

Chapter 5
The Pirates of Sangir

Changa opened his eyes to a lateen sail fluttering against a cloudless sky. Panya came into view, her face motherly with concern. Her lips moved but he heard nothing. He smiled and his lips moved to answer. He had no idea what he was saying.

Panya snarled and slapped him. Sound exploded in his ears and the world came back to him. Wood creaked beneath him, the urgent voices of his crew welcomed. He was thankful for Panya's blow despite not knowing what he said to deserve it.

"Don't ever speak to me that way again!" Panya warned.

Changa lifted up on his elbows, his mind swimming. "The spice, it was the spice talking, not me," he apologized.

Panya look at him suspiciously. "At least you're awake."

"How did I get here?"

Panya pressed a cup of brown liquid that tasted as bad as it smelled. He forced down the brew and handed the cup back to her.

"The Tuareg led a party into the jungle to find you three days after you departed," she answered as she refilled the cup. "They found the remains of the Han in the moss field. A day later they discovered the temple."

The potion was working, clearing the spice fog from his head.

"How did they get past the spice?"

"Some didn't. The first men to scale the temple wall fell to their deaths when the spice took hold. The party escaped the temple and the Tuareg sent for me. I made a potion to counter the spice. Even with that only the Tuareg kept enough sense to get you away from the temple entrance."

Changa attempted to stand but his head spun.

"The spice is its own protection," he said. "There will be no profit from this venture. At least we still have cargo to trade."

"Not exactly," Panya replied.

Changa's stomach became queasy. "What do you mean?"

Panya stood and backed away from Changa. "The fleet is gone."

"You mean gone ahead, right?"

Zakee appeared with the Tuareg, the young Arab's face as grim as the Tuareg's eyes.

"She means gone as in stolen by pirates," he answered.

Changa slammed his fist into the deck and jumped to his feet. "Stolen by pirates? Impossible!"

Mikaili joined them, scowling as always. "It's possible all right, especially if those pirates are Sangir."

"Who are the Sangir?"

"A whole damn nation of pirates!" Mikaili spat. "I'm talking about families, clans, villages, cities, every damn one of them. Don't get me wrong, they have their share of feuds. But nothing brings them together like a chance to claim a huge prize, such as a treasure fleet blundering around the sea."

Changa sat back down. "I still don't see how they stole an entire fleet. How many ships did they sail?"

"None," Mikaili answered.

Changa glared at his captain. "This is not the time for

jokes, Mikaili."

"He tells the truth." Zakee stepped before Changa in Mikaili's defense. "They came on a moonless night under the cover of fog. The dead could not have been quieter. They came in hundreds of boats wearing loincloths and brandishing wicked knives with blades that curved like a snake. Our lookouts never saw them approach. We did not suspect a thing until they swarmed onto the deck. If it were not for Mikaili's nervousness and the Tuareg's diligence we would not be here. We fought them off and drove them back into the sea but our brethren were not as lucky. Burning ships lighted the night and the cries of dying men echoed over the sea. Panya raised a wind and we outran them. Mikaili steered us to you."

"We must get those ships back," Changa said.

"We have our dhows and our lives," Mikaili countered. "That's enough. It's time we went home."

"If we go back to Sofala now we'll have nothing. Everything we've built since leaving Mombasa will be gone. I'll have to disband the crews and sell the dhows."

Changa did not say the most important reason he could not return to Sofala without goods to trade. It rested in the quiet promise of an eight year old boy that watched his father executed and his mother and sisters dragged away to become the wives of the man who swung the axe that killed his father. He made a promise that day he meant to fulfill, and he needed the wealth of a merchant to do so.

A moment passed as everyone considered his words, each struggling with their own motives.

Mikaili stepped forward. "Sangir is hundreds of islands with thousands of decent harbors where a pirate can hide, but there is only one harbor that can hold a ship the size of the treasure junk. I can take us there."

Changa surveyed everyone. He saw no challenge or fear in their eyes.

"Take us to Sangir, Mikaili," he announced. "We have a treasure to reclaim."

The city of Topan skirted the edge of a wide, deep harbor on a hilly island that claimed the same name. Hidden among a maze of islands, it was considered a safe haven; not that the Sangir feared its discovery. Their reputation as fierce fighters kept their enemies at bay. The Malaccan Strait belonged to them; what they didn't receive in tribute they claimed at the point of their jagged sewars.

The men rowing quietly across the harbor knew nothing of the Sangir's reputation nor did they care. Their future rested in the hull of the towering treasure junk rocking on the black waves, surrounded by lesser junks and dhows captured with it. Sangir guards, never very diligent in their own waters were less so due to their three day celebration of recent good fortune. Those unlucky enough to pull duty slumped against the ships' masts, empty bottles of *arrack* surrounding them. They never heard the bahari scale the sides of the massive junk using the same hooked bamboo poles the Sangir favored. Once on board the bahari worked their way through the vessels, dealing silent death on every level. Minutes later the invaders waved white cloths visible only to the broad shouldered Bakonga in the crow's nest of the *Sendibada*, his eyeglass trained on the captured ships.

Changa swung his eyeglass to the men creeping towards the warehouse near the boat docks led by Zakee. They formed a perimeter around the structure as Zakee entered. The young prince emerged from the warehouse waving a red kerchief.

Changa put away his eyeglass and climbed down to the deck. His men circled him, each clad in black armor and brandishing black blades, awaiting his orders.

"It's time," he said.

They loaded the boats and rowed into the black river oozing from the island's interior into the languid sea. Theirs was the most dangerous task. The plan required them to transverse two miles of dark jungle to the fortified hill holding the Sangir treasure house. It was a diversion sure to bring every able Sangir running in their direction. They would have to fight until Zakee freed the ship crews and took them to the ships. Then they would escape back to the *Sendibada*, if they survived.

Mikaili was the first to set foot on land.

"This way," he whispered.

"Are you sure?"

Mikaili scowled and plunged into the trees. They moved fast despite the darkness and soon found themselves looking up a steep hill crowned by a square white building with a flat palm roof. A sturdy fence of narrow tree trunks encircled the hill base, each trunk capped with a wide rusted iron spike. Guards paced wearily behind the posts with sewars and spears, their eyes focused on the city, not the wall of blackness that was the jungle.

Changa crouched beside Mikaili.

"The guards are slaves," Mikaili whispered. "The Sangir post them to protect the treasure house from their own. They are not the problem. The true obstacle is the fence. The posts are trees grown close then trimmed to the shape you see. They contain a sap that hardens the wood like iron when the trees die."

"How do we get through them?" Changa asked.

"There is a gate on the other side but the key is kept by the headman of the ruling clan. The way through the fence is also our way to draw the Sangir from the city." Mikaili smiled. "The sap that hardens them makes them burn like oil."

Changa grinned as he unfastened a throwing knife and hurled it at the barricade. The knife spun and struck one of the trees, the sound drawing the attention of a guard. He was walking towards the sound when the second knife struck the first. The metal sparked and the post ignited. The guard yelled as the flames hopped from post to post, encircling the hill in a flaming halo.

Changa charged from the wood like a buffalo. He grunted as he slammed into a smoldering post. It crumbled under his force and he tumbled into the midst of the startled guards. He jumped to his feet then cleaved two guards before they snapped from shock. Mikaili and the others poured through the gap, surrounding the guards and cutting them down. Those lucky enough to escape the bahari's sudden attack fled up the hill to join their brethren protecting the treasure house. Changa led his men upward, waving his Damascus over his head. The guards formed a ragged line, sewars and spears ready. Mikaili pushed his way in front of Changa and yelled at the guards in a strange tongue. The guards backed away, cutting glances at each other and the old captain. Changa raised his hand and his men halted. Mikaili continued walking towards the guards, his voice calmer. A guard stepped forward, a short fierce-looking man with black hair and a voluptuous moustache. The two exchanged intense words and the guard returned to his cohorts. He shouted a few words to his comrades and they put down their blades in unison. They ran down the hill and disappeared into the jungle.

A stream of torches flowed from the city towards the hill.

"Here they come," Changa said. "We'll meet them at the gate."

He led his fighters down the hill. The Sangir made no

effort for stealth or deception; they ran headlong down the path, screaming and brandishing their blades. Changa and his men took position at the path before it expanded to surround the hill. He stood in the center flanked by three bahari on either side. The other men stood close behind, ready to fill a gap in the line if a man went down or was wounded. Changa held throwing knives in each hand, his bahari held their orinkas. As the Sangir came into view the bahari hurled the war clubs low, cutting down the front ranks. The rear ranks tripped over the wounded, torches falling from desperate hands and setting those on the ground ablaze. The charge wallowed in confusion, buying Changa and his comrades a few seconds more. But the Sangir recovered and the fight was on.

Changa slashed the first man across the neck and kicked him back into the mass. The second man went down spinning from a blow across the jaw, the third howling through broken teeth from a blow of Changa's sword hilt. The rest became a blur of steel, flesh and blood. The bahari held the line at the mouth of the path, beating back the endless swarm of Sangir. Sweat and blood burned Changa's eyes; his arms ached with each swing of his sword. The Sangir came on despite their casualties.

A ragged chorus of conch horns bellowed from the harbor. The Sangir broke off their attack, running back down the path to Topan. They were after Zakee now; Changa's part of the plan was complete. He looked to either side of him and bloodied bahari looked back, tired and triumphant. They were not the same men that began the fight with him. He stepped back and stumbled over wounded and dead, bahari and Sangir. Apparently some Sangir had worked their way through the jungle and almost succeeded flanking them. Zakee's discovery had saved their lives.

"Gather the dead and wounded," Changa ordered. "We're

going back to the ship. It's up to Zakee and the Tuareg now."

Changa was helping a wounded bahari to his feet when the man spoke.

"Where is Mikaili?"

Changa looked around. Bahari were leaving, using the torches of the dead Sangir to light the path back to the river and the *Sendibada*. Mikaili was not among them. Changa helped the wounded bahari to another man and searched the dead. The results left him relieved and puzzled; Mikaili was not with the dead, yet he was not among the living.

He grabbed his knives and ran down the road to Topan. Anger overruled fatigue; Mikaili had slipped into the city. Why, he didn't know. Whatever his reason for disappearing, he had put everyone's life in jeopardy. Changa would find him and get him back to the *Sendibada*. Once they were in open water he would kill him.

Changa slowed and crept into Topan. The entire town seemed to have run to the docks. Dirt streets emerged from where he stood into a mass of dilapidated bamboo huts. He picked a road and followed it into the city, frustration contorting his face as he searched for sign of Mikaili.

The ring of clashing steel drew Changa deeper into the city. He followed the sound down a cluttered road, stepping into an expansive section surrounding a cluster of stone buildings. Mikaili fought a barrel-chested man with gray hair and thin limbs. Their knives sparked as they struck, the old men struggling with surprising speed despite their age. Mikaili kept pace with his adversary, but it was obvious to Changa the man was toying with his captain.

Changa's throwing knife spun from his hand towards Mikaili's adversary. The old man turned and batted it away, his face surprised and angry. Mikaili jumped at the distraction, driving his knife into the man's gut. His satisfaction was momentary; the old man slashed Mikaili's shoulder as he fell away.

"Damn you, Mikaili!" Changa ran to his captain, catching him and easing him to the ground.

Mikaili struggled to breath, blood flowing through his fingers.

"He was the one, Changa," he managed to say. "He was my master."

Changa placed a sympathetic had on Mikaili's shoulder, easing the old captain down against the hut to bandage his wounds.

"So that's why you know so much about the Sangir."

Mikaili smiled then winced. "I won't bore you with the details of how I came to be so far from my beloved mountains, but one day I found myself a captive to these people. I served them for seven years before I managed to escape aboard a Champan grain ship delivering supplies to Topan. In Champa I worked as a loader until I earned and stole enough gold to buy passage to Calicut. From there I worked my way back to Mogadishu. I vowed never to sail again and, most of all, never to sail east. It seems I broke both those promises. But it was worth it to sink a blade into that bastard's gut. I hope God will forgive me."

Heated voices reached Changa's ears. The Sangir were coming back.

"Can you walk?"

"Yes."

"Can you run?"

Mikaili's expression was not encouraging. Changa searched about frantically and found what he needed. He bounded to a nearby hut, jerked the torch from its mount and ran to the shed, emerging with a ragged push cart. He gripped Mikaili and put him into the cart. He lit the torch then shoved it into the old captain's hand.

"Hold on tight!"

Changa grabbed the push cart handles and ran. Mikaili gripped the torch with one hand while using the other to stay in the jumbling cart as Changa sped through the city and into the jungle. Sangir cries rode heavy on Changa's ears and he ran faster, his thick legs bounding through the bushes, branches, and thorns. Pain bit his back but he charged on.

The jungle gave way and the *Sendibada* loomed before them. Changa stopped at the bank and dumped Mikaili into the river.

"Swim!"

He dove and swam like a madman. The Sangir ran into the clearing and were met by a storm of crossbow bolts that drove them back into the safety of the trees. Changa and Mikaili reached the ship and a boat splashed down before them. No sooner had they climbed in did it ascend under the watchful eyes of the *Sendibada*'s bahari. They helped Mikaili and Changa onto the deck, Changa shouting orders as soon as his feet touched wood.

"Strike the oars and get us down river!" He was making his way to the helm when a sharp pain stopped him in his tracks. He spun about to see Mikaili holding a bloody kris knife.

"A parting gift from the Sangir," Mikaili said. "It was sticking from your back."

Changa grinned. "I'll tend to it later. Get your shoulder tended to and get us out of here."

The oarsmen earned their gold, rowing the *Sendibada* quickly down the river and into the open sea. They continued rowing on a steady course until Topan appeared as a speck on the horizon. Mikaili stood at the helm, his wounded shoulder bandaged and his mood lifted by a bottle of spirits. He grinned as Changa arrived.

"Thank you for saving my life."

Changa shrugged. They stood side by side in silence, Mikaili steering them to the rendezvous. Changa relaxed as he saw the treasure ship sails rise over the horizon. The full fleet came into view soon afterwards, the *Hazina* and the *Kazuri* flying their signal flags.

"Take us to our friends, Mikaili." Changa turned to leave the helm.

"Where are you going?"

Changa turned his head slightly. "To bed," he replied. "Wake me when we get to China."

End Kitabu II

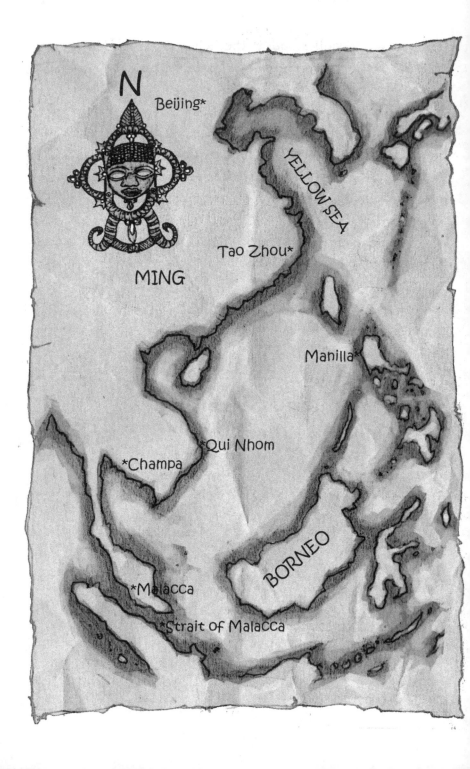

Kitabu Chatatu:
(Book Three)

The Emperor's Ransom

Chapter 1
Three Eunuchs

The Smoking Dragon towered over the chaotic docks of Qui Nhom, spreading its shadow over the southernmost port of the Champa kingdom. The enormous bi-level establishment catered to the well-to-do merchants of the city, a private club for the successful. Burly guards armed with swords and crossbows stood at the door and paced the perimeter, for despite its prosperity Qui Nhom was not safe. Champa was a loose collection of states united by their constant wars against the Annam kingdom to the north and the Khmer throne to the east. The result was a slave trade fueled by prisoners of war and merchandise gained by plunder. Everyone and everything in Qui Nhom was for sale.

Changa, the Tuareg, and Mikaili waited nervously at the door of the inn. Changa's hand twisted at the hilt of his Damascus, his wary eyes following the guards. He'd made a mistake coming here. This was a dangerous place. He and his men could be swallowed up into this mass, never to be seen again. He had let his greed lead him into a trap.

He turned to his men. "Let's go. Draw your swords."

"Wait," Mikaili said.

"For what? This place is a snake pit. The letter was a ruse to bring us into port. There could be slavers swarming my dhows as we speak."

"Our dhows won't be touched and neither will we,"

Mikaili assured him. "Do you think I would be here if there was trouble? The owners of the Smoking Dragon are honorable and powerful men. If they wanted to take us they would have done so the moment we sailed into the harbor."

Mikaili patted Changa's back, flashing his ragged smile.

"Relax rafiki. They will come soon."

The metal door slid open noiselessly, revealing a woman clothed in layers of sheer golden silk, her black hair cascading down onto her slim shoulders. Her deep brown eyes widened briefly then narrowed as she regarded the trio. She lingered on Changa then pressed her palms together as she bowed.

"Welcome to The Smoking Dragon, Bwana Diop," she said in perfect Swahili. "I am Mei Lien. Please follow me. My masters are anxious to meet you."

Changa entered the Smoking Dragon. The building was empty, the tables before him clear except for a row at the rear of the room. Three men dressed in emerald robes stood before them, their hands folded and heads bowed. The woman led them to the men then floated away, disappearing through a beaded curtain behind the banquet table.

The men raised their heads. The man in the center stepped forward and bowed again, his smile creasing his cherubic face, his eyes almost invisible.

"Welcome, Sultan Changa," he said, his shrill voice unusual for such a stout man. "I am Minsheng Liwei. These are my brothers, Minsheng Rong and Minsheng Shen. We are honored to meet the friend of Zheng San."

The mention of his former colleague cast a shadow over Changa's face.

"Thank you for your invitation. I am sorry to inform you that Zheng San is dead."

Liwei shook his head slowly. "Yes, we have heard as much. We all knew Brother San's obsession for the spice would one day kill him. Still, we are saddened at his loss."

Changa pinched his chin. "How did you know so soon? We only arrived yesterday."

"Sailors talk, my friend, and words fly faster than eagles. The word of Brother San's death came to us through merchants from Pelembang. We also heard of your great victory over the Sangir. Every ship passing through the Straits owes a great debt to you, Bwana Diop."

Rong waved his hand towards the feast. "Shall we?"

Changa folded his arms across his chest.

"Food can wait. Why have you summoned me?"

"A very direct man," Shen observed. He clapped his hands and servants appeared carrying an elaborate lacquer table and high back chairs. They sat; Changa, the Tuareg, and Mikaili opposite the eunuchs.

Shen continued. "We have no intentions of claiming Zheng San's treasure junk. We knew brother Zheng sought a foreigner to aid him on his quest for the spice. Apparently you are the one he chose. Are you sure there was an agreement between you?"

"Yes, of course," Changa answered. He relaxed and leaned back into his chair. "Our journey for the spice was unsuccessful, but we still have much to trade."

The eunuchs shifted about, nervous glances passing back and forth. Shen finally stopped the dance with a bow.

"I'm afraid that won't be possible," he said.

Changa raised in his seat, his hand falling back to his sword hilt.

"What do you mean, not possible?"

"Much has changed in the Middle Kingdom since Zheng

San's departure. I'm sure he spoke to you of Brother Wang Zen?"

"Yes. He is the emperor's advisor."

Shen lowered his head. "Brother Zen was a great man, a master among masters. But his dreams reached beyond his abilities. He led an army with the young Emperor against the Mongols. He was one hundred thousand strong to their twenty thousand, so he was sure of victory."

"He was a fool!" Rong spat. "He didn't listen to his generals and attacked the Mongols after a month of hard marching. The Mongols charged our army then fled after a brief engagement. It was a classic Mongol ruse. Our soldiers broke rank to finish them, ignoring the cries of their generals and listening instead to Wang Zen's ignorant encouragement. The barbarians turned about and slaughtered our soldiers like pigs."

Shen glanced at Rong. "Brother Wang was killed, some say by the Mongols, others say by his own generals. The emperor was captured. His uncle rules now, and sways to the words of Chongli and his hosts."

"What does that have to do with my cargo?" Changa asked.

Liwei raised his hand. "We eunuchs serve the emperor in every way. We provide his every need, from sweeping the steps of the Forbidden City to administering his royal holdings. We control the merchant trade, bringing the wealth of the world to his feet. We are not nobles; we owe everything to him. We have sacrificed our manhood to serve him.

"Chongli and his kind serve their own interest but say they serve the Kingdom. They bend the new emperor's ear with claims of immortality while poisoning him with lies against our counsel."

Liwei stopped talking, his voice trembling. Rong and Shen

placed their hands on his shoulders, whispering into his ear.

Shen continued. "We have been stripped of all power. Brother Ma Shun, commander of the Imperial Guard, attempted to defend us but was killed by Chongli's followers before the eyes of emperor. Our brothers have scattered into the countryside or fled to the harbors. Many have left the Kingdom, vowing never to return."

"The new emperor has banned all trade," Rong said, finally answering Changa's question. "Your dilemma is a double blow. Your goods will not be accepted because you are a foreigner, and you would be arrested if you appear in any harbor with Zheng San's fleet."

Changa slammed his fist on the table and everyone jumped to catch their goblets.

"I sailed thousands of leagues and risked my life for this? Tell me there is another reason you sought me!"

"There is, Bwana Diop," Rong confirmed. "Our contacts in the north tell us the emperor lives. The Mongols have sent several emissaries to the Forbidden City asking a ransom for his release but his uncle refuses to pay. He is emperor and has no intentions of releasing the throne."

"We are willing to pay," Shen continued. "We'll pay their ransom and help the true emperor regain his throne. There are many still loyal to him and the imperial guard simmers after the death of Ma Shun."

"But we have no way to get the ransom north," Liwei confessed. "We are watched within the empire. The northern borders teem with soldiers anticipating a Mongol invasion."

"So you want me to deliver your ransom to these Mongols," Changa concluded.

"Yes," the eunuchs replied.

Changa looked to his cohorts. The Tuareg's eyes were doubtful; Mikaili's entire being was negative as usual.

"You say your home is closed to foreigners. What makes me so special?"

"You are not just any barbarian," Shen answered. "The sailors have dubbed you the Black Sultan, the master of Africa and the slayer of the Sangir. You are famous!"

"Your companions are famous as well," Rong chimed in. "The mysterious covered man, the young Omani prince and the beautiful priestess that shares your bed and gives you the strength of the Four Winds."

Changa bit his lip to keep from laughing. He could imagine Panya's expression if she heard herself described as his lover.

"People will make exceptions to see you and hear your tales," Liwei said. "Changa Diop will be welcomed by all."

"I'm still risking my life. It seems to me this scheme is worth more than the privilege to unload my ships."

"An emperor would be indebted to you," Liwei answered. "If you free him the wealth of the Middle Kingdom would be open to you."

Changa grinned and Mikaili moaned.

"I need some time for I cannot speak for my crew. They follow me on their own accord, each of them free to make their own decisions, especially when it involves risking their lives. I must present this opportunity to them before giving you a final decision."

"We understand, Bwana Diop, but we must have our answer quickly," Shen advised. "There are too many eyes and ears in this city and most are easy to buy. We don't know how much time we have."

"Our guards will escort you to your dhows," Rong said.

"Please consider our proposal, Bwana Diop. You are our last hope."

"Thank you for the invitation." Changa stood and bowed. "You will have my answer by nightfall."

No sooner had the trio stepped out to the inn did Mikaili yell, startling the curious folk waiting to glimpse the Sultan.

"I can't believe you're considering this!"

Changa smiled at his navigator. "The chance to have an emperor in your debt is a rare opportunity. This could more than make up for the spice debacle."

"You can't trust these eunuchs," Mikaili argued. "They think nothing of those not of their kind. Once the emperor is free they'll deny everything. What will you do then, Sultan?"

"I'm not stupid, Ethiopian. I know damn well I'm a means to an end. If the crew agrees to take this on I'll follow the eunuchs' plan until I get the emperor. Then the rules will change."

"I'll have no part of this!" Mikaili shouted.

"Of course you won't. I want you to take the treasure junk someplace safe. If you don't hear from me in six months set sail for Sofala with the next monsoon. Mulefu will make sure everyone is paid."

"God punishes me for my past sins!" Mikaili exclaimed.

The Ethiopian sought the eyes of the Tuareg.

"If you ever thought of opening your mouth and talking some sense in your captain's head, please do it now."

The Tuareg glanced at Changa, turned back to Mikaili and shrugged. Mikaili threw up his hands. He walked in silence, his sullen eyes wandering between Changa and the Tuareg.

They reached the docks, boarded their boats and returned to the *Hazina*. Panya and Zakee waited eagerly on deck.

"So when do we trade?" the amir asked.

"We don't," Changa replied. He walked past them both and went below deck to the mess hall. They gathered around the table as the mess help brought them beer and hard bread. Changa explained the situation to them between swigs and bites. When he finished he braced himself for Panya's assault. Instead of a blistering interrogation, she smiled.

"If you feel this is right we should do it."

Changa's mouth gaped as her words registered. "Are you sure?"

Panya's smile broadened. "You told us we would take our dhows from the Sangir and we did. I have no reason to doubt any of your decisions."

Changa took a moment to savor Panya's change in attitude.

"Mikaili will take the Han ships out of the harbor. Prince Zakee, you will stay with the dhows."

"Begging your pardon, Changa, I would rather accompany you on this adventure. Mikaili can manage."

"Listen to the boy," Mikaili said. "He's right for the first time in his life."

Changa placed his hand on Zakee's shoulder. "I need you to stay with Mikaili to make sure he doesn't sail off without us. We may be gone as long as a year."

"I'm no fighter and I am not a thief," Mikaili declared. "There's an island one to two hundred leagues south of this cesspool that has enough fresh water and game to sustain us the duration of your safari."

Changa scratched his chin. Zakee had become a member of his crew, but he hadn't forgotten the amir's promise. There was a substantial ransom waiting for him in Oman and he didn't want to risk it. The young noble proved himself in battle, but something about this journey was making the Bakongo wary.

"You can come with us later. Tonight you stay with Mikaili. The Tuareg and Panya will return to the Smoking Dragon with me. The eunuchs wish to discuss the details of our journey."

"Take care, Changa," Mikaili warned. "If these eunuchs turn their back on you, no one will come to your aid."

The interest spurred by Changa's presence was mild compared to the commotion caused by Panya. People fought to see the legendary sorceress behind the power of the Swahili king. Changa failed to tell Panya the story. He hid his smile as some people fell to her feet and attempted to touch her clothes while others ran away with fearful looks on their faces. The crush of the curious was becoming serious when the eunuchs' henchmen arrived. They yelled as they beat back the onlookers with wicked bamboo staffs that left red welts wherever they landed.

Changa and Panya were greeted by the smiling face of Mei Lien.

"Welcome again Bwana Diop and Tuareg. Welcome, priestess," she sang. "My masters have retired for the day and left you in my hands. I will make sure needs are met until you meet with them again."

They were swarmed by a noisy group of brightly dressed women, their dainty hands separating them from one another and playfully guiding them to separate rooms. Before Changa could utter a protest he stood naked before a tub of steaming water. The women fell silent as they stared at his physique, some amused and others in wonder. He smirked and strolled to the tub, giving them a good show before climbing into the soothing liquid. To his surprise the women shed their clothes and joined him, laughing and shrieking as they scrubbed him clean.

Panya's bathe was serene. She stripped her clothes away

layer by layer, revealing the perfect body men across Africa fought to possess and that Changa somehow manage to ignore. The touch of warm water on her sepia skin was a gift she didn't deserve but enjoyed.

The Tuareg chased the servants away with the flat of his takouba. He entered his room, locking the door behind him. He was pleased the eunuchs had been observant. New blue robes hung beside his bath; a prayer rug rested nearby. He carefully unraveled his turban, exposing the face no man had seen since his initiation into manhood and indulged himself in a long bath and serene solitude.

Panya and the Tuareg were waiting with the eunuchs when Changa finally emerged from his bath. His bathing partners hovered around him, clinging to his massive arms and giggling like children. Shen waved his hand and they disappeared into the shadows, much to Changa's disappointment.

"Bwana Diop, I suspect the bath was to your liking?"

Changa adjusted his clothes. "You have a very polite way of telling someone they stink."

The eunuchs' smiles barely hid their embarrassment. "We apologize if we offended you," Shen replied. "We meant no harm."

"No harm done, Master Shen."

"Good. Come, we must discuss our plan."

The eunuchs led them to an oval table at the center of the meeting room. A canvas map covered the tabletop. The land masses, rivers, and waterways were unfamiliar to the three travelers, although Changa knew Mikaili would have no problem recognizing them. The decision to keep him with the ships was hard, but his navigation skills were more valuable to him than his knowledge of the Han. Mikaili was the only person capable of taking them back to Sofala.

Liwei stood over the map with a narrow bamboo pointer.

"Our people at the wall tell us the Mongols have agreed to free the emperor for our ransom. You will sail first for Quangzhou; from Quangzhou you will sail north to Shanghai. Our brothers there have arranged for a caravan to take you north to Mongolia."

Changa looked at the map, disturbed by the distance.

"This won't be as easy as it sounds."

"Of course not," Liwei agreed. "The emperor's spies are everywhere and the Confucians are more numerous. Every city you pass is a risk. There are bandits along the roads and soldiers at checkpoints in every town, not to mention those damn tax collectors at every turn."

Changa rubbed his chin. "Once I reach the Mongols and free your emperor, how will I be paid?"

"You cannot imagine the gratitude of the emperor if you complete this task," Shen said. "The wealth in your dhows pale in comparison to the emperor's treasure."

Changa frowned. "I'm sure the emperor will be generous upon his return to the throne. But I won't risk my life and the lives of my crew on a promise."

The eunuchs looked at each other, nodding as their eyes met.

"We have a junk filled with porcelain and silk waiting for you in Shanghai. Consider it your down payment."

Changa's smile brightened the room. "It is settled then. When do we leave?"

"Three weeks," Liwei replied. "We need time to confirm our plans with our brothers."

The weeks sped by as the Sofalans prepared for the

journey. Changa indulged in food, gambling and the pleasures of his bathing partners, while Panya made forays into the port city under the watchful eyes of the Tuareg and her bodyguards. The curiosity of the locals made her trips difficult but she insisted on the daily journeys to familiarize herself with this new land. Her Han improved rapidly as she conversed with the peddlers, priests, and shamans. Oya, her orisha, was here, though her presence was weak among so many non-believers. Still, it was enough to aid her if needed.

Two days before their departure Changa's indulgences finally abated. He slept alone, his snores reverberating throughout his room. Thousands of treks away from home, the memories of Kongo emerged in his mind, surrounding him with dense forest and pungent smells. He trudged the muddy roads with the narrow legs of a boy, man-shackles around his ankles and wrists, the wooden yoke biting into his narrow shoulders, his pain numbed by emptiness and vengeance. His blistered feet rose and fell in rhythm with his despondent companions. His weary eyes stared into the thick forests pressing the narrow trail and the darkness glared back. There was no refuge in the trees for the tebos followed, waiting for their chance to snatch him away and carry him to his death. His foot fell and the mud cracked like wood, waking him.

Changa's eyes sprang open and he heard the wood crack again. Silhouettes flickered by the door gaps and the smell of smoke seeped into his room. Changa's eyes adjusted and he found his bag of knives. He extracted a knife, his fingers grasping the throwing knife's leather wrapped handle.

The door crashed open and Changa flung his sheets and throwing knife at the invaders. The first man cursed as the sheet enveloped him then cried out when the throwing knife struck his chest. Changa sprang across the room, grabbing his Damascus as the second shadow leapt past his dying companion. He twisted and blocked the blade aimed at his chest with such force the weapon flew from his attacker's hand and into the wall on the opposite side of the room. The man kept coming, snatching two daggers from his waist sash. Changa backed away, knowing that daggers in the hands of a skilled fighter were deadlier than any sword. He ignored the man's weaving hands and dancing footwork, concentrating on the faint glimmer in his eyes. Follow the eyes and follow the man, the old pit fighter saying went. No one knew brutal pit lessons better than Changa.

He ignored the left hand feint then dodged the right hand knife, slashing the man's thigh. His howl filled the room as he staggered back toward the door. Changa sprang after him, slapping away a feeble jab and driving his foot into the man's stomach. The assassin rolled into the hallway, his hand clutching his gut. Changa chased him; he lifted his Damascus to finish the man but was blinded by black smoke billowing from below. The cloud shrouded him, burning his eyes and throat. He coughed, staggering from the sudden loss of air. The smoke cleared for a moment and Changa managed to open his eyes. The Smoking Dragon burned, fires scattered throughout the inn.

His assassin attempted to stand, using the rails along the atrium for support. Changa ran up to him and landed a hard side kick to his chest, sending him over the rail and into the thick smoke. He ran down the hall to Panya's room then kicked in the door. She stood on her bed, swinging her staff side to side, driving back the two assassins creeping toward her.

"Hey!" Changa yelled. The killers turned and his Damascus swung in a wide arc, disemboweling both men. They fell to their knees grasping their wounds, blood and entrails seeping through their fingers. Panya leapt over them, landing against Changa. He caught her with his left arm, pressing her close to his chest. Her arms wrapped around his neck. Changa spun and ran into the hall.

He put Panya down and they ran for the stairs.

"Where are the others?" Panya shouted.

The Tuareg emerged from the smoke, takouba in one hand, scimitar in the other, both blades dripping blood. He nodded and the trio bounded for the stairs. The lower level was in chaos, servants running about screaming, smoke obscuring vision and burning eyes and throats. The Tuareg grabbed Changa's arm, tugging him toward the exit.

"Not yet," Changa said. "We have to find the eunuchs."

A woman Changa recognized as one of his bathing partners ran up to them, tears running down her smudged cheeks, her elegant silks torn and singed. She clutched at Changa's garments, babbling and crying.

Changa turned to Panya. "Ask her if she's seen the eunuchs."

Panya took the woman's hands and spoke to her slowly. Words spilled out of the woman's mouth.

"She's talking too fast," Panya said. "I can't understand her."

Changa grabbed the woman by her shoulders and shook her to silence.

"Ask her now."

Panya talked to the woman and she answered calmly, her fearful eyes staring at Changa's angry face.

"The eunuchs are in the back of the inn!"

Panya spoke to the woman again and she led them through the smoke to the rear of the inn. The door to the eunuchs' chamber sagged from its hinges. The eunuchs lay on the floor in their own blood. Panya went to them, checking them for signs of life.

"Liwei is alive," she said. "The others are dead."

Changa grabbed the man, throwing him over his shoulder like a sack of grain.

"Let's get out of here!" he yelled.

They ran across the room and out into the streets. Bundles of straw blazed against the tavern walls, dead sentries strewn about with arrows protruding from their torsos. Changa and the others took cover behind the nearest house, searching the rooftops for bowmen. The Tuareg was the first to emerge. He looked up and down the roadways then waved to Changa and Panya. Changa shifted Liwei on his shoulder and they ran for the docks.

Their luck failed just before the marketplace. People scattered as they approached, revealing a score of masked men in gray, wide swords held high over their heads with one hand, the other hand extended, palms facing the Sofalans. Changa put Liwei down and drew his Damascus. Panya walked towards the warrior with her staff, but Changa stopped her.

"Stay with Liwei," he ordered. "Don't let anyone near him."

He charged the assassins before Panya could protest, the Tuareg beside him with both blades spinning before him. The duo smashed into the masked men; Changa ducked a swing at his head as he kicked the man's feet from under him and slashed him across the back as he fell. He grabbed a throwing knife and flung it into the back of an assassin approaching the Tuareg from behind. A yell from Panya warned him of his next attacker. Changa blocked his thrust with his wrist knife then slammed his hand into the man's throat, lifting him into the air and throwing him aside with a broken neck.

Three assassins remained as Changa rejoined the Tuareg,

three men that apparently decided their pay was not worth their lives. They had been sent to kill eunuchs, not battle two men that fought like tigers. They looked at each other in silent agreement then fled into the darkness.

Panya stood over Liwei, an assassin at her feet, blood oozing from his head. A rivulet of blood trickled from under her sleeve to her little finger. Changa ran to her but she waved him off.

"I'm fine. We have to hurry. Liwei is dying."

Changa lifted the eunuch and they resumed their run to the docks. Onlookers swarmed the dead assassins behind them, searching the bodies for valuables and tussling over the weapons. Others rushed the burning inn with buckets of water. No one dared approach the Sofalans. Their terrifying martial arts display against so many assassins was enough to keep the peasants away.

Zakee and a force of Kazuri bahari greeted them on the main road leading to the docks.

"We saw the fire. What's going on?"

"The Smiling Dragon was attacked," Changa replied. "Either someone knew the eunuchs were planning something or they knew a fortune was hidden inside the inn."

Zakee stared at Liwei's limp body.

"Is he a eunuch?"

"He's the only one alive."

Panya intervened. "He won't live long if we don't get him on board and treated."

The young amir unsheathed his sword. "Follow me."

He charged and the *Kazuri* bahari followed, swinging their blades and dispersing the crowd. Changa and Panya followed them to the docks and onto *Hazina*. Changa took Ziwei below to Panya's cabin, easing him down into her bed. Panya's hands flew across her shelves, grabbing vials and bottles then stacking them on the table beside her bed.

"Will he live?" Changa asked.

"I think so."

"Good. This plan won't succeed without him."

Panya glared. "Get out, Changa."

The Sofalans sailed out the harbor into the sea, continuing until the city torchlight was barely visible over the horizon. Changa finally rested, sitting down on the deck, his back against the bow. A beam of moonlight slithered across the lapping waves as a light wind stirred the sails. Doubt drifted into his thoughts as he watched the stars, a feeling as unfamiliar to him as the surrounding waters. They could end this quest tonight, sail back to Calicut and take their chances. At worst they would break even with the current cargo and they would be much safer. The eunuch's scheme was a great risk; at the same time it offered the greatest reward. He could purchase an army of Samburu and return to Bakonga, fulfilling his lifelong promise. His mother and sisters would finally be free. Usenge and his tebos was another matter.

Panya startled Changa when she appeared on deck, wiping her hands with a bloody cloth.

"He'll live," she said as she sat beside Changa. "He asks for his brothers."

Changa went to the eunuch. Liwei turned toward him as he entered the cabin, his face bunched in pain.

"They tried to kill us?" he whispered.

Changa nodded.

"It had to be the monks. They must have discovered our plan."

Liwei struggled to rise and Changa gently pushed him back on the bed. "You're hurt, Liwei. You must rest."

Liwei grasped Changa's wrists. "I must consult with my brothers. This was unexpected."

Changa looked away, the next words difficult to say. "Liwei, your brothers are dead."

Liwei's eyes went blank and closed. He laid still, his mouth forming words without sound. Moments later his body relaxed and he sat up.

"We must sail for Quangzhou immediately. Brother Li Chang will help us."

"Can you show us the way?" Changa asked.

Liwei scratched his head. "Shen was the best navigator, but I have sailed to Quangzhou many times. I will have to do."

"Then we will set sail tonight."

Changa burst onto the deck, a satisfied scowl on his face.

"Okay you sea rats, step lively! We have a destination!"

The bahari cheered. The time had come to make Qui Nhom a memory. Their real adventure was about to begin.

Chapter 2
The Invitation

Quangzhou appeared over the horizon like the face of a kind stranger, welcoming the battered Sofalans into her calm harbor. A lazy sun lounged above the bustling seaport, its visage obscured by drifting smoke. The Han Sea had finally relented, releasing the small fleet from her capricious grip. The ships limped into harbor, their crews thankful for the respite. The sour mood that had spread among the haggard seamen dissipated as the port drew closer. It wasn't home, but it was close enough.

Changa and Panya smiled at each other on deck, the Tuareg nearby in stoic silence. Zakee joined them, grasping the railing and emitting a loud exhale that reflected everyone's feelings.

"I hope never to see a storm again! Shaitan's hands are surely under these waters."

"Just give me solid ground," Changa agreed.

Panya's smile waned. "This safari is cursed."

Changa frowned. He hoped Panya's normally negative tone was gone, but the storm had apparently rekindled it. She stared at Changa, waiting for a reply. He said nothing, his eyes fixed on the harbor.

Liwei drifted in among them wearing a brilliant yellow robe displaying dancing dragons and prancing horses. Though he'd recovered physically from the attack on the Dragon, his gaunt face and distant eyes revealed his mental wounds had not yet healed. He folded his hands behind his back, leaning his upper body over the railing.

"We are here," he whispered. Liwei's eyes glistened as he gazed upon the harbor. "Shen would be happy. Quangzhou was his home."

Changa decided to change the subject. "Where will we find your brother?"

"He administers the royal warehouse."

The eunuch removed one of his rings, an elegant jade oval carved in the shape of an elephant. He extended it to Changa.

"I cannot go with you. It is too dangerous. Show the ring to Li Chang. You will be safe."

Changa was skeptical. "If you are in danger then so is your brother. Are you sure he still controls the warehouse?"

Liwei grasped Changa's wrist, pulling him closer. He put the ring in the Sofalan's palm and closed his fingers around it.

"Please help us, Bwana Changa. I know our situation means little to you, but we eunuchs have nothing to give but service to the emperor. We have lost our manhood; we can leave no family to remember us and praise our names. If we cannot serve, we cease to exist."

Changa frowned, angry with the conflict waging inside him. This deal grew riskier with every step, the profit less attractive with each day past. Yet he understood Liwei's plea.

"Panya, Tuareg, come with me," Changa said. "The rest of you keep an eye out and the sails ready."

Quangzhou was a collage of colors and faces, a diverse mix of people and cultures throughout the East. Like all merchant ports it vibrated with commerce, an energy that put Changa at ease. He had been in the lands of the East long enough to tell the difference between its people, and Quangzhou teemed with them.

Hans, Malays, Champans, Siamese and others sprinted about selling the endless flow of goods inching through the stifling streets. The ever present Arab could not be missed, always in the middle of the negotiations. The Imperial warehouses overlooked the constricted lanes, broad structures filling up blocks along the edge of the harbor. All goods entering the empire had to pass through their massive wooden doors. The eunuchs controlling them took a portion as tax after assessing the value of the goods. An unscrupulous man could make himself rich in such a position; Changa suspected much of the eunuchs' wealth came from what they skimmed.

Li Chang's small warehouse occupied a lot hidden by the bulk of its brethren. Merchants formed a line stretching from its modest entrance into the street, some holding small packages, others pushing carts filled with small wooden barrels. Bodyguards stood close by, their suspicious eyes evaluating every passer-by. Those eyes settled on the trio as they bypassed the line, heading directly to the entrance.

Changa stopped before a pair of imperial soldiers flanking the entrance.

"We are here to see Li Chang." Changa showed the guards Liwei's ring and the guards stepped aside.

The line of merchants continued. The walls on both sides were stacked with chests, some opened to reveal incredible amounts of jewels and trinkets. The procession ended before a large mahogany table, the thick base supported by legs carved to resemble jumping carp. Heavily armed guards stood on either side of the table flanking a man who despite his flowing robes resembled a boy. His bulbous head tottered on a long thin neck, his eyes larger than most of this land. He placed raw emeralds on a golden scale with delicate hands as a servant wrote down the totals in a massive ledger.

Changa cleared his throat and Li Chang looked up, frowning at the interruption.

"Who are you?"

Changa answered with Liwei's ring. Li Chang's eyes bulged and he jumped to his feet.

"Guards! Guards!" he yelled.

Changa's sword was halfway out of its sheath when he caught the motion in Li Chang's head. He pushed the sword down and raised his hand to his companions. The Tuareg's takouba had drawn blood, his blade resting in a bloody crease on the closest guard's neck. His scimitar was pressed against the belly of the other guard. Zakee stood dumbfounded, his mouth wide in shock. Guards surrounded them, taking their weapons and leading them to a sparse room behind the table. Li Chang followed, his arms folded behind his back.

"Hua and Juang will stay with me," he said. "Clear the warehouse. There will be no more taxation today."

Chang waited until the door closed behind the guards before speaking again.

"Where are the three? Are they well?"

Changa folded his arms across his chest. "Are we prisoners?"

Li Chang bowed. "I'm sorry but this was necessary. Hua and Juang are loyal to me. The others were sent by the emperor. They watch us all these days. It's only a matter of time before they round us up and kill us."

"Liwei is safe, but his brothers are dead," Changa said.

Li Chang paled and his hands cover his face.

"What happened?"

"Assassins attack the Dragon. We barely saved Liwei before

the inn burned to the ground."

"Many of my brothers outside the empire have been slain," Li Chang lamented. "It is more difficult inside. The emperor is too dependent on our services to get rid of us quickly. He must make us useless before he can slay us all."

Li Chang stepped closer to Changa, looking up and down his frame.

"You are the one they have chosen to deliver the ransom?"

Changa nodded.

"Good, we must hurry." He led them to the rear of the room and pressed his fingers against a broken stone in the wall. A door opened into a narrow alley, the rancid smell rushing in with the humid air.

"I suggest you wait until dark to return to your junks. Hua will take you to a safe place until then. I cannot leave the warehouse until sunset and my home is watched constantly. I will get what you need. Make sure you tell Liwei to take special care. Chongli is behind this purge and his eyes see where others are blind."

Hua stepped across the alley and opened the door to the opposite building. The aroma of food usurped the alley odor, stirring Changa's stomach.

"We'll wait for you until morning. If you fail to show my men and I will leave."

"I'll be there," Li Chang promised.

They hid in the rear of the restaurant, gorging on the delicacies surrounding them. Without a window to the outside they had no idea how long it had been dark when Hua finally returned and led them into the streets, checking before letting them emerge into the night. The taverns along their route swelled with shore men, their raucous chatter spilling into the night. Changa and his men looked at each other and grinned. Though they did not understand the language, they knew the moment well. Changa imagined himself among them bragging on his exploits against the Sangir and shouting down the skeptics.

Their journey to the dock was uneventful, the dhows a welcomed sight. Zakee ran up the plank and into the startled arms of Panya. Liwei emerged on deck, visibly disappointed.

"Li Chang is not with you."

"He's watched by imperial guards," Changa replied. "He had to sneak us out tonight. He warned us to be careful. Someone named Chongli is involved."

Liwei's eyes widened. He squatted on the deck, his head in his hands.

"It's over, we're finished," he cried.

Changa pulled the eunuch to his feet.

"What are you talking about? Who is this Chongli?"

"He is Zhengtong's closest advisor, the most powerful man in the empire. He is also fangshi."

Changa folded his arms across his chest, waiting for an explanation.

"Before the enlightenment of Confucius there were the fangshi," Liwei continued. "They are the diviners of the future, the wielders of magic and the holders to the secrets of immortality. The Han lived in fear of them, even more so than the emperor. The First Emperor consulted his fangshi before every important decision. It is said the Tang rose to power because of the fangshi, not their armies.

"The fangshi claim they know the secrets of immortality and that they can predict the future. For a time, they could. But as they gained wealth and power, their talents diminished. They fell into disfavor and were banished from the imperial court, forced to struggle for a living among the superstitious peasants.

"It is said that Chongli refused to accept banishment. He set out with a junk of his most loyal slaves and disciples, determined to find the Island of Immortals. From them he would learn the secrets of immortality and return the fangshi to a position of respect. But he vanished, until now."

"It sounds like a charlatan using a legend to his advantage," Changa commented.

Liwei looked at Changa, his eyes glistening.

"I apologize, Changa. We shouldn't have involved you in this. Take your dhows and go home. You'll find the merchants of Vijayanagar eager to trade with you. You can still salvage this journey."

"It's too late for that," Zakee announced, gesturing to the shore. Imperial soldiers marched up the main road towards the dock, scattering the frightened merchants before them.

"Weigh anchor!" Changa shouted. "Get us out of here, Mikaili!"

"Too late," Mikaili replied. "We're trapped."

Changa rushed to the opposite side of the dhow and saw the source of Mikaili's despondence. A fleet of ships weaved into the harbor flying the dragon standard of the emperor.

"Their warships worked their way into the merchant boats," Mikaili growled. "They have no cannon, but those men fumbling about on their decks are no bahari."

Changa cursed. He turned his frustration on Mikaili. "How did you let this happen? You were supposed to keep a lookout on the harbor!"

Mikaili responded, more surprised than angry. "Me? Let this happen? If you listened to me we'd be halfway to Calicut. This is your mess, Changa, not mine!"

Changa ignored Mikaili's retort as he tried to think of a way out. He could try running the blockade but he chanced losing one or all of his dhows. If there was a slim chance to get them free, he would take it. If there was no chance for a peaceful solution, they would fight.

A vessel approached, a bright green oddity resembling a floating palace. Eight rowers maneuvered it through the harbor traffic to the bow of the *Sendibada*. A man in flowing red robes emerged from beneath the tiered roof, unrolling a scroll. He read in a deep voice that carried across the waves to the Sofalans above.

Liwei listened, his eyes growing larger with every phrase. The orator completed his pronouncements, rolled up his scroll and folded his arms, apparently waiting for a response.

Changa dropped a hard hand on the eunuch's shoulder.

"Well, what did he say?"

"He is a messenger from the emperor. You are requested to attend an audience before the Son of Heaven in the Forbidden City. You are to set sail immediately."

Changa's council formed around him. For the first time he saw fear in everyone's eyes except the Tuareg. His silent friend was stoic as always, his eyes complacent.

"We have no choice," Changa explained to them all. "If we fight we'll lose. We didn't come this far to die."

Mikaili rolled his eyes. "Do you think if we go to see this emperor we'll live?"

"You have been summoned by the Son of Heaven," Liwei interjected. "If he wished us dead, we would be."

"What would he want with us?" Zakee asked.

"We'll find out soon enough," Changa answered. "Liwei,

tell your brethren we accept the emperor's invitation. We would be honored to visit him and his city."

Liwei bowed. "I am sorry for all of this, bwana."

"Quit apologizing," Changa said. "We're in a hole with only one way out. Let's hope this is it."

Chapter 3
The Wokou

The sea continued to punish the Sofalans, battering the dhows and their imperial escort as they sailed north to Beijing. Stops for fresh water and supplies were brief and communication between the ships non-existent. Changa worried about his crew, their fearful faces revealing their doubts about this safari. None of them had been so far away from Sofala except Mikaili. The taciturn navigator steered the *Kazuri* silently, occasion-ally touching the Coptic cross hanging around his neck.

Changa did his best to keep them focused on their duties, but he couldn't prevent the doubt seeping into their minds like seawater through their sewn hulls.

The ocean's temper waned, replaced by a wind colder than any the Sofalans had ever experienced. The bahari fell ill, their worn clothing unsuited for this cold clime. Changa convinced the imperial fleet to make an unscheduled landfall to purchase adequate clothing for his crew. The Han leader agreed to make landfall at the next port, a city named Taozhou.

The city perched over a deep harbor gouging into the surrounding green mountains. A massive wall skittered along the ridge, a grim gray gate the entrance in or out.

"This is more a fortress than a city," Changa commented.

Liwei nodded in agreement. "These are dangerous waters. Wokou are numerous here. They are bandits from across the sea.

They are devils, every last one."

A pair of imperial warships led them into the harbor, bearing the dragon banners of the emperor. Changa noticed the faces of the Han; they were not comfortable. The silence was broken by the sound of distant drums. Men rushed across the ramparts and took position inside the towers. The wooden shutters creaked open.

Changa recognized what they were doing.

"They're arming cannons!"

"Impossible," Liwei said. "We are among an imperial fleet. I'm sure they recognize us."

A cannon's roar echoed against the distant hills. The shot splashed before the fleet, a plume of gray water rising before them. The Han officers yelled, waving their banners furiously. Another cannon fired, its shot splashing closer to the lead junk. The flagmen rushed to the prow, his arms snapping the flags. His counterpart on the wall signaled back and the two engaged in an exchange that carried on too long. The dialogue ended abruptly, the fleet flagman dropping his flags and reporting to the imperial admiral.

"We are dropping anchor," Liwei translated. "The city commander refuses to let us any further into the harbor. Wokou have been spotted and he doesn't trust us."

"Can the admiral order the commander to let us in?"

"Fortified town commanders have special privileges granted by the emperor," Liwei explained. "Under peacetime our admiral outranks the commander, but since the Wokou threatens the rank shifts to the city commander."

The gate creaked open and a small delegation emerged. They boarded a large rowboat and rowed out to the fleet, joining the admiral on the deck of the *Kazuri*. The city commander had come personally, accompanied by a militia consisting of farmers with weapons from the imperial arsenal. Although their plain clothes spoke of their position, they stood proud beside the commander.

The commander's face was solemn as he spoke to the admiral, a striking contrast to the admiral's trembling impatience. The fleet commander extracted a jeweled scroll from his coat and handed it to the commander. The commander took his time unrolling the scroll, adding to the admiral's agitation. He read slowly, nodding his head with each word. He rolled up the scroll, handing it back to the commander. The admiral questioned the commander and the commander barked a reply. The city delegation left, climbing into their boats and rowing back to the city docks.

The admiral ranted until the Taozhou delegation disappeared behind their gate. He stormed off the deck, signaling for the fleet to proceed into the harbor.

"The commander has allowed us refuge for one night," Liwei said. "They will provide provisions and clothing, but we will not be allowed into the city."

"I admire Han hospitality," Changa joked.

"The commander is a practical man," Liwei explained. "He wants us gone before word of our presence reaches the Wokou. They would surely come for what we carry."

"We don't have much," Changa admitted.

"The Woku value our ships as much as our cargo," Liwei explained. "These ships could add greatly to their arsenal. The commander is concerned they would come for the ships then attack the city."

"I don't care so long as we get fresh clothes for my crews," Changa revealed. "Tell the admiral I'm willing to offer trade for the best clothing they can spare. I have a feeling we'll need them."

"You will indeed," Liwei agreed. "It's winter in Beijing."

"What does that mean?"

"It means it will be colder than this."

The imperial fleet finally docked. With only a day to rest and repair the Han and the Sofalans rushed to their duties. Panya and Liwei led the Swahili delegation meeting with the city leaders. Provisions and clothes were brought out of the city as promised. Oxen drawn wagons brimming with food, medicines, and other goods emerged from the walls. The people of Taozhou feared Wokou, but they apparently were brave enough to take advantage of a trade opportunity. The barren dock transformed to an open market in moments, Han and Swahili mingling for profit.

Evening came early to Taozhou as the gentle sun disappeared below the mountain rim looming behind the city. Fog crept in from the east with the dark, damping what little light the night torches could manage. Changa returned to the *Kazuri* with the clothes he purchased. Ivory made a significant difference; the imperial sailors stared enviously at the Sofalans draped in their new, thicker garments.

Changa worked his arms back and forth, trying to force his jacket to fit. He heard laughter and turned to see Panya grinning.

"Your size seems to be a problem," she said.

"At least I'm warm."

Panya came so close that they almost touched.

"Changa, are you sure about this safari?"

"I haven't been sure about anything since we landed in Champa," he confessed. "We should have headed back to Sofala after the spice debacle."

"Why didn't we?"

Changa hesitated before answering. "It's a feeling. We need to be here."

"I sense it, too," Panya said. "My connection to Oya is weak here so I cannot focus clearly. But something here is not as it should be."

Changa frowned. "Don't start with the spirit talk. It's not what I meant."

Panya hands rested on her hips. "What do you mean?"

He shrugged. "I'm not sure."

"You must understand something, Changa. When we drank Kintu's potion we changed. We are linked to the ancestors like no others can be. We have become more sensitive to a world beyond ordinary men. Your feelings may be more than uneasiness."

Changa wasn't listening. He was looking into the dark beyond the harbor.

"Listen!"

Panya looked out into the harbor. "To what?"

Large bright objects shrieked over them and exploded into the city walls, blowing stone into the sky. Drums and bells responded along the walls mingled with the frantic voices of the guards.

Changa ran to the alarm drum, pounding with all his might. Bahari clamored onto the deck armed with swords and crossbows. The dhow trembled as the cannon ports opened and the cannons rolled forward. The same sequence was repeated on the *Sendibada* and the *Hazina*. The Han junks performed a similar maneuver, dropping sails and weighing anchor, signaling each other with a flurry of waving torches.

Changa grasped Panya's shoulders. "Get to the Hazina. Tell Doraja to get my ships out of the harbor."

Panya knocked his hands away. "No. I'm staying with

you."

"No you're not!" Changa's booming voice drew everyone's attention. Panya stepped away, her eyes fearful. Changa cursed under his breath, angry at himself for the outburst.

"Please Panya, go to the Hazina," he said in a calmer tone. The Tuareg approached, his eyebrows bunched with concern as he looked at both of them.

"Go with her," Changa ordered his friend. The Tuareg nodded then focused on Panya. She gave Changa a long look then rushed to the boats.

Changa turned his attention to the bahari gathering around him.

"We must give the Sendibada and the Hazina a chance to escape the harbor. Let down the sails and get the oarsmen ready."

Another volley of rockets streaked overhead, hitting the walls again. Taozhou answered with a barrage from their dragon cannons, tongues of fire lapping from the mouths of the stylized barrels. A fire flash in the darkness brought a smile to Changa's face.

"Strike the pace," he yelled. "Let's give these Wokou a Sofalan welcome!"

The oars struck the ocean in rapid time, the *Kazuri* loping out to sea like a cheetah. Her bahari perched on the masts with loaded crossbows while below the gunners held their fuses for the first sign of a broadside. Changa braced himself by the bow, a throwing knife in each hand, his cautious eyes darting side to side. Zakee manned the stern, his eyes searching the darkness behind them.

"Where are the others?" Changa shouted.

"Right behind us!" Zakee shouted back.

"Good. Let's hope they don't follow us to the bottom of

this wretched harbor."

The Wokou appeared. The fleet was small, twenty ships in all; each rigged for battle and plunder. The flotilla was an agglomeration as diverse as the wretched souls manning them. No sooner had they come into view did the bahari open fire.

"Send them some light!" Changa yelled.

The archers lit their arrows and fired them into the darkness, some falling harm-less into the water but most finding their mark. Burning sails reflected off the water, illuminating the other ships.

"There's our path, rafikis!"

The oarsmen plowed forward a few more strokes before the *Kazuri* swung to port, exposing her guns. They fired in unison, smashing the nearest junk to pieces. The starboard oarsmen stopped and the port side resumed, turning the dhow to port. The starboard gunners fired, blowing away the junk advancing from the right. Changa scrambled from side to side, dodging arrows flying from the darkness while directing bow fire. The Wokou converged on the flagship, surrounding it in a ring of breaking and burning wood.

Changa yelled out to Zakee, "Where are they?"

Zakee ducked an arrow before yelling back, "They're out of the harbor!"

"Good. It's our turn!"

The drummer changed the rhythm and the oarsmen changed their stroke. The *Kazuri* lurched forward, its cannons firing at will, the archers trading fire with the encroaching Wokou. Changa and the others drew their swords, waiting for boarders. They came in a sudden rush, swinging from ropes and clamoring hand over hand across grappling lines. Changa caught a jumping Wokou mid-air and threw him back against the junk and into the sea. More Wokou fell onto the deck, far too many to repel. The archers threw their bows aside, drew their blades and slid down from their perches into the fray. Changa held the bow, slashing, hacking, kicking, and punching, a black storm whirling amongst a determined foe.

A terrible sound engulfed the *Kazuri*. The deck lurched and Changa fell onto his back. The entire ship listed starboard and he rolled into the bulwark. He grabbed the railing and pulled himself up. A pillar of smoke rose from a gaping hole in the deck. Bahari and Wokou dead lay tangled amidst the wooden debris. The cannons of Taozhou roared in the distance, their lethal packages landing among the junks, the *Kazuri* an unintended victim. Changa allowed himself a brief moment of sadness then set about saving his men. The Wokou fled, sure of the *Kazuri's* fate. Changa dashed to the bow and found Zakee lying on his back, his shirt bloodied. His chest moved erratically as he moaned. Changa stumbled to the deck drum and pounded a rhythm every bahari knew but dreaded to hear. They responded in a daze, trudging to the sides and jumping into the black waters. Changa dropped the batons and lifted Zakee onto his shoulder. He took one last look at his burning dhow, climbed onto the railing and jumped.

Chapter 4
The Heart of Zanj

Changa heaved Zakee onto the dock then grasped the edge as he gathered his strength. The swim had been a hard one, a struggle against the shifting waves and dangerous debris. As he lifted himself up a horde of hands pulled him onto the dock. He rolled onto his back, his chest burning with fatigue, his energy spilling into the wood under him.

"Bwana Diop, are you well?"

Liwei stared down on him with concern.

"That's a damn stupid question to ask!" he snapped.

He lay still for a few more minutes, his body slowly adjusting to his current situation. He heard voices, Han and Swahili, some urgent, others painful. Most had survived, but the *Kazuri* was gone, its final resting place the bottom of a foreign harbor.

Changa sat up. Bahari were sprawled along the dock, Han healers working their way through them. Three Han surrounded Zakee, their voices tight and agitated. Changa came to his feet and went to his injured friend.

"Will he be okay?"

"He's badly injured," Liwei replied. "He will need much rest and care. The general will allow us into Taozhou. Your actions impressed him. You are all welcomed."

"How did you survive?" Changa asked Liwei. "I didn't see you escape the ship. As a matter of fact, I didn't see you on the ship."

"I was never on board," Liwei confessed. "The dock master is a brother. He took me into the city when the attack began. I watched everything from the ramparts."

"Did the Sendibada and the Hazina escape?"

"Yes and no. They fled the harbor, but they were surrounded by the imperial fleet. Yours was the only ship that fought. I'm afraid they are on their way to Beijing."

Changa's thoughts went to Panya. She was alone among his crew for the first time since joining him. The situation could affect their discipline, putting her in danger. But the Tuareg was with her. Changa was sure of his silent friend's integrity. He would protect her, to the death if necessary.

"We have to follow them. Will your brethren give us a ship?"

Liwei bowed. "Bwana Changa, please listen to what I have to say. If we leave now we could not overtake them. You and your men are in no condition to sail anywhere. Even if we were to make it to Beijing, without imperial escort we will not be received. Our best chance to save your friends is to continue our safari to the Mongols and free the true emperor. He is the only person that can save your friends now."

"They could be dead by the time we reach your emperor."

"They could be dead now," Liwei said.

"No, they're still alive," Changa said confidently. "If they were dead I would know. I would feel it."

Liwei didn't question Changa's certainty. He nodded and remained silent.

"What about your ransom?" Changa asked. "Is it here?"

"No," Liwei confessed. "Li Chang sent it ahead when the imperial soldiers appeared. We will find it at the Long Wall."

There was still hope yet to salvage. The loss of the *Kazuri* was hard but nothing compared to the loss of Panya and the Tuareg. This was no longer a situation of profit or honor; Changa had to save his friends.

"We'll follow your plan," Changa said reluctantly. "There are items we need to retrieve from the Kazuri that will help us on our safari."

Liwei beamed. "Thank you, Changa. You will not regret your decision."

Changa and his men entered the city. Square stone houses topped with two tier roofs and clay shingles flanked narrow streets thick with people and livestock. The people were farmers, simple folk whose hard wrinkled faces and dark skin reflected their dependence on the gifts of sun and soil. The Sofalans were led to a large building in the city center. Beds were set up for the wounded, the Han eager to care for the brown-skinned warriors that fought valiantly to save their city. Changa made certain all his men were tended to before accepting any attention. He was led to a small cot where a small thick man with a warm smile tended to him. He drank a tea whose fragrance dulled his pain and restored his strength.

Liwei shuffled up followed by the city commander. Changa stood and bowed.

"Changa, this is Qi Jiguang, Commander of the Taozhou defenses."

Qi Jiguang bowed. He spoke with a pleasant voice that reflected his calm countenance. Liwei listened intensely, his eyes closed and his head nodding with each word.

"The commander thanks you for your help against the Wokou. He is honored by the presence of the Black Sultan. Whatever you wish he will provide as well as he can."

"I am humbled by his words," Changa replied. "Tell him I wish only rest and care for my men and provisions to continue my journey."

Qi Jiguang laughed as Liwei translated. The commander's reply made the eunuch smile.

"The commander says if all his requests were so simple his life would be useless. You will be given everything you need."

Changa bowed. "I thank you."

Qi Jiguang bowed and left the makeshift hospital.

"You have made a powerful friend," Liwei observed.

Changa shrugged. "We'll see how far his friendship extends."

"I don't think you'll be disappointed."

Liwei's words proved prophetic. The farmers of Taozhou pampered the Sofalans, nursing them while providing for their every need. Some invited the recovering bahari into their homes. Changa found himself living with the general. The home reminded Changa of the family compounds of Sofala. A grand stone entrance greeted him, opening into a large courtyard. Changa was led across the courtyard to a room opposite the gate. There was a spacious bed covered with fine cotton sheets and silk, bordered by a large writing desk and clothing chest. Changa dropped his gear and collapsed into the bed hoping for a good night's rest. Instead his mind swam with doubt. He wanted to find Panya and the Tuareg and get his men home. He was tired; he'd lost half his crew and all his dhows. He didn't understand this land or these people. His instincts didn't apply to this land. He had no choice but to help Liwei for now. If they were successful they would claim the emperor, but would they see their friends again? Would he see Panya again?

Two months passed before Changa and his men were fit to

travel. Their respite in Taozhou refreshed them mentally as well as physically and gave them time to acclimate to the land, its customs and its people.

The time had come to continue their trek. Commander Jiguang was generous with his provisions as promised. The Sofalans were given three wagon loads with food, pack mules and riding horses. Each man received a mare and two stallions for the journey. The party set out at sunrise, the farmers present for their adopted brothers' departure. The Sofalans descended into the verdant valley, following the narrow dirt road through the farmlands and into the mountains.

Changa and his companions were not prepared for the rigors of the mountain passes. The group encountered trails so steep the wagon had to be unloaded and the provisions carried by hand. Part way through the gray peaks winter wind broke through, bringing blinding snow and bitter cold with it. The party persevered, led by mountain guides supplied by the general. Six miles of trail took four days of treacherous travel.

The winter persisted as the mountains relented. The path wound downhill, expanding into a snow covered valley. They found shelter in a small village at the base of the peaks, sharing their provisions with the impoverished villagers. The people were polite and curious; some ran their fingers across the Sofalans faces, looking to see if their brown color remained.

After two days the party moved on. Winter followed them north like a starving wolf, pushing the Sofalans to the brink of endurance. The sky was icy blue, so clear the sun burned their eyes. New snow covered the hard ground, a virgin white blanket hiding the dingy ice from the past weeks. Changa was growing use to the harsh weather, though he still longed for Sofala's humid heat.

On the afternoon of the third day the party crested a precipitous rise and was confronted by a vast valley dense with evergreens, their weak branches sagging with clumps of snow. The undergrowth was clear of ice, emitting a sweet warm breeze.

Liwei joined him. "We will leave the road here. There is a trail that takes us around the valley."

"Why not follow this road?" Changa asked. "The weather seems pleasant among the trees."

"Some places are not meant for men," Liwei answered. "We won't lose much time following the other trail. We are close to the wall now, which means we are close to my brothers and the ransom."

Changa and his men followed Liwei and the Han around the forest. The path snaked into a crowd of low wooded hills, their broad summits capped with snow. The band crested the mounts at dusk and was confronted by an astounding site. A massive wall loomed before them, undulating over a ridge that disappeared into the eastern and western horizon. The empty ramparts hovered over them, its shadow bringing premature darkness over the lands beneath it.

"This is the Long Wall," Liwei said.

Changa was speechless. He tried to imagine the massive amount of material and men required to build such a structure. He also tried to imagine an enemy so terrible that such a structure was needed to keep them out.

"We will camp in the hills tonight," Liwei told Changa. "There is shelter within the Wall, but imperial guards patrol the ramparts and may come upon us. We'll be safer in the hills."

They suffered a long night battered by the relentless winds. Changa lay cocooned in heavy woolen blankets and pelts but could not sleep. His bleary eyes stared at the Wall, his mind musing on the adventures ahead. He was anxious to secure the ransom, free the emperor and return to Sofala. This safari had gone on long enough. Even the thought of tebos did not deter his conclusion. He was ready to go home.

The sun rose with its usual weakness, barely stirring the travelers from their frozen slumber. Changa gathered his provision quickly, ready to begin the latest leg of their dismal journey. Liwei approached him and bowed.

"I am deeply sorry, bwana Diop. It is true we haven't taken the most direct route to the Wall but we must be discreet. I am sure the Emperor's men are searching for us. The brothers helping us do so at their own peril. Many of them will lose their lives when they are discovered. Please understand that I don't take your sacrifice lightly. My own brothers have already paid too high a price."

Changa was embarrassed by Liwei's speech. This man was watching his entire life destroyed. His future, the future of his brotherhood, depended on a single hope.

"Let's go to the village," Changa said. "The sooner we arrive the sooner the both of us can save our friends."

The descent was far quicker than the climb. A sense of urgency flowed through them all, sparking a pace that was reckless but necessary. That pace quickened when the guides spotted smoke rising over the evergreens from the direction of the village. Changa was the first into the clearing. The village remnants smoldered before him, the stench of burned flesh and wood pervasive. Nothing stood; ashes and charred bones littered the ground. No one was spared.

Liwei looked upon the scene, leapt from his horse and fell to his knees. The other Han did the same, some scooping up the ashes and smearing them on their faces and clothes.

"Bahari, search the area!" Changa barked. He walked to Liwei, draping a friendly harm around his shoulders.

"This is no time to grieve, my friend. We must find the ransom soon. What does it look like?"

Liwei didn't answer. He banged his head against the ground, his sobs so deep he coughed. Changa grasped his shoulders and lifted him to his feet.

"Listen to me!" he shouted. "We can do nothing for these folks but we can save our friends. You must tell me where to find the ransom."

Liwei wiped his face with his sleeve.

"It's over. Even if I knew where the ransom box is, what good will it do? The village is destroyed. The ransom is surely gone."

Changa's men returned with glum faces. Nafasi stepped forward and bowed.

"Everything was burned. We found tracks leading away from the village into the forest."

Changa had to make a decision. If he was to risk the lives of his men he needed to know if following the tracks was worth the risk.

"Liwei, what is this ransom?"

Liwei straightened his robes and cleaned his face with the sleeve. He closed his eyes for a moment before he answered.

"Three hundred years ago the Han were overrun by a people beyond the Long Wall called the Mongols. Their empire stretched from the China Sea to the land of the whites. Their leader, Chingis Khan, ruled his empire from Karakorum. During the height of its strength Chingis's son Ogedei presented his father with the greatest gift he ever received. It was called the Heart of Zanj, a diamond as large as a man's fist and as perfect as the sun.

When the Khan died the Heart was lost. His sons scoured the entire empire but failed to recover the precious treasure."

Changa could not contain his astonishment. The Heart of Zanj was a legend among the Swahili, a jewel so precious no one dared to believe it existed. The legend told of a diamond pulled from the breast of the Satima Mountains by a god so ancient no one remembered his name. He took the Heart to the East to hide it from his jealous brethren. It was said when the Heart returned to the Satima, the mountains would rise to rule all men and peace would reign over all.

"You possess the Heart?"

Liwei closed his eyes. "Possessed it is the more appropriate statement."

Merchant lust burned in Changa's chest. Acquiring the Heart would make him the richest man in Swahililand. He could damn the emperor and head home. There was still the matter of Panya and the rest of his crew trapped in Beijing and Prince Zakee recover-ing in Taozhou, but he was sure the Heart would bring more than enough gold to save them all. But who would buy it? Better still, who would try to steal it? His life would become a constant vigil to protect the jewel from everyone, even his own men. He would give up his freedom for a prison of wealth.

"Gather the men, Nafasi. We'll follow the trail and find the Heart."

"No, Changa," Liwei urged. "Do not go there. Let the jewel be."

"Whoever or whatever destroyed this village took the Heart into those woods. I intend to follow."

"If you enter the forest you will break a covenant made long ago between these people and the creatures that dwell within."

Changa looked around. "It seems the covenant's been

broken."

"It is our doing. We shouldn't have brought the Heart so near to it. Even it understands the value of such a treasure."

"We're going after the Heart, Liwei. I've seen many strange things in my life, but nothing that couldn't be handled with determination and a sharp sword."

Changa led his men into the woods. Warm humid air enveloped him and a memory emerged, a vision of himself as a boy staggering through the jagged Ethiopian peaks, a heavy yoke lashed to his narrow shoulders. His breath burned; each gasp like fire in his chest. But his captors wouldn't let him rest. They prodded him forward, threatening to kill him if he fell. So he stumbled on, his fatigue replaced by an angry determination to live until they day he faced his enslavers as a free man.

Changa pushed the memory away, concentrating on the charred footprints leading deeper into the trees. The evergreens edged closer on either side, hunched over the path like curious old men. The air warmed so Changa discarded his coat along the trail. The forest grew denser, the gaps between trees filled with ferns and vines, flora more suited for a warmer clime.

Searing heat burst toward Changa and he threw up his arms as he shut his eyes. Flames smashed his chest, knocking him on his back and stealing his breath. He was lifted and thrown upward through the branches, landing on his side in the thick under-brush. The heat rushed toward him again but this time he reacted, throwing a knife with his free hand in the direction of the source. Something screamed; a sound unlike anything he'd ever heard, a voice that burned like the fire around him. Changa gripped the trunk of the nearest pine, pulling himself up despite the sharp pain in his side. Steam rose from his body and his clothes smoldered, fabric falling away piece by piece. The evergreen smoked then burst into flames around him like torches. The world became an inferno; yet he did not burn.

The flame thing approached him warily. Changa tried to make out an image but his mind couldn't grasp the monstrosity before him. It shifted with every second, each form unique from the previous. The only constant was the heat. Suddenly it charged, hot tendrils lashing at his face. With no chance to flee Changa attacked, jamming his left arm into the flames and grasping for some type of hold. Pain raced up to his shoulder as he smelled his flesh burn. He shoved his arm deeper and found substance. He gripped it and the fire wavered. Changa pulled his sword from the scabbard, drawing it back as he aimed its point where his other hand gripped the wriggling fire. With a desperate yell he plunged his blade into the living inferno. The fire shuddered. Changa gripped his hilt with both hands, shoving the blade deeper into the tempest. A shriek burst from the being, the force blasting Changa away in a wave of vicious flame. He fell into a clump of tree limbs and leaves, his charred body smoldering. The temperature of the air around him plunged, enveloping him in frigid oblivion.

His men surged around him, their frantic voices annoying him despite his searing pain. He looked at his left arm and watched the burned skin flake off. The pain subsided, the feeling rapidly replaced by the numbing cold.

"Give me a coat," he croaked.

Nafasi took off his coat and wrapped it around Changa. Changa pushed the Kazuri commander away and stood, surprised at how strong he felt despite his wounds. He walked to where the body of the fire creature lay. A Han lay sprawled on a pile of burned grass, Changa's sword lodged in his thick throat. He lay nude, his entire body covered with tattoos resembling Han calligraphy.

"He was a shaman, no doubt," Changa surmised. The surrounding bahari nodded their heads in agreement.

"Search the area," Changa ordered. "Find the box"

The bahari searched the trees, none of them surprised that Changa recovered so quickly from his battle with the shaman. They seemed to have expected it. Changa inspected his body again as he removed his borrowed coat. The charred skin was gone, replaced by a layer of pink peppered with dark brown spots that expanded before his eyes. In moments his arm was healed. Kintu's elixir had helped him once again.

A bahari interrupted him.

"Bwana, we found nothing."

Changa put the coat back on and jerked his sword free from the shaman's neck.

"It's here somewhere," he said. He found a narrow trail leading deeper into the woods.

"Come. Let's see if our flaming friend has a home."

They followed the trail into the forest. Ice formed on the evergreens, the mystical heat subsiding with every second. The trail widened, pushing back the trees to reveal a glimpse of an opening ahead. The road spilled into a broad clearing occupied by the shaman's domain. A gray wall rose from the blackened earth, the courtyard gate facing them. The party crept through the open gates, swords and throwing knives ready. Loot from the ravaged village was piled in the center of the courtyard, singed remains of the once prosperous town.

As they approached the pile people emerged from the rooms along the walls. Their ragged clothes hung from their filthy shoulders, their faces gaunt and sad. Most were women; the males among them were boys.

One woman approached Changa, her blank eyes locked

on his. She reached out, touching him with one finger. She drew it back and studied it then touched him again. This time she ran the finger from his forearm to his hand. The others came closer, touching the bahari the same way.

"They have never seen black men before," Liwei said.

Changa turned to see the eunuch and his men entering the courtyard. They pressed close to each other, fear in their eyes. Liwei spoke to the woman and she backed away. She answered the eunuch and bowed.

"She is the head wife of the shaman. She and the others were offerings from the village. The shaman accepted them as wives in return for sparing the village. The children are his."

She spoke again, smiling at Changa.

"She thanks you for freeing them," Liwei continued. "She is thankful your burned skin protected you from his fire."

"Ask her about the Heart," Changa replied.

Liwei asked and the woman grasped Changa's arm. She dragged him to the room opposite the gate. They stepped into the shaman's bed chamber, an opulent space filled with large porcelain jars and extravagant mahogany furniture. A wide canopy bed draped with sheer silk rested opposite the entrance. The woman towed Changa to the bed then pulled the sheets aside, revealing a jade box carved in the shape of a coiled dragon. Its bared ivory teeth exposed a forked tongue created with a string of brilliant rubies. Gray pearl eyes glared while flakes of gold seemed to shimmer with anger down the creature's back, ending at its tail. The box itself was a treasure.

Changa sat beside the box and opened it. The Heart of Zanj rested in a bed of royal blue silk, glimmering with the light of perfection. A diamond the size of a man's fist exquisitely cut to resemble a human heart, the sight of the jewel held Changa's fascination. He closed the lid and handed the box to Liwei.

"Take it before I change my mind," he growled.

Liwei looked relieved. "You have done us a great service, Changa."

Changa shrugged. "Your emperor owes me, Liwei. I intend to collect."

Chapter 5
Chongli

Panya pulled her coat tighter as the *Sendibada* sailed into Beijing Harbor. The Tuareg stood beside her, oblivious to the frigid air, his arms folded across his chest as always. The *Hazina* sailed close by, Daraja, Mikaili's first mate, steering the dhow as close as he dared. The imperial fleet encircled them, guiding the Swahili ships into the crowded harbor.

She missed Changa. She imagined him standing beside her, his stoic face gazing at the sprawling city as if he'd visited a thousand times. Then he would smile at her and go about his business, barking orders on the deck while she followed behind with her worries and concerns. He handled her like everyone else, brushing aside her arguments and occasionally fussing when she became unbearable. But he cared about her; he would die for her or any member of his crew.

The Tuareg touched her shoulder, drawing her from her thoughts. A barge approached, a wide flat bottomed craft flying bright yellow banners and skirted with flowing red silk. Emerald green dragons embroidered into the silk undulated with the wind. A delegation of elderly men draped in plain gray robes occupied the stern, flanked by drummers rapping out a steady rhythm.

"I believe this barge is for us," Panya said. "Come, let us meet the Son of Heaven."

Panya had chosen her outfit carefully, well aware of the seriousness of her meeting. She wore her favorite dress, a silk wrap that complimented her bosom and hips while clinching tight around her small waist with a thin gold chain. An amber necklace draped from her neck, a talisman disguised as a jewel. Her father gave the precious necklace to her as a wedding gift and she thanked him by running away. She closed her eyes, running her hand back and forth on the smooth resin as the images of Yorubaland filled her troubled mind. Ife appeared, its white washed buildings and wide avenues lined with broad leaf palms bustling with proud black skinned people. She inhaled the aromas of the market, the sweet ripe fruits, pungent fish and savory meats. Oyewole's face appeared, his wide white smile like a crescent moon, his rough hands pulling her along to see his latest prank. They were true twins, inseparable and imperious. Among the Yoruba, crossing twins was to invite bad luck, so they were allowed every indulgence.

They were good children in spite of the special treatment. Her brother became her protector as they grew older, though his attention was rarely needed because of her own skills. He was the only man she felt truly safe with until she became a member of Changa's crew.

Panya, the Tuareg, and a squad of bahari from the *Sendibada* descended the catwalk into the barge. The monks stared at Panya, their mouths forming little circles. One of the monks, the youngest by the look of his thin moustache, came and bowed.

"Lady Panya, I welcome you on behalf of the Son of Heaven. He is thankful you arrived safely. His heart was heavy upon hearing the fate of the Sultan."

Panya hesitated as the unthinkable flashed before her eyes.

"I am grateful for the emperor's concern, but I'm sure the Sultan is fine. He was detained in Taozhou. He will join us soon."

The monk gave Panya a distressed look.

"We pray that is the case."

He gestured to a padded seat in the center of the barge.

"Please, sit," he urged. "It is our emperor's wish to serve you with care."

Panya bowed and sat. The seat was truly comfortable, so much so that Panya felt guilty for the luxury. She looked into the eyes of the bahari and detected no negative feelings. They accepted Changa's hierarchy with no question.

An imperial escort awaited them at the docks. Panya was led from the barge to a wagon just as elaborate. She envied the Tuareg and others; although they walked beside the wagon, they had clear view of the city. She peeked through the silk curtains and was in awe. Beijing was the largest city she'd ever experienced, crowded with people wherever she looked. The wealth of the Middle Kingdom was on display, from its wide paved roads to the countless homes, palaces, and buildings casting a constant shadow over them. Musicians preceded them, their music more a warning than entertainment of the gathering crowds. The Tuareg and the bahari managed to keep their composure despite the pressing curious that reached out to touch the dark-skinned strangers among them. Panya could decipher some of the babble rising from the crowd, some of it complimentary, some of it less so. Overall, the Chinese were as fascinated by the Sofalans as the Sofalans were with them.

After a long procession they reached the emperor's palace, the Forbidden City. The complex filled the city center, its thick walls looming over the surrounding buildings. They entered through the south gate, emerging into the imperial courtyard. Panya's procession halted before a building which was a palace in itself.

The young monk greeted her as she climbed out of the wagon.

"Please enjoy this guest house for the night. Your men will be quartered with imperial guards."

"The Tuareg remains with me," Panya said.

The monk bowed. "As you wish."

A short, wide man shuffled up to the monk and bowed deeply. The monk looked at him with contempt.

"This is Guangli. He will see to your needs while you are the emperor's guest. The emperor will receive you tomorrow."

The monk left Panya and the Tuareg in the hands of Guangli. The eunuch led Panya and the Tuareg up the steps, opening the doors to the gates of the guest house.

"I'm pleased to serve you," Guangli said in good Arabic.

"Thank you for your service," Panya replied.

Guangli moved closer to them both.

"I must speak quickly," he said in Swahili. "You are in danger here. You must leave as soon as possible."

Panya kept her face unemotional as she answered. "We've done nothing. Why are we in trouble?"

"It is not the emperor, it is the fangshi. He is the true reason you are here."

"How can we leave now?" Panya asked. "We are in the Forbidden City."

"I'll do what I can," Guangli answered. "Stay alert. You must be ready when I come."

Guangli went to the room opposite the main gate, sliding the door aside to Panya's room.

"As I said, I will do what I can."

Panya and the Tuareg entered the room. The promise of its

opulent comfort was dulled by the eunuch's warning. The eunuch reappeared in the door of the bedroom, breathing hard.

"I almost forgot. Changa and the others are well. They travel north to meet the Mongols with the ransom. Let us pray their mission is successful."

Guangli hurried down the stairs and disappeared. Panya and the Tuareg looked at each other, riveted by the eunuch's parting words.

"I knew he was still alive," she whispered.

The Tuareg nodded his head, but concern lurked in his brown eyes.

"I know they still must complete the journey," she conceded. "At least he lives. That is enough."

They explored the house together and decided which rooms to occupy. The Tuareg selected the servant's room which fitted his status for the moment. Panya's room was clearly meant for the master of the house. A large bed occupied the center, draped by a sky blue silken drape decorated with white cotton clouds and dragons. She pulled the drapes aside and collapsed on the cushions. No sooner had she closed her eyes when she was awakened by a persistent tapping on her door. She opened her drowsy eyes to the Tuareg and Guangli standing before her. The eunuch was flanked by two young women dressed in peasant gray pants and jackets.

"I apologize for the intrusion, Lady Panya. I assumed you would wish to take a long bath after your journey."

"You're a thoughtful man."

The women went to the rear of the house and prepared the bath. Panya disrobed and entered the water, succumbing to the warm sensation. The scent of familiar herbs filled her senses and she closed her eyes. Weariness settled in, a combination of worry and fatigue dragging her into a deep dreamless sleep. When she awoke the women were gone. A towel rested by the bath with a yellow silken robe festooned with red lotus blossoms. In her room her clothes rested on her bed. She dressed, her peace slowly replaced by a growing nervousness. The house was quiet, a stillness that seemed unnatural for such a large palace. She went to the Tuareg's room and found him sound asleep, his veil covering his face even at rest. She backed out and went into the main courtyard.

She was startled by a man draped in a golden robe standing before a long table holding a feast. At first glance he seemed young despite his bald head and long moustache. He emitted a ka that rivaled Kintu's, smiling as he motioned Panya to the table.

"I hope you're hungry," he said in perfect Swahili. "My servants were a bit overzealous in their presentation."

"You are Chongli," she said.

The fangshi smiled and nodded.

"Please, Panya, sit. We have much to discuss."

Panya went to the table and sat. Chongli sat in the seat opposite her.

"My visions were true. You are beautiful."

Panya glanced at the food covering the table. She was famished but her apprehension was far greater than her appetite.

"I was expecting an audience with the emperor," she finally said.

Chongli laughed. "The emperor would never entertain an audience with foreigners. He is a Confucian. He believes there is nothing of importance beyond the bounds of the Middle Kingdom."

Panya fought to keep her composure despite Chongli's disturbing revelation.

"You don't seem to agree," she said.

"Of course not." Chongli picked up a steamed dumpling with his chopsticks and popped it into his mouth.

"I sent the ships to bring you here. I expected the sultan to be with you."

Panya picked up a dumpling and ate it. The taste made her moan. She had almost finished it when she tasted a familiar herb. Chongli was attempting to drug her. She pushed the plate away and he smiled.

"You are perceptive. The others will sleep for a time, long enough for you and me to speak."

"What do you want, Chongli?" she asked.

"Let me tell you a story," he said, ignoring her question. "I think you'll find it interesting."

He ate another dumpling. "I was born five hundred years ago in Lang-ye on the Shandong peninsula," he said in perfect Yoruba. This time Panya could not hide her shock. Chongli smiled and continued.

"Lang-ye is a spiritual place, the home of all fangshi. My father was the greatest fangshi of his era and he taught me all he knew. It was only a matter of time before his talents would be noticed by the emperor. The Son of Heaven sent for us when I was a young man eager for the chance to prove myself and achieve my own success. The royal family gave me the perfect opportunity. My father and I became rivals, both of us trying to best the other with our predictions and advice to the royal family. When it became clear we were of equal talent, the emperor decided to enter our competition.

"There is an island to the east where the Eight Great Immortals live. They exist in constant meditation, free of the physical demands of mortality. It is said that if a person could reach this place, the immortals would share their secret. The emperor is a man like us all, and like us he desires to live forever. He granted my father a fleet of his finest junks with the order to find this island. He had one year; if he failed, it would be my turn. My father took the challenge and sailed to the east. A year passed and he didn't return. After six more months I was sure I would never see my father again. Two years to the day of my father's departure I was summoned to the palace. The challenge that was given to my father was given to me.

"Our journey was doomed from the start. Storm after storm beset us, destroying our junks one by one. The men begged to turn back but I refused. I threatened the men with all the power I could summon, driving them on to our unknown destination. The day arrived when even I lost hope. On that day I and my crew huddled on one battered junk, a massive typhoon spinning towards us. We were too tired to go on and too fatigued to run. We made our prayers to the ancestors then waited to join them. The typhoon swallowed us and our ragged junk was thrown like a child's toy. Men fell overboard and disappeared into the churning black waves. The sea lifted us into the sky and smashed us. I awoke among the debris, washed ashore on a white sandy beach. My crew was dead. I was alone."

Chongli filled a bowl with soup from his side of the table. He set it before Panya.

"Go ahead, I know you are hungry. I assure you it is untainted."

Panya took a sip. The concoction was drug free and delicious, the warm sour liquid soothing her inside and out. She finished the bowl before looking up into Chongli's pleased face.

"You say your junk was crushed, yet you survived."

"Barely," Chongli confessed. "I was broken like a stick and delirious with pain. I don't know how I ended up on the shore away from the waves, but my pain subsided as soon as my back touched the sand. The soil seemed alive, shifting my body, aligning my broken bones as some unseen force mended them. How long the healing took I cannot say; when I awoke I was restored. I stood and gazed out into the ocean. The storm still raged in the distance, waves spawned by its malevolence crashing against the shore. When I turned to see my landfall a different scene greeted my eyes. Palm trees swayed as far as I could see in either direction, bulging with coconuts and other fruits. The treetops rustled with exotic birds, their songs melding into one soothing chorus. The forest marched inland, gradually rising for miles until the trees relented to gray stone peaks jutting into a canopy of white clouds. I studied my surroundings again and I knew I had reached my destination, the Island of the Immortals.

"I set out immediately, plunging into the forest with no regard for the dangers that might lurk within. If I was the type of man who sought adventure in the wild I would have been disappointed. No beast threatened my progress; no great obstacle blocked my path nor did fatigue enter my limbs and slow my stride. Hunger never burned my stomach or slowed my thoughts. The beasts I encountered were just as strange as the flora. The birds never ate the fruits. Monkeys swung overhead with no regard for the feast surrounding them. The island seemed to sustain everything with its energy.

"I climbed the mountain during the day and rested at night, tucked in some niche or cave. I counted seven sunsets before I reached the clouds, three days to penetrate them and another week before I saw the summits. A narrow path cut through the peaks and I followed it eagerly. To my surprise the white capped peaks surrounded a wide green pasture. Eight men in white robes sat in the center in a circle, their eyes closed in blissful meditation.

As I stood above them I realized my journey was complete. I was looking upon the Eight Immortals.

"I descended into the crater, working my way thought the foliage to the field. The force of their meditation flowed through me as I approached. When I sat beside them I was immersed in their peace. I lapsed into a state of perfection, submerged in ultimate serenity. But my intrusion did not go undetected. Peace was shattered by pain, the Immortals flooding my mind with displeasure. I was the intruder, unworthy of their lofty communion. I jumped to my feet and fled, running through the glade and scrambling down the mountain, never stopping until I reached the forests below, driven by the relentless despair in my head.

"The world transformed. Hunger gnawed at my stomach. The forest rattled with sound, the birds and primates attacking the fruited trees and each other in a ravenous frenzy. Insects assailed my exposed flesh; vines that had once caressed now bit with wicked thorns. I had upset the balance instilled by the Immortals and the island became more dangerous than the wildest forest of the Middle Kingdom.

"My encounter with the Immortals affected me in an unexpected way. My body was endowed with strength; my mind brimmed with the wisdom of ages. I used this new power to construct a small junk and fled the immortal island, braving the angry seas and winds to escape the terror I created.

"I returned to a different China. The Qin dynasty had long passed; the fangshi had died away, reduced to ridicule and fortune-telling for the poor. The empire was shaking away the dregs of Mongol rule. No one noticed a lone man limping into the harbor in a ragged junk."

"And now you sit beside the emperor and command his

household," Panya completed. "You have all that you desire."

"Not quite," Chongli replied.

Chongli placed his chopsticks on the table and rose from his chair. He came to Panya's side of the table and took her hand.

"I am only one step away from the throne. Zhengtong is a puppet with no vision. He and his monks wish only to plow fields and worship their fathers while an entire world waits to be conquered. No nation can withstand the might of the Middle Kingdom. Our army is ready to march on the Mongols and I will lead them."

Chongli's announcement caught her off guard.

"The Mongols?"

Chongli smiled. "Yes, I know about the eunuchs and their plan. Our army masses in the north awaiting my arrival. It is unfortunate Changa will be among them when we attack. I hope he dies honorably."

Chongli seemed to sense her tension. He applied slight pressure on her wrist and she relaxed immediately.

"I've been alive hundreds of years and never have I met a woman such as you. You possess a link with the spirits. I can feel it. With you beside me I can claim the title Son of Heaven knowing my sons will have the strength of their father and mother. Our children will rule the world from sea to sea."

Panya smiled to keep her mouth from dropping. Chongli was powerful, an altered spirit, but he was also mad. He continued to touch her wrist sending waves of pleasure throughout her body. Suddenly he stopped, dropping her arm as he stepped away.

"I have overwhelmed you. I apologize. We will talk later. My men will arrive tomorrow and escort you to my home beyond the city. I hope you will seriously consider my offer."

Panya watched Chongli stride across the courtyard until he disappeared through the gate. Her composure crumbled; she jumped from her seat and fled to the false safety of her bedroom. She feared Chongli, the way he could manipulate her feelings with his touch, bringing desire in her when she cared nothing for him. She knew if she went to his home she would be trapped. Oya's magic could not protect her. She had to escape.

The Tuareg burst into her room with both swords drawn. His eyes were first angry then concerned.

"I am fine," she lied. "We must leave this place. Chongli knows of the eunuch's plan. We must warn him!"

The Tuareg sheathed his swords and folded his arms across his chest. He looked around the room and back at Panya.

"Tomorrow will be our best chance," she said. "Chongli plans to send me to his home. We will have to try then. You must find Guangli. We cannot escape without his help."

The Tuareg disappeared, returning quickly with the eunuch. Guangli, still groggy from sleep, rubbed his eyes and yawned before bowing.

"I'm sorry I haven't come to you, Sultana. A sickness seems to have spread throughout the palace. The emperor himself is bedridden."

"Chongli is responsible," Panya said. "He was here. He knows of your plan. He's sent an army north to confront the Mongols."

Guangli's eyes widened. "I must act quickly. Don't worry, Sultana. I will not fail you."

The eunuch scurried away. Panya looked into the Tuareg's eyes for assurance but found none.

"I know what you think," she said. "This land stinks with conspiracy but we have no choice but to trust him. If he fails we must be ready to take our own chance. Sleep well, we will need our energy tomorrow."

She woke to ringing bells. Her servants knelt at the foot of her bed, their heads bowed.

"Sultana, we have come to help you prepare for your journey."

"I don't need help," Panya replied. "I will be along soon."

Panya dressed in her traditional clothes despite the fine garments sent by Chongli. She tucked various herbal mixtures about herself then strapped a dagger to her waist. Her wrist knives resembled bracelets; their edges covered the with leather bands matching her amber necklace. She checked herself then entered the courtyard.

Chongli's escort greeted her; over one hundred men on black horses lined behind a splendid wagon. The Tuareg sat before them on a tall stallion, seeming quite comfort-able despite the situation. No Sofalans were present. One of the soldiers dismounted and approached her, his eyes on the Tuareg.

"We have been sent by Master Chongli to escort you to his home."

"Where are my men?" she asked.

"They were sent back to your ships to await your return. They will be taken care of."

Panya stiffened at the hidden meaning of the soldier's words.

"Tell Master Chongli I am grateful for his special attention. I would be terribly disappointed if anything happened to my men."

The commander gave her a sly smile. "I will be sure to deliver your message to Chongli personally."

Panya entered the carriage and the group set off. She kept

her window curtain closed; she had no desire to see the sprawling city that had become her prison. Her only indication they were out of the city was the increased jostling of the wagon as it transitioned to the rough country road through the farmlands.

The day drew to a close, sunlight dimming through the drawn shades. Panya fought sleep and despair as the chance for rescue slipped away with the setting sun. Then the wagon lurched, swerved right and careened into something hard. She tumbled out of her seat, slamming into the wagon side. Stunned, Panya groped about for the door with one hand while searching for her dagger with the other. The wagon door jerked open and the Tuareg reached in and pulled her free. A battle raged around her, imperial troops against masked attackers. The Tuareg half dragged her to two horses at the road edge. Guangli sat on the third horse looking about nervously.

"Quickly, Quickly! We must go!"

The Tuareg pushed Panya up onto the horse then jumped on his mount with an agility that surprised her. The three of them galloped down the road through the fighting, the Tuareg killing anyone that drew near. They galloped north; once they were sure they were not followed Guangli led them into the woods. The trio dismounted and led their horses through the thicket along a narrow trail. Guangli seemed to know where he headed despite the darkness.

The trees finally gave way to a clearing. Guangli unpacked his horse and built a fire.

"We are far from the main road," he said. "Our fire cannot be seen. We'll travel north to the Long Wall and meet our allies."

"Why did your men attack us?" Panya demanded.

Guangli looked away, visibly embarrassed.

"They were not my men. They were bandits. I didn't have

time to purchase mercenaries, so I went to Frog Street. I spread the tale of a rich and beautiful princess being escorted to the house of Chongli. Then I waited."

"That was dangerous," Panya said. "We could have been killed!"

Guangli bowed. "I am sorry, Sultana. It was the best I could do."

The look in the Tuareg's eyes said he agreed. Panya stomped away from them both and unpacked. She was angry with Guangli's hasty plan and anxious to reach Changa. Later that night she tried to sleep but Chongli's image persisted. When sleep finally took her she saw herself naked in Chongli's arms, his lips closing in on hers. She attempted to break away from the dream, struggling to open her eyes. Then she cried out the name of the only man who would protect her.

"CHANGA!"

The Bakongo's face emerged through the confusion, shattering Chongli's image. She embraced his memory, pulling him close. She held onto him the entire night and all the following nights as the trio fled to the Long Wall. Panya's preoccupation with her dreams let the grandeur of the Long Wall go by unnoticed. They entered the land of the Mongols during a brutal snow storm, sheets of snow streaming sideways with the bitter wind.

"Oya! Your daughter calls!" Panya shouted. "Ease your fury against us so we may join our friends."

The local spirits responded to her plea with increased ferocity. Guangli struggled to her side.

"There is shelter ahead. Follow me."

They joined hands, following the eunuch through the blinding storm. The house emerged abruptly before them, its entrance half covered with snow. They forced the gate open then struggled to close it behind them. The walls eased the wind to their relief. A barren courtyard lay before them, decorated by tree husks and shrubs long dead, their withered branches glistening with dangling ice and snowflakes.

The Tuareg was the first to realize they were not alone. He eased his takouba and scimitar free, motioning to Panya with his head. Panya gripped her staff and stepped beside him, her eyes probing the frigid shadows. Guangli took heed and unsheathed his sword, tossing his scabbard to the ground. He scampered before the Tuareg and called out in a tongue unfamiliar to the Sofalans.

The men emerged. There were ten of them, stocky figures wrapped in heavy black coats that reached to the brims of their scuffed riding boots. The coat collars joined the flaps of their conical fur caps, obscuring their faces. Each held a short, thick bow nocked with arrows aimed at the trio. One man advanced on Guangli, distinguishable from the others by a single red tassel dangling from the center of his cap. The two exchanged words and Guangli handed the man several pouches. The man raised his hand and the others lowered their bows.

"Everything is fine now," he said to Panya. "They are Mongol outriders. They were expecting us."

"Will they take us to Changa?" Panya asked.

Guangli nodded. "They have food, water and extra horses. You journey will be much easier from here."

Panya lowered her staff. "You're not going with us?"

Guangli bowed. "I have travelled too far as it is. Chongli will suspect my hand in your escape. I must return to Beijing and do my best to delay his pursuit."

Panya's uneasiness was obvious. Guangli touched her hand and smiled.

"Don't worry. The Mongols have been paid. They are barbarians but they are men of their word. You and the Tuareg are safe."

Guangli turned to leave but Panya grasped his hand.

"What about you, Guangli?"

The eunuch smiled and patted her hand. "I will be with my brothers, whatever my fate."

They left the house together then parted ways, Guangli riding south; Panya, the Tuareg and the Mongols north into Mongolia. Though she didn't know the destination, Panya was at ease. She knew once they reached it, her mind would be at peace. She would be with Changa.

Chapter 6
Beyond the Wall

Changa couldn't imagine cold any worse than northern China, but he had never been to Mongolia. A different cold existed on the plains, a cold fueled by frigid winds that struck with a force unobstructed by hills, mountains, or trees. Some days the wind blew so strong the travelers sought relief by lying against the frozen ground, choosing a static cold over the frigid maelstrom. Changa was not much a man for spirits, but he prayed with his men for the winds to end.

Two weeks beyond the Long Wall the party saw the first glimpse of the Mongols. The nomads kept their distance, following the interlopers just beyond the horizon. The days passed and the horsemen grew less wary, coming close enough to be seen by a man with a keen eye. Changa was not impressed. They were short, broad men with hard wrinkled faces. Their horses seemed no better, small beasts with large heads and shaggy coats. The men wore conical leather caps with flaps protecting their ears. Ragged silk sleeves covered hard arms protruding from their fur lined leather vests. Quivers filled with arrows bounced against their horses' flanks. Changa counted ten, not enough to be a threat under normal circumstances.

The horsemen followed them until dusk then rode away into the darkening horizon. The night camp was silent as the weary travelers set up their ragged tents for another bitter night on the frozen plains. Changa bundled himself with thick woolen blankets and huddled with the others around the anemic fire. He took his turn on the outside of the human ring, the relentless wind seeping into the tent and pushing against his broad back.

He awoke to trembling earth. Changa flung his blanket aside and charged from the tent, the bahari close behind. A pulsing wall of Mongol horsemen charged the camp, swords waving over their heads. Changa ran to the center of the camp, throwing knives in each hand.

"Form a circle! Porters in the center! Warriors form the perimeter!"

The Sofalans responded rapidly, the Han lagging until Liwei translated the orders. The Mongols circled them, taunting and brandishing their swords and bows, occasionally firing an arrow at their feet. For what seemed like hours they ringed the beleaguered group. Suddenly they ceased, their bows drawn and loaded.

One man emerged from the horde riding a white mare. He wore a white fur coat which fell to his knees, the collar trimmed in ermine. His cape was adorned with diamonds; a silk cape hung from his shoulders. His face was rugged yet handsome; his coal black eyes scrutinizing the group and then lingering on Changa.

"Eunuch, step forward!" he commanded.

Liwei shuffled to the man and prostrated before him.

"Honorable Jochi, I am humbled to meet you," he said. "We have searched long for you."

"Not long enough," Jochi replied. "Your men are freezing and starving. A few more days I could have pulled the ransom from your frozen hands."

Jochi turned his attention to Changa.

"So this is the one that defeated the Sangir?"

"Yes, honorable sir," Liwei replied. "He is Bwana Changa Diop, Sultan of Sofala."

Jochi dismounted and strode to Changa. He stood a head shorter that the Bakonga, but he was clearly not intimidated by Changa's size.

"The word from beyond the wall says you slew the fire wizard."

Changa nodded.

Jochi smirked. "My khan is eager to meet you, Bwana Changa."

Jochi raised his hand and the Mongols lowered their bows. They supplied the travelers with new cloaks and coats, much to their relief. The Sofalans chose the cloaks, the coats being too small for their larger frames. The nomads offered them horses which they accepted reluctantly because of their small stature. After a few miles of riding they gained a healthy respect for the strong beasts.

The horde made swift progress across the monotonous landscape, the cold wind less fierce in the larger group. The grasslands took an abrupt plunge into a steep valley carved by a wide, lazy river. White conical huts peppered the riverbank intermingled with pens holding sheep and horses. Hundreds of Mongols went about their daily chores as if it was the warmest day of the year. They were led to a group of huts further down the river.

"We'll wait for the other clans, and then we ride to Kara Korim. You will meet the Khan and your emperor there."

"The emperor is not here?" Liwei asked.

"Of course not. He is a respected guest of our khan."

"A guest can leave when he chooses," Liwei replied.

Jochi approached the eunuch, his smile disappearing. "There are different types of guests, eunuch. Your emperor and his pet invited themselves into our land with a sizable escort.

We welcomed them with swords and arrows. Truth be told, if we returned him to the Forbidden City his uncle would kill him. You know this as well as I."

Jochi's smile returned. "We are the reason he is still alive. The khan will release him once he receives the Heart, but I fear we will be releasing him to his death."

"That will not happen," Liwei said.

Jochi glanced at Changa and his men. "Forgive me if I don't believe you. You'll need more than a handful of Zanj mercenaries, even if one seems blessed by the gods."

Jochi nodded to Changa. "We leave in the morning." He spurred his mare and rode away.

Liwei came to Changa. "Don't listen to him. Our allies will be waiting for us when we return. The northern army is still loyal to the emperor as is the southern provinces. Our only opposition lies in the imperial guard and the units surrounding Beijing."

"It doesn't matter," Changa replied. "The lives of my friends depend on the emperor. He'll regain the throne if I have to sit him on it myself."

Morning brought more horsemen. By afternoon thousands of them swarmed the camp like summer flies. Hundreds of ox-drawn wagons followed them, loaded with weapons, food, and gers. Jochi gave the order and the Mongols broke camp. By noon they were riding north. They rode swiftly across the plains, the miles flowing under their hooves like a rushing river.

The journey to Kara-Korim took three weeks of hard riding. The Mongol capital was more ruin than city, crumbled white walls surrounded by a multitude of gers.

Changa pulled his horse beside Liwei. "This is their capital city?"

Liwei nodded. "Long ago Kara-Korim was one of the great

cities of the East. The Mongols controlled an empire stretching from the Middle Kingdom to the lands of the whites. Chingis Khan forged the nomads into a fierce army that knew no rivals. The city was just a large camp during Chingis's reign, but his son Ogedei had grander plans. He transformed Kara-Korim into a true city. Those ruined walls once towered over the grasses. Four gates guarded entry on each side. Ogedei's palace was constructed outside the city, a grand building built in the Chinese style."

"So what happened?"

"Divisions among the Mongols made them weak. A new dynasty rose to power in China, the Ming. They drove the Mongols from our land and followed them to Kara-Korim, where they destroyed it. It has remained so for two hundred years."

Changa spat. "It's not much to look at."

"This land does not only hold a city. It has always been sacred to the Mongols, a place associated with power."

Changa rubbed his chin. "If that's so, I believe this gathering is for more than just ransom. There's a deeper purpose here."

"The return of the Heart is a great occasion for these folk."

"Believe what you will, but it's more than that, Liwei. I think we might be too deep in the snake to escape."

They followed Jochi's horde into the ruins. Scaffolding framed the outside walls of most buildings, workers shuffling back and forth as they replaced old stone with new ones cut from the nearby mountains. Green tiled roofs protruded over the low sections of the wall. A platform rose before the main gate, each corner punctuated with yellow triangular flags marked by a single red spiral.

"It is the mark of the khan," Liwei said. "He is claiming

this city. I'm sure he'll be challenged for that honor."

"Not if he possesses the Heart of Zanj," Changa replied.

If weather was a sign of the spirits Kara-Korim was indeed a sacred place. The jagged mountains surrounding the plains turned back the frigid winds. The crisp climate was a welcomed change, balmy compared to the sharp air that dogged them since passing the Long Wall. Some Sofalans even dared to remove their cloaks; a few minutes exposed to the cutting wind convinced them otherwise. A river flowed through the foothills, its strong currents providing the power for the numerous iron furnaces belching black smoke into the sky. A few settlements followed the water's edge but most congregated around the ruins.

Jochi approached Changa soon after he secured his *ger*. The Mongol commander rode his horse up with a smile, apparently pleased by the height advantage.

"You will accompany me to the palace."

Changa nodded. "I'll get Liwei."

"No." Jochi's expression lost its mirth. "The eunuch stays. He should be grateful I allowed him to come this far."

"You have something against Liwei?"

Jochi leaned forward. "He is a eunuch. That is enough."

Jochi called out and a warrior appeared with a horse definitely not of Mongol stock. The beast was tall at the shoulder but bulkier than an Arabian. Its gray coat was heavy, but it was a fine animal.

"I thought this would suit you," Jochi said. "At least you can ride without your boots scraping the grass."

Changa followed Jochi to the palace. The decrepit condition of the building became more evident as they neared. The scaffolding swarmed with Persian and Han artisans replacing worn stone that traveled up the Silk Road three hundred years before. The palace gate was the only complete section remaining; two metal doors flanked by heavily armored guards. On Jochi's signal they pushed the doors open, revealing a narrow tunnel running through the stone base supporting the two tiered pagoda roof above. The tunnel opened to the main courtyard. Five palaces and two storehouses occupied the grounds, each under repair.

The largest palace was nearly complete, its only flaw the faded outside wall. They dismounted and climbed the broad stairs to the elaborate wooden doors. The doors swung open, revealing a cavernous foyer inhabited by a massive tree constructed of pure silver with four sculpted lions lounging at its base. Four gilded serpents dangled from its tarnished branches, their bodies coiled as if ready to strike. At the top of the tarnished limbs stood an angel, her slender arms lifting a silver trumpet. A man stood before the fountain, his back turned to Changa and Jochi. A splendid ruby hued silk robe trimmed in sable fell from his shoulders, covering the rest of his form.

Jochi fell to his knees and touched his forehead to the marble floor.

"My khan, the sultan is here."

Tumen Khan turned to face them. He was younger than Jochi, his moustache barely rooted in his smooth face. His eyes sparkled with ambition, the smirk on his face suggesting more wisdom than his young face displayed.

"Bwana Diop, welcome to Kara Korim." The perfect Arabic he spoke resonated within the chamber.

He turned back to the statue. "When my father Chingis made Kara Korim his capital, it was just a collection of gers. He was content for despite his conquest he was still the nomad and had no use for cities. But I had seen the cities of China and the West. I promised that if I was chosen khan I would build a city worthy of my empire. When I was chosen, Kara Korim finally became the gem it deserved to be."

He stepped away from the silver tree. "Mare's milk once flowed from the mouths of these lions, cara cosmos, bal and rice mead spewed from the throats of the serpents. My guest drank their fill, for the fountain never ran dry. Such was my wealth in those days. Such was the wealth of the Mongols."

Tumen approached the skeptical Sofalan. "You ask yourself how can I speak of things long past as if they happened only yesterday. I stand before you now as Tumen, but before I was Ogedei, son of Chingis, second Khan of the Mongol Empire."

"I am honored," Changa replied.

"No, it is I who am honored. Because of you I possess the one item that eluded me in my past. I have the Heart."

Tumen bowed to Changa. "Tonight warriors from throughout the plains will gather before my palace. Merkits, Jalays, Taichuds, Talars; all the people of the plains will unite once again under the banner of the Mongols. Once they see the Heart, they will know the time has finally come for the Mongols to reclaim what was once theirs."

Tumen faced the tree. "My tailors are preparing you an appropriate uniform for tonight's celebration. You may leave."

Jochi escorted Changa back to camp. Liwei waited, his eyes expectant.

"Did you see him?"

Changa took off his cloak and tossed it on the ground.

"Yes I did. He's young for a leader. I think he's crazy, too."

"I don't care about the khan. Did you see the emperor?"

Changa sat on a wooden stool and took off his boots. "No. Tumen Khan was alone."

Liwei began pacing. "Has he betrayed us? No, the Mongols are nothing if not honest. We brought him the Heart. He will give us the emperor."

"There's a ceremony tonight," Changa said. "I'm sure the emperor will be there. I think we'll get our answers there."

A frigid night settled on Kara Korim, bright stars flickering in the massive sky. The Sofalans huddled in Changa's ger, nervously eating a meal of sheep. Their situation was precarious at best, surrounded by warriors whose intent was unknown. The eunuchs had underestimated the Mongols intentions. There was more to the ransom than freeing the emperor.

A warrior entered the ger with Changa's clothes draped over his arms.

"Your clothing, Sultan."

Changa took the garment and the warrior exited. It was an excellent green robe made of the finest silk. He donned the outfit and joined the Mongol escort waiting for him.

A field of torchlight surrounded the palaces, the khan's platform materializing in the wavering light as they approached. White banners hung from each corner, stirred by a slight breeze from the mountains. Tumen Khan sat in a gilded throne flanked by body-guards in full Mongol military regalia. Another man sat beside the khan, his red dragon robe barely visible under the flickering torches.

Changa's escort led him to the perimeter of the throng. A pathway bordered by white wooden stakes wormed its way to the platform base. Mongols flanked either side.

"The khan wishes you to come to him alone with the Heart," one of his body-guards said.

Changa removed the Heart case from under his robe and spurred his mount. He rode slowly past hundreds of Mongols, men standing like statues in the cold darkness, the only movement the wavering torch flames. Jochi greeted him at the platform and took the reins of his horse. Changa dismounted and handed the Heart to Jochi.

Jochi pushed it away. "The khan wishes you to bring him the Heart."

Changa cursed as he climbed the wooden stairs to the platform. Tumen Khan waited in a splendid emerald robe trimmed with sable, a leather conical cap studded with gold on his head. The emperor sat beside him in a plain high back chair, his cotton robe well made but no comparison to the khan's wardrobe. He seemed not much older than the khan but the contrast was striking. Tumen stood before his people with confidence, the emperor cowered in his seat, his fearful eyes on the khan.

Changa kneeled and extended the box to Tumen. The khan took the Heart and turned to the crowd as he lifted the lid. He scooped the enormous jewel from its cradle, lifting it high for all to see. The crowd bellowed, their voices reverberating through the platform. The emperor clasped his hands over his ears and closed his eyes. Changa saw him and shook his head, visibly disappointed. The eunuchs risked their lives for this boy?

He began doubting his reliance on the Han. The thought crossed his mind to throw his lot in with the Mongols but he dismissed it. He knew something of the Han; the Mongols were still a mystery to him.

Tumen lowered the Heart and the crowd hushed.

"Now do you believe?" he shouted.

"We believe! We believe!" they responded.

Tumen waited until the din subsided before he spoke again.

"We come together as we did long ago, setting aside our

differences for a great dream. White walls once surrounded a city of thousands on this very spot. The markets thrived with people from every land, merchant carts brimming with goods from throughout the world. This palace was once the home of Ogedei Khan, its warehouses holding the wealth of his empire. I know this because I was there. I rode with Chingis Khan, trampling the bones of my enemies under the hooves of my mare. I am Ogedei!

I have returned to lead my brothers once again. This Heart, the wonder once possessed by my father is my claim to that right.

Will you ride with me, my brothers? Will you follow me to the ends of the earth?"

Thousands of torches jerked side to side, the Mongols waving them furiously as they answered their khan.

"To the end of the Earth! To the end of the Earth!"

Tumen signaled the emperor to come forward. The boy stood slowly, steadied himself and toddled to the khan.

"Two years ago we rescued Emperor Zhu Quizhen from the control of the mad eunuch Wang Zhen. We have protected him from his uncle who instead of rescuing his nephew took the throne for himself. In return for our help the emperor pledges his loyalty to the Mongols. The soldiers loyal to him will rise up and march beside us to dethrone Zhengtong and restore the rightful Son of Heaven to his throne. What nation can stand against the Middle Kingdom and the Mongols combined?"

The Mongols cheered again. Tumen looked at Changa.

"Rise my friend," he whispered.

Changa stood and carefully took his place behind the khan.

"And last, my brothers, the Sultan of Zanj, the defender

of the Swahili, the protector of the Heart, and the vanquisher of the Sangir stands with me. He has come a thousand li to give his honor to your khan. He will lead his armies from the west and we will encircle our enemies like the Great Hunt. They will be ours for the taking!"

Changa looked into thousands of jubilant faces. These were men with a purpose, weapons forged by the harsh winds ready to march in the name of Tumen Khan. The eunuchs had been duped. They believed they were rescuing an emperor. Instead they were reviving an empire.

Tumen allowed Zhu Quizhen to accompany Changa to his ger. There was no need to fear escape by either men and the khan seemed tired of Quizhen's uneasy company. Liwei waited, pacing and wringing his hands. He saw the emperor and fell to the ground in submission.

"My emperor, you are free!"

Changa stepped past him, throwing his cloak to the ground. "Not exactly."

Quizhen went to Liwei and pulled him to his feet.

"Please rise, my friend. Among the Mongols we are equal. We are all prisoners."

Liwei stood reluctantly, confusion in his eyes. "What is happening, Changa?"

Changa sat on his stool and took off his boots. "The Mongols won't free any of us. That was never their intention. When Tumen captured the emperor he had what he needed to fulfill his dream. He knew the discord it would cause in the kingdom. Killing the emperor would legitimize his uncle's claim to the throne and bring the emperor's wrath down on the Mongols. Keeping him alive would split the empire and give him time to amass the Mongols."

Changa tossed his boots atop his robe. "Tumen's a respected chieftain but he needed something to unify the tribes. Defeating them would take too long and weaken his future army, so he gambled. He sent the word he would free the emperor for a ransom. I believe he expected enough wealth to buy his brothers' loyalty. The Heart was beyond his wildest dreams."

"You think he lies about being the reincarnation of Ogedei Khan?"

"No, I think he believes it. Look at what has happened in such a short time. Some shaman somewhere fed him that notion to gain his favor. It doesn't take much to make a vain man believe in his own greatness."

Liwei looked stricken. The emperor stood beside him, his young face empty. They both stared at Changa as he dressed in his own clothing.

The emperor cleared his throat. "Sultan Changa, what should we do?"

"I'm no sultan, boy," Changa spat. "I'm just a fool who followed his greed too far. Give Tumen what he wants. Promise him your soldiers and your support. Send Liwei to gather your forces and wait for Tumen to march on China."

"I cannot fight the khan!" the emperor exclaimed. "He will crush us!"

"Pardon my interruption, emperor, but I think you are stronger than you know," Liwei said. "Though brother Wang was respected, he was not well versed in military matters. I have studied the ways of war all my life. The Mongols can be defeated."

"You must fight Tumen," Changa added. "If you allow him to place you on the throne you will be his puppet for as long as you live."

The emperor sat. "What you say seems true, Changa. If we succeed the Son of Heaven will be indebted to you."

"I just want to free my friends and go home," he answered. "This safari has gone on far too long."

Chapter 7
The Great Hunt

Chongli sat in the center of a circular pagoda, his legs folded under him, his arms resting in his lap. His eyes closed; his chest expanded and contracted in a low, deliberate rhythm. Candles flickered in recesses carved into the stone wall; incense smoke rose from the metal pots surrounding him, the smell and smoke weaving patterns in his incantations.

Panya had escaped. He was disappointed but not troubled for he would have her again. She was strong, much stronger than the others. He was sure she could survive his attentions and bear his child. What happened to her after the child was no concern. While Panya's body would give him a future gift, her mind surrendered something more immediate. When Chongli distracted the young priestess with images of amorous intent, he probed her thoughts for details of the one who served as her rock of defiance, the man that traveled with the eunuchs to save the deposed emperor.

And what a unique man he was. Born with the ka of a king and touched by the essence of an ancient spirit, his power was more than he realized. Fear held him from his true potential. Chongli dissected the images but could not find its source. He would have to look elsewhere.

Chongli's eyes tightened as his breathing deepened. He separated from his mortal shell, rising through the rafters of his temple and into the darkening sky. He dispersed, breaking into spiritual motes that scattered into the Earth's canopy. He lingered, savoring the vastness

*of the planet, the hunger to rule the millions of lives pulsing under
his gaze rising within him. This was not the reason for his quest; he
focused his power on the land of Changa's origin. There he located
Changa's weakness in a being whose ka burned as bright as his own
but drew his power from a different source. This being had a name,
Usenge. His spiritual shields were too strong for Chongli to penetrate
from such a distance, but he was certain this man was the well of
Changa's fear. He drew back from Usenge, rising to rejoin his body
when something caught his attention. It seemed Usenge was a man of
resources as well. Creatures roamed Changa's land, misshapen servants
to the Bakongo sorcerer. They searched for Changa, their intentions
clear. Chongli's power was weak in his current state, but there was
enough power for one task. He focused on one hunter, using his skill
to lay a path to its prey. The being responded, beginning a swift and
deliberate journey across the sea. Chongli withdrew himself and his
eyes snapped open. An exhausted smile came to his face. Changa Diop
would die.*

Morning in Kara Korim began before sunrise with blaring
horns and clanging gongs. Changa jumped from under his blankets
cursing. His eyes cleared to the image of Jochi standing at the ger
entrance, his ever-present smirk annoying Changa even more.

"The Great Hunt begins. You will ride with the khan."
Changa roused his comrades. He had no idea what this Great
Hunt was or what it involved, but the fact that the khan was
attending made it important. Changa went to Liwei, prodding
him with his scabbard until he stirred.

"Wake your master," he ordered. "We have been
summoned."

Liwei crawled to the young emperor and shook him gently.
Changa watched as Liwei assisted the displaced monarch like a

parent with a child. The relationship between them was more than loyalty; the eunuch cared for Quizhen.

The two of them joined Changa.

"Where are we going?" Quizhen asked.

"I have no idea," Changa confessed. "Jochi called it the great hunt. Whatever it is, it's our opportunity. Jochi won't allow Liwei to come with us. He can slip from the camp and return to the kingdom while we hunt."

The emperor stared at the eunuch. "Can you do this?"

"I must," Liwei replied. "I am not a physical man like Changa but I will find my strength in his example."

"You're the strongest of us all," Changa said. "You led us this far. You will lead us back."

Changa, the emperor, and his men rode to the palace. Tumen Khan's clan gathered below the platform, surrounding Tumen's elaborate wagon. The other Mongol tribes gathered before Kara Korim, meshing into one massive horde. They followed a small group of hunters into the grasslands north of the river, riding until they reached a perimeter of flags disappearing into the horizon in both directions. The Mongols separated, riding single file in both directions. The warriors formed a line behind the flags, taking great care not to go beyond them. The khan's wagon approached the line, his entourage waiting behind the wagon. Changa made his way to Jochi's side.

"What is this Great Hunt?"

"It is a test of Mongol unity," Jochi said. "It will insure we are ready to reclaim our empire."

Tumen emerged clad in full Mongol armor, a yellow flag gripped in his right hand. He mounted his mare, riding the short distance to the line and raised his flag. The flagmen responded, banners rippling down the line, eventually disappearing into the distance. Minutes later the flags lowered and the Mongols breached the flag line in unison. They marched at a steady cadence, driving animals before them; their ranks close to prevent any escape.

They progressed with precision, a human line eighty miles long advancing in perfect time, communicating across the miles with flags. The hunters spent the entire day on the march. At nightfall they made camp, half the army sleeping while the others stood guard over their prey.

For two weeks they kept the line, driving the growing mass of prey before them. On the fifteenth day the flag signals changed. The center line halted as the flanks continued to march, encircling the terrified menagerie. Rabbits, antelope, oxen, wolves and other creatures ran about in bewilderment. The larger beasts tried the line and were driven back by Mongol shouts and waving lances. No animal was harmed despite any injury it inflicted on a Mongol. A man too wounded to hold his place was quickly replaced.

Changa was in awe. He watched Tumen enter the circle with a gilded bow, a single jeweled arrow in his hand. He looked over the captured game, sizing up each animal with an experienced eye. He loaded his bow, drew back and fired. The animals fled from his target, an impressive stag that tumbled onto its side, the arrow protruding from a well-place shot to the heart. The air hummed with bowstrings as the Mongols claimed their rewards. Some men rushed in with lances to take their prey. Some used their barc hands, wrestling down their prey with mortal results for both man and beast.

A hideous cry ripped through the cacophony, ending the wanton slaughter. Mongols ran for the safety of the human palisade, dropping whatever bounty they held. A beast pursued them, a massive feline whose dense white fur was creased with black stripes. The cat's roar raised the hairs on Changa's arms. Its pale eyes focused on the warrior and his hand fell to the hilt of his sword as a familiar and foreboding sensation settled on him. A tebo lurked within this beast. How it found him in this land he could not fathom, but he knew its intent. It had come to claim him.

"The gods send a sign!" Tumen exclaimed. "How many generations have lived and died without ever seeing the Ghost?"

The other Mongols did not share Tumen's joy. Changa saw terror in their eyes as they fled the beast, their fear spurred by some belief unknown to the burly Bakonga. Even Jochi backed away, his usual smirk gone from his face.

The khan goaded his nervous mount into the circle, taking a lance from a nearby hunter and advancing on the tiger.

"Tumen, stop!" Changa shouted. He galloped after the khan, an unsettling feeling growing in his gut. Tumen saw only another trophy to claim, but Changa knew the truth in the cat's black orbs. It would take more that a prick from the khan's lance to bring down this creature. Only he could kill this thing, if it did not kill him first.

The khan lowered his lance and charged the Ghost. It bounced aside and pounced, its paws wide and claws extended, its jaws wide and fangs exposed. Changa's first throwing knife struck the beast's shoulder with little effect, but the second knife caught it in the neck. The tiger bunched around the blade, slamming into Tumen's mare. The khan fell and crashed into the ground. Changa's horse balked, refusing to get closer to the thrashing cat. He hurdled from the horse, running to the khan with his Damascus drawn. The tiger regained its feet, swiping away the knife lodged in its neck. It strode between Changa and the khan, a threatening growl escaping its fangs. Their eyes met, man and demon, two predators looking for a sign of weakness. Changa cut his eyes away and the Ghost pounced. Changa sidestepped and swung his blade, slicing the cat's paw. It howled and swung its other paw. Changa turned, catching the blow on his back, his sword flying from his hand. The Ghost dug its claws into Changa's coat, pulling the Bakongo to its open jaws. Changa slammed his fist on the cat's snout as he snatched another throwing knife from his bag. He let the beast pull him close, using the momentum to drive the blade into its neck and he drove his open hand into its bottom jaw. Changa yelled as he slammed the cat to the ground.

He pushed the blade deep into the cat, driving the blade into its backbone. The Ghost jerked still. Changa rolled off the beast, his breath coming in painful gasps. He rolled onto his hands and knees and crawled to the khan.

The Mongol leader lay still. Changa touched his face and he moaned.

"He needs help!" Changa shouted. The Mongols stood still, refusing to come closer. The Sofalans responded, running to them both. Their action broke the Mongol trance and the khan's bodyguards joined the Sofalans.

The khan's bodyguards rushed him away. Changa's men lifted him to his feet and he pushed them away, his energy returning quickly. He thought of Panya's words about Kintu's gift and shook his head in wonder. His men grinned, once again witness to the Bakongo's abilities. They waved their weapons as they chanted his pit name.

"Mbogo! Mbogo! Mbogo!"

The Great Hunt ended in a celebration for the Black Sultan. The remaining game was slaughtered and offered to Changa and his men. The Sofalans returned to Kara Korim leading a train of borrowed mares loaded with provisions. The surprises continued in the camp. They were led to a different area populated with larger and finer gers. Each Sofalan was given his own ger, servants, and horses.

The emperor accompanied Changa to his ger.

"You made a powerful ally," he said.

Changa shrugged. "I saved the khan, but may have dug us a deeper hole. Did Liwei leave?"

"Yes." The emperor lowered his head. "I pray he is able to gather my forces."

Changa entered his ger and was greeted by an unexpected sight. Panya and the Tuareg stood in the center of the tent flanked by Jochi and another warrior. Panya dashed to him, throwing her arms around his shoulders and kissing him. Changa stumbled back, knocked off balance more by the kiss than Panya's lunge.

He wrapped his arms around her small waist and pulled her close, his senses filled by her presence.

Panya pulled away from him, her eyes full of joy and relief.

"You're safe," she whispered.

Panya glanced toward the Tuareg. Changa eased Panya down then strode to his friend, surprising him with a great hug.

"Thank you, my friend. Thank you."

The Tuareg nodded, his brown eyes glistening.

"They were sent by a eunuch from the palace," Jochi interjected.

"They are my friends. We were separated in Taozhou."

"We must talk, Changa," Panya said. "The Han are marching north. They know the eunuchs' plan. They know everything."

"How is that possible?" Jochi demanded.

"Chongli," the emperor answered. "There are no secrets to

the fangshi."

Changa frowned but Panya nodded.

"He's right. Chongli is leading the Chinese army. He's coming for me and you."

"What are you talking about? Why should we worry about this fangshi?"

Panya sat Changa down with the others and described her ordeal, holding his hand the entire time.

"We must tell the khan," Jochi concluded. "Come with me."

They rode to the palace. Tumen Khan was holding council before the silver tree when they entered. He saw them and waved them over, meeting Changa with a hug.

"You decided to join our council," he said.

Changa bowed. "I have come to talk."

Tumen's eyes had shifted from Changa to Panya and the Tuareg. Changa noticed and stepped aside.

"This is Sultana Panya and my personal guard, the Tuareg."

Tumen smiled. "A beautiful empress and a strong companion. You are truly blessed."

"We were separated in Taozhou during the Wokou raid," Changa continued. "Panya and the Tuareg were taken to Beijing while I and the others remained in Taozhou."

"Your friends are very resourceful to have escaped the Forbidden City," Tumen said. "I shouldn't be surprised after your display at the Great Hunt. That is why I wish you to join me as a member of my council."

"I'm flattered, Khan. If you respect my advice then hear it now. Panya tells me the Chinese know your plan and are marching north as we speak. They are lead by Chongli."

Tumen's eyes widened. "The fangshi is leading the army?"

"Yes. They will reach Kara Korim in days. I suggest you pull back your *ordus* and avoid the Chinese until they tire of the chase and go home. You can strike later when your army is full strength."

Tumen's face was impassive. "The omens are strong for victory. Our shamans have read the signs and your victory against the Ghost confirmed their predictions. We will not run. The Mongols have always been outnumbered and we have always won. This will be no different."

Changa wanted to wrap his hands around Tumen's neck and shake some sense into him.

"At least save the energy of your men. Let the Chinese come to you. Pick your place for battle and let them trip your snare."

"That is good council, Sultan. Jochi, send out word to the noyans. Sultan, please join us and share more of your council." Panya and the others returned to the Swahili camp while Changa joined the council. He returned to his ger after sundown. Panya was waiting.

She grasped his hand and led him to a pile of furs, removing his cloak and weapons along the way. Changa was puzzled by all the attention. This was not the Panya he lost in Taozhou.

They sat close on the furs.

"What did the council decide?" she asked.

Changa stretched out on the furs. "They will choose a battlefield close to the city to meet the Chinese. Their plan is good."

"What about Chongli?"

"We'll deal with him when he gets here."

Panya's face showed an emotion Changa thought he would

never see from her.

"You're afraid of this man," he said.

"He is a demon, Changa."

"We've faced demons before."

"Not like this," she replied. "Chongli is not what you think. He appears like any other man. But his soul is corrupt. His time among the Immortals made him too human. His appetites know no limit and he has the power to feed them. No one can stop him from getting what he wants."

"And he wants you," Changa said.

Panya gripped his arm. "He senses Oya's power in me. He thinks our children would be Immortals and grow to rule the world."

Changa's hands were warm. His eyes narrowed as he leaned closer to her.

"What did he make you do?"

Panya looked away. "Nothing, but he was inside my head. He took memories no man had a right to, twisting them into something horrible. I could hide nothing from him."

"I'll kill him," Changa stated plainly.

"You may not be able to."

"He must have a weakness. You must have noticed something."

Panya snaked her arms around his waist and pressed her head against his chest.

"When Chongli entered my head the only way I could get rid of him was to think of you."

"Me?"

Panya pressed tighter against him. "You are the strongest man I know. I thought of you and me together on the Sendibada sharing your cabin. No one dared approach me because of you."

The kiss was unexpected but the lovemaking was deliberate. They shared each others bodies like lovers too long apart. When they were done they slept in each others arms, savoring the warmth beneath the furs.

By morning the emotion of the night had fled. Changa woke alone. When he opened his eyes he saw Panya sitting against the ger wall, her knees drawn up, her arms wrapped around them.

He stood, the blankets falling away from his nude form. "What is it? What's wrong?"

"Last night was wrong," she said.

He stepped toward her but she put out her hand.

"No, Changa, please stay away from me."

Changa was dumbfounded. "I didn't force this on you. You came to me with your words. I won't lie; I have thought of us together, but you know I have always respected you."

"I'm not accusing you of anything," Panya assured him.

"I'm just not sure why we made love."

"Because we wanted to. Isn't that enough?"

"No, it's not enough. I fled my home because I refused to marry a man I didn't love. I swore to Oya I would be no man's wife unless my heart and my head agreed on the choice."

She stood before him, her face resolved.

"My heart chooses you but my mind does not."

Changa didn't expect her words to upset him as much as they did. She seemed to sense it for she came toward him as he dressed. "Changa, I didn't mean…"

Jochi entered the ger. "Sultan, Tumen Khan awaits you."

Changa hesitated, gazing at Panya a moment longer.

"Let's go," he said.

Changa followed Jochi to the crest of the hill situated

between the river and the mountains. The Mongols of Kara Korim prepared for battle. Wood from the river's edge had been hauled in for the construction of catapults and manogels. Grindstones hissed against sword blades while bowmen replaced their worn bowstrings and replenished their arrow supplies.

The khan greeted him with a bow. "It is good to see you, Sultan. I hope you enjoyed your reunion with the Sultana."

Changa bowed, forcing a smile to his face.

The khan waved his hand across the landscape below him.

"This is where we will defeat the Chinese. What do you think?"

"It's a good position. They won't extend their line beyond the river or the mountain and the position allows you to observe their movements."

"Then we agree," the khan said. "Our scouts informed us that the Chinese have a massive army, about fifty thousand men."

The khan spat. "First the eunuchs, now the sorcerer. No matter; they'll all die the same way."

Changa remained in the khan's camp as the Mongols took their positions. Despite the flurry around him Changa's thoughts went to his friends. He wondered how Zakee was recovering, if Mikaili still waited on his secret island for their return. Panya concerned him the most. The encounter with Chongli had changed her. She was vulnerable, unsure of herself. He doubted the reason for their tryst. He wanted to believe she wanted to be with him, but she was different. He finally saw the sense in her decision. They should stay away from each other until this safari was over.

By nightfall the Mongols were ready. The hill had been

transformed into a fortified maze, bristling with weapons, horses and men. Changa retired to his ger, hesitating before entering.

Panya's items were gone. He tried to sleep but his persistent worry about her wouldn't let him rest. He dressed and went out into the camp; he found her standing on the platform before Tumen's palace, oblivious to the stiff wind pulling at her cloak. She didn't seem to notice him climbing the stairs to stand by her side.

"He's very close," she whispered.

"Come back to the ger," he urged.

They were quiet for a moment, both consumed in thought. Panya finally broke the silence.

"Changa, make me a promise."

"What do you wish?"

"Promise me you'll kill Chongli."

"I'll try."

Panya gripped his shoulders. "Promise me, Changa. I won't be free of his touch until he's dead."

"You said he was immortal."

"He is to everyone but you."

Changa laughed. "So now I'm a god-slayer."

Panya's serious face stifled his humor.

"Every time you defeat an adversary, you gain his ka. First there was Bahati, then the drug slaves and the Sangir."

"The fire priest, too," Changa added.

"Fire priest?"

Changa told Panya about his encounter with the fire mage.

"You didn't think it strange that you withstood his fire?"

"Mind tricks," Changa said.

"These things are real, Changa, all of them. You travel a

path of destiny and Chongli stands in the way."

"Enough about Chongli," Changa said. "Tomorrow will take care of itself. Tonight I'm cold and my ger is warm. Are you coming?"

Panya nodded. "There will be no lovemaking tonight."

Changa shrugged. They walked to the ger, grasping hands along the way. They were kissing as they entered the ger.

Changa awoke with Panya still in his arms, pleased that she didn't run away like before. He shifted and she pressed against him, a soft moan escaping her lips.

"You have my heart," she said.

"Do I have your mind?"

The ger flap swung open before she could answer. Jochi stepped inside.

"It is time, Sultan."

He untangled himself from Panya and went to his armor. Panya followed, neglecting her own clothes. She handed him his garments and armor as he dressed, her face solemn. As he secured his knives and sword, Panya tucked his talismans and gris gris about him.

"Remember your promise," she said.

She draped an amber necklace over his head. Changa looked puzzled, waiting for an explanation.

"It belonged to my father," Panya explained. "He gave it to me as a wedding gift. It has protected me. Hopefully it will protect you."

Changa ran his fingers across the smooth warm stone and smiled. "I'll return it soon."

Panya said nothing. As he left the ger he heard her whispering a prayer to Oya.

Chapter 8
The Battle of Kara Korim

The Chinese army rose over the horizon with the morning sun, their advance slow and deliberate. Red Dragon banners fluttered over the ranks as the marching drums doled out a morose rhythm. The Mongols watched from their hill, their faces bare of any emotion. Skirmishers rustled at the base, their mares jostling for action. Behind them the heavy cavalry waited in rigid discipline. Changa sat on his mount in the company of the khan and his elite at the hillcrest surrounded by his bahari. Tumen Khan sat astride his white mare clad in white garments and silver armor, the Heart of Zanj hanging from his neck on a thick gold chain.

The emperor stood beside the khan, clearly shaken by the sight before him. His army approached not to save him, but to kill him. Changa shook his head. By the end of the day it was likely Tumen Khan would be the sovereign not only of the Mongols but the Chinese as well.

The khan nodded toward Jochi. The general raised a red flag and the catapults responded, hurling their massive payloads into the Chinese ranks. Jochi raised a second flag and the manogels joined the barrage, unleashing their massive arrows with deadly effect. The Chinese continued to advance; soldiers in the rear moving up to take the space of those smashed by the projectiles.

Jochi watched the bombardment stoically, waiting patiently as the Chinese army pressed forward. When the army reached the edge of the ruins Jochi waved the two red flags, unleashing the skirmishers. The silence was shattered by the cry of hundreds as they sprang forward in perfect unison, galloping for the Chinese center. Chinese voices were heard for the first time, urgent tones shouting orders to the ranks. The Mongols veered away left and right, firing into the ranks as they rode parallel to the Chinese line. The Chinese answered with their crossbows. The Mongol fire was far deadlier and the Chinese line faltered. The skirmishers rode back and forth, firing as they went and working up a shroud of dust and debris.

Jochi raised three flags and the heavy cavalry charged under the cover of the skirmishers' dust, their destination the Chinese right flank. They were approaching the open field when the skirmishers emerged from the dust pursued by Chinese horsemen.

Leading the riders was Chongli riding a massive black stallion, bare-chested despite the cold. He fired a crossbow, dropping a Mongol with every shot. As they closed on the fleeing Mongols Chongli dropped his crossbow and drew his sword. A skirmisher too close was cleaved in half by one swing of the immense blade, his torso falling away from his mare while his legs clung to the saddle. The skirmishers scattered, fleeing in terror from the onslaught of the fangshi and his riders.

Tumen yelled and charged. Changa, the bahari, and the escort joined their leaders and the entire horde rushed down the hill, a flood of men and horses converging on the Chinese attack.

Tumen reached Chongli before Changa. From the beginning of their duel it was obvious the young khan was overmatched. The fangshi hammered at the khan, his relentless attack taking a deadly toll on the man's desperate speed. Jochi and his men fought to reach the khan but Chongli's men kept them at bay by sheer numbers.

Changa charged towards the duel. The first man blocking his way spun away with a throwing knife lodged in his forehead.

The second man managed to avoid a killing blow from the second throwing knife, the spinning blade bouncing off his helmet. Changa's sword was more successful, lopping off the man's head as he rode past.

He didn't see the rider galloping to intercept him. His only warning was a victory yell the man uttered; sure the Sofalan would feel his steel. Changa ducked the reckless swing, pressing his head against his mare's neck as the blade flashed overhead.

Their mounts collided, throwing Changa into the air. He crashed against the frozen ground, rolled and came to his knees to see another rider bearing down on him, crossbow raised for a killing shot. Changa waited, his keen eyes focused on the man's trigger finger. He rolled aside as the man fired, the bolt whizzing over his head and burrowing into the ground. The man disappeared, replaced by a bloody sword and a black mare carrying the Tuareg.

A swarm of horsemen encircled Changa as he clamored to his feet. Nafari brought him his mare. Changa jumped onto the horse and they charged towards the khan.

They arrived too late. Tumen Khan lay in the grass, Chongli's sword buried in his chest, blood flowing onto his damaged armor. Chongli ripped the blade out and waved it over his head triumphantly. Changa hurled his last knife, the blade streaking true to the fangshi's head. The impact knocked Chongli aside, his sword tumbling from his hands. He grabbed the blade hilt, fell to his knees and collapsed beside the dying khan. Changa rode up to the bodies, leaping from his mare and rushing to the khan's side. He was bending closer to the khan when someone spoke to him in Bakongo.

"He is dead, Changa. There is nothing you can do."
Chongli stood, the throwing knife still lodged in his head. He gripped the handle with both hands and tore it free.

"Panya said you were strong. She was right to think of you."

He tossed the throwing knife at Changa's feet. Changa watched in fascination as the wound healed.

"I hoped the tebo I summoned would finish you but you are stronger than I expected. I would be right to fear you; any normal man should. But as you can see, I am no normal man."

Changa blocked Chongli's swing, striking back with a thrust that cut a crease on the fangshi's cheek. The wound healed as soon as it appeared. He stepped away from Chongli's next swing and then launched into a furious attack. The fangshi was skilled but it was his healing ability that kept him alive. Changa struck a number of blows that would have killed other men but Chongli continued to fight.

They broke away as the battle swirled around them, both men circling for an opening. Chongli smiled, his breath heavy.

"Yes, Changa, I should be dead. You didn't believe Panya when she told you I was immortal. Do you believe now?"

Changa said nothing, saving his breath and gathering his strength. No man walking on this earth was immortal. Every living being could die. He couldn't strike the man fast enough to kill him before he healed. But there was another way.

He charged the fangshi, holding his guard low. Chongli reacted, slashing at Changa's neck. Changa caught Chongli's wrist and wrenched the sword from his hand. He drove his elbow into Chongli's jaw, smiling as he heard bone shatter. He ducked

Chongli's desperate swing, stepping behind him as he swept his feet from under him. The fangshi fell flat on his chest into the grass; Changa dropped his knees into Chongli's back. He took Panya's necklace and wrapped in around the fangshi's neck.

Chongli grasped at the necklace and the amber stones flared. The fangshi screamed and jerked his hands away. The necklace emitted a pulsing light that flowed from stone to cord, the glare increasing whenever Chongli grabbed at it. Changa felt nothing as he tightened his grip. Chongli reached back desperately, his long nails tearing Changa's skin as he attempted to break his grip. Gradually the fangshi's struggles slowed then ceased. His head drooped forward; Changa kept his grip making sure the fangshi was dead before dropping him into the grass. The light faded from the amber jewels and the necklace went cold in his hand.

Changa stepped away from Chongli's body. His men still surrounded him, a circle of Chinese bodies before them. Beyond them the Chinese army was in full retreat, the Mongol heavy cavalry close behind with waving swords and loaded bows. Nafari and the Tuareg rode up to him with his mount, Nafari's words repeated by Tuareg's expressive eyes.

"Bwana Changa, are you well?"

Changa mounted his horse. "I'm alive, that's well enough."

"The man they call Jochi seeks you," Nafari said.

Changa found Jochi kneeling and chanting with Tumen's elite by the body of the khan. He waited until the ceremony was complete before approaching Jochi. The Mongol commander stood and waved him forward.

"You are khan now," Changa said.

"No, my friend," Jochi replied. "This was Tumen's dream, not mine. I followed him because I believed he could accomplish it. He gave us hope of greatness, a chance to be the people we once were. It didn't matter if we succeeded. The chance was enough."

Jochi mounted his mare. "Take the emperor back to China.

There is nothing left here."

Changa looked one last time at Tumen's body and his eyes narrowed. "Where is the Heart?"

Jochi smiled. "It seems to have been lost again. I feel this time it will never be found."

Jochi winked and galloped away. Changa and his men found the emperor and Liwei still atop the hill, the emperor crying tears of joy while Liwei patted his back.

The emperor looked up at Changa and jumped to his feet, running to him and falling to the ground before him.

"You are blessed by the gods! I am nothing before you!"

Liwei joined the emperor and lifted him to his feet. "Thank you, Changa."

Changa shrugged. "We must leave now. Tumen is dead and the Mongols have no leader. Jochi won't bother us but the others may not be so generous."

They found horses for the Chinese and hurried back to their camp. Panya emerged from his ger, dressed for the road.

"He is dead," she said.

"Thanks to your necklace," Changa replied.

"The necklace only amplifies the power of the one possessing it. That is what my baba told me."

Changa stepped towards her, the necklace in his hand. Panya stepped away.

"You keep it. It contains Chongli's ka. It is part of your magic now."

Changa put on the necklace and stepped toward her again.

She raised her hands to stop him.

"No, Changa. Something is different."

"What are you talking about?"

"The feelings, they're not the same. When you killed Chongli everything changed."

Changa looked at her dumbfounded. "My feelings haven't changed."

"But mine have. I believe when I used you to fight Chongli's control I shifted the sensations he wanted me to feel for him to you. Now that he is dead…"

"So you feel nothing for me?"

Panya looked at him, her eyes remorseful. "I feel much for you, Changa. But not that way, not yet."

"Pack your belongings," he said abruptly.

"I'm ready."

Changa turned to his mare when Panya touched his shoulder.

"I'm sorry, Changa."

Changa hesitated. He wanted to convince her that her feelings were true, not the conjuring of some mad priest. But there was no time. The Mongols were beginning to fight among themselves for the spoils of the battle. It wouldn't be long before they began searching for the foreigners in their midst.

"Let's go. Everyone is waiting."

The others stood on guard, their eyes darting about for interlopers. Changa looked over his crew and scowled. They had lost good men on this safari, but all in all they had done better that he expected.

"Okay, Liwei. Lead us out of this wretched place."

The eunuch nodded and they rode away to the Long Wall, the ruins of Kara Korim fading away in dust and smoke.

* * *

The farmers of Taozhou struggled with the abundant harvest of an excellent season. The rains had been plentiful, the earth fertile and the growing season pleasant. Best of all, the Wokou did not come. With an uninterrupted season their barns overflowed with food. There would be plenty for all and more remaining for trade with neighboring seaports and passing ships, which meant more money to spend on luxuries and repairs.

Changa and his cohorts emerged from the mountains, exhausted from the long journey from Mongolia. They stopped at the first farm they encountered, overwhelming the farmer and his family with the company of not only the valiant Sofalans, but the true emperor as well. They spent the better part of an hour pulling the startled family up from their ceaseless bowing, preferring fresh water and food to praise. The wife snapped from shock first, ordering her brood around the farm to gather food for her royal guests. The farmer ran to his bell, banging it like never before. Farmers came running from miles away, summoned by an alarm usually meant for fires. Instead they were greeted by the beginnings of a celebration. They ran back to their homes and returned with more food and more people. The only sounds louder than the growing crowd were the bells ringing throughout the valley.

Cannons rumbled in the distance in answer to the bells, signaling the approach of Qi Jiguang and the city garrison. The commander and his soldiers galloped down the main road, banners flapping and trumpets blaring. They pushed their way through the mass to the courtyard where Changa, the emperor, and the others received praise and gratitude. Qi Jiguang finally emerged before them, flanked by two familiar and welcomed faces; Prince

Zakee and Mikaili.

The two waited until Jiguang and the emperor had exchanged pleasantries before rushing to their friends. Zakee pounced on Changa, wrapping his arms around the man's neck and almost toppling him.

"Praise to Allah!" he shouted.

Changa pried him off. "A little too joyful, don't you think, Zakee?"

"How can I contain the joy of seeing friends long thought dead?" He attacked the Tuareg the same way, babbling in Arabic to his mentor and friend. He approached Panya more conservatively in respect to her modesty, though his hands quivered.

"The sun still blushes at your beauty," he said.

"I see your words are still sweet despite your wounds," she answered.

Mikaili's approach was more casual. He looked Changa up and down, a smirk on his scarred face.

"You're a hard one to kill, aren't you?"

Changa swatted the captain's shoulder. "Sorry to disappoint you. You wouldn't make a good rich man anyway."

"It was a good dream, though."

Changa's tone turned serious. "Where are my dhows?"

"In the harbor. Qi Jiguang sent word to us. Apparently your loudmouth Arab told them where we were hiding. We set sail soon afterwards. We've been here three months. Three months too long, I say."

Changa took a swig of beer. "We lost the Kazuri."

"I know," Mikaili said. "They told us what you did. That was a damn waste of a good dhow. Only a merchant would do something that foolish."

A farmer stepped between them, slapping Mikaili on the

shoulder and handing him a beer. Mikaili snarled and took a swig.

"She was a fine dhow, but she was just a dhow. You're all alive, that's what matters."

He rubbed his cross and Changa smiled.

The celebration continued into the night before a massive bonfire, the farmers doing their best to rival the finest shows of Beijing. Changa fellowshipped with his men and the Chinese, but his eyes always returned to Panya. She seemed to be enjoying herself. Zakee sat beside her as he always managed to do, filling her ears with stories and compliments. Occasionally she looked his way and their eyes met. Her smile would become uncertain and she would turn away to engage in conversation with Zakee or anyone close. Chongli had done damage to her. It would take time for her to recover and she would have that time at sea. Changa shrugged and drank more beer. The safari back to Sofala would be a long one.

The next day held the greatest surprise. The winds were shifting; it was time to sail west. Changa and the others went to the docks and were greeted by the sight of their entire fleet with one notable addition; the *Kazuri*.

Changa stood stunned for a moment then rushed onto the reincarnation like a giddy boy, the bahari close behind. The dhow was the same in many ways; where it was different it was better. Changa ended his jaunt behind the helm, running his hands over the smooth wood.

"The farmers began rebuilding her as soon as you left," Zakee said. The prince and Mikaili stood behind him, both men smiling like proud parents.

"They went into the mountains for the wood. Their best swimmers found the wreckage and made measurements. They were nearly complete when Mikaili arrived. He supplied them with the details."

"She's better than before," Mikaili added. "No offense, but the Chinese are better shipbuilders than the Swahili."

"We shall see," Changa replied.

Blaring horns announced the arrival of the emperor. Changa met the young monarch on the docks and bowed. The Son of Heaven was different among his own. He stood straighter, the uncertainty in his eyes replaced by a confident stare. Liwei stood beside him, his hands hidden in the sleeves of his robe. He shuffled forward and looked into Changa's eyes.

"I wish to express the gratitude of our emperor for your help, Bwana Diop. Our kingdom is forever in your debt."

Changa bowed again. "I'm glad to see the emperor among his people. I hope he will return to his throne soon."

Liwei shoulders slumped as sadness seized his face. "I know I promised you a grand payment for your help, Changa, but as you know the emperor claims only a title. It will take time for us to regain the Forbidden City."

Changa shrugged. "I have my friends, my dhows and my cargo. After what we've been through I consider that payment enough."

"The emperor never breaks a promise," Liwei said. "On the day he regains the throne a treasure shall be yours, my friend. I will deliver it to you myself."

Changa smirked. "I'll be waiting,"

The Sofalans boarded their dhows. Changa manned the helm of the resurrected *Kazuri*, anxious to begin her maiden voyage. The entire city crowded the docks, hundreds of hands waving and hundreds of mouths wishing them a safe journey home. Changa looked to the *Hazina* and saw Panya standing on the deck. Their eyes met and she smiled before turning away. Time would heal her, he thought.

"Nafari!" he barked. "Drop the sails! It's time we went home."

End

The Safari Glossary

Amir – prince

Assegai – spear

Baghlah – a Swahili merchant ship (dhow)

Bene – King

Benematapa – An East African kingdom, home of Great Zimbabwe

Damascus sword – Changa's sword made from the legendary wootz steel of India

Dhow – Swahili for ship

Fisuname – Hyena man

Gris-gris – magical items worn for protection

Hazina – "treasure"

Junk – Chinese for ship

Kazuri – "small and beautiful"

Koloshe – A cave creature

Lobola – bride wealth

Mabaharia – sailors

Mamba – crocodile

Mogadishu – Northernmost Swahili city

Mombasa – Swahili port city; Changa's second home

Nahoda – sea captain

Quilin – A mythical Chinese creature resembling a giraffe

Samburu – An East African people related to the Masai

Sangir – pirates of the Malaccan Straits

Sendibada – "I'm always before everyone else"

Sewar – an Indonesian short sword

Sirocco – desert wind

Tebo – an evil spirit

Tembo – elephant

Wokou – Japanese and Chinese pirates

Yoruba – A people of West Africa residing in the area now known as Nigeria

The Safari Continues in 2011!

Changa and his cohorts begin their return home. There are more unexpected adventures in store for them as Changa continues his path toward fulfilling his promise and his revenge. A taste of Changa's Safari: Volume II.

Kali's Daughter

She stood on the balcony of the hunting palace and gazed into the night, a warm breeze teasing the ends of her sheer gown. The night was as black as her hair, the stars flickering like tiny torches in the distance. For the first time in her life she felt safe. Her prince promised her he would protect her, and he had kept his word. The hunting palace was one of his father's largest, a huge collection of buildings surrounded by high thick walls and dense forests.

She turned to gaze on him, his naked body stretched out across the cushions, his brown skin glistening from the sweat of their lovemaking, his details obscured by the mosquito net. She did not love him but she was certain he loved her. It was easy for her to make men love her. Her beauty attracted them like a bee to a brilliant flower and her ways made them promise her all they could give. She wanted only one thing, protection. It was a gift every man was eager to give, but it was the one thing that never endured.

The sensation began at the small of her back, running up her spine to her head and emerging like fire in her eyes. She jerked her head around and ran to the balcony, her face distorted with dread, hoping she would not see what her senses warned. Scores of hands appeared on the edge of the wall followed by turbaned heads as the interlopers pulled themselves up. She stood frozen as they dropped into the courtyard one by one. Yells and screams rose to her ears and she answered with a painful howl.

The prince struggled up. "What is it?"

She ran to him, tearing through the mosquito netting, her eyes crazy with fear.

"They are here! They are here!" she screamed.

"What are you talking about? No one is here but us and my men."

"Thuggee! Thuggee!

Terror flooded the prince's eyes. He jumped from the bed and ran across the room, grabbing his sword as the door crashed in.

The invaders charged with yellow scarves in their calloused hands. They saw her and hesitated, then turned to the prince standing naked with his sword.

"If you leave now you have a chance to live," he said.

They attack him like starved wolves. The prince fought well, but they were too many. They dodged his swings and thrusts waiting for the right moment. One of them finally broke through his guard, slipping behind the prince and throwing his scarf around his neck. As the prince reached for the scarf another attacker ripped the sword from his hand and grabbed his feet. A third man grabbed the prince's head, snapping it forward as the second man pulled his feet away and the scarf wielder pulled opposite. They strangled him in seconds, dropping the body to the ground absently. He had taken her from them. He had to pay.

She watched her husband murdered and felt nothing. It was ending as it had before. Was there anyone one who could protect her?

They approached her and she backed away towards the balcony.

"Stay away," she whispered.

They fell to their knees in unison. One of them stepped forward, a gaunt man with a dense moustache and dark eyes. A dingy turban encircled his head, held together by a brilliant ruby pendant. He extended his hand to her, a reverent smile on his face.

"We have come to take you home, goddess," he said. "Please accept these sacrifices as our gift."

"NO!" she screamed. "Why can't you leave me alone?"

She stomped the floor and the room shook. The others lifted their heads, fear in their eyes. Their leader stepped away.

"Please, goddess, we do not mean to offend you."

The anger came from inside, coursing through her like a swollen river. Her skin darkened like the night sky, her pupils disappearing into a searing white glow.

"Why won't you leave me alone!" she hissed.

The men scrambled to their feet and ran for the door. She smiled, raised her arms, and danced.

Acknowledgements

Big thanks as always to Charles R. Saunders, my sword and soul brother. Thanks for the continued friendship, encouragement and support.

Other thanks to my gang of thieves: Carole McDonnell, Valjeanne Jeffers, Ronald Jones, and Eugene Peterson. Thanks for reading the manuscript and expressing your views.

A special thanks to Winston Blakely for the wonderful illustrations. Don't get to comfortable. We have three more books to go.

CPSIA information can be obtained
at www.ICGtesting.com
Printed in the USA
LVHW09s0507221018
594365LV00001B/18/P